Praise for Gloria Nagy's *Unapparent Wounds*

"Well written, tough, and glib."— Los Angeles Herald Examiner

"Nagy's style is fresh, her pace brisk, her humor delightful."— LA Times Book Review

"Written with pizzazz and insight ... It has style and is in no way run-of-the-mill"— West Coast Review of Books

Radio Blues

"Gloria Nagy is one terrifically funny talent. Roll over Woody Allen!" —Alexandria Penny

"A new comic genius has landed on earth. *Radio Blues* is sensational." — John Naisbitt Author of *Megatrends* and *Reinventing the Corporation*

A House in the Hamptons

"More than a summer page turner...Ms. Nagy has slapped her well-heeled characters beyond what they thought they could bear, by making the unexpected manifest." – The New York Times

"Tom Wolff, take note... A staggeringly honest book about a special piece of the American Dream." – Playboy magazine

"Hilariously pierces the Seaside Social Set right through their Patagonias."— Los Angeles magazine

"Gloria Nagy's style is fresh, her pace brisk, her humor delightful." —Los Angeles Times

"Who says money can't buy happiness?...Spend a few days in A House in the Hamptons." –The Cincinnati Enquirer

"Bubbling with plots and personalities...colorful, thoroughly likeable characters... fast paced and funny." —Booklist

"Number one on your summer reading list. Honest...teary...hilarious... the thinking person's fun fiction. Gloria Nagy is a comic genius with heart."
—Patricia Auberdene, author of *Megatrends 2000*

"Seashore of the Vanities...no beach bag will be complete this summer without a copy." —*Trump* magazine

"Fabulous entertainment—and a quintessential summer read...combines a savvy urban sensibility with a sharp, sassy sense of humor to create a superb comedy of manners." –*Kirkus Review*

"Amusing, hip, highly readable...keen observation and psychological insight."– *Publisher's Weekly*

"A *House in the Hamptons* is selling faster than NO. 25 sunscreen." – *USA Today*

"Quicker than a gelato meltdown, mortality tips a designer hat at the best social gatherings. Temptation arrives wearing knock-you-down perfume and clingy white cashmere...there is a sense of history...mixed with social satire on the east end."–*The New York Times*

Virgin Kisses

"A stunning accomplishment—funny and sad, erotic and ultimately very moving. Gloria Nagy's dazzling portrait of the sex-obsessed narcissist and his eager victim will make readers tremble with the rage and sadness of recognition."
—Gael Greene

"*Virgin Kisses* is like a nightmare Woody Allen would have on a very bad night—the humor is quite literally hysterical."–*Time Out*

"Gloria Nagy's gift is to move you as she elevates the ultimate joke into tragedy, marshaling absurdities for a final triumph."–*New York Magazine*

"A lacerating, literate, funny, and obscene expose."–*Vogue*

"Nagy is a tremendous writer who tiptoes along the fragile line between the believable and ridiculous but never makes a false step."–*The Californian*

Natural Selections

"With searing wit and compassion, Gloria Nagy's Natural Selections taps into the issues of the eighties with fascinating precision. I couldn't put it down."
—Bonnie Straus, *Hour Magazine*

The Beauty

"Question: What is enticing, thrilling and can cost you a day or a weekend? Answer: Gloria Nagy's new novel, *The Beauty*."—Norman Lear

"If every good novel is a mystery story, this particular mystery story has lots of other tasty novelistic virtues going for it—a sense of mischief, sharp social observation, doses of complicated wisdom. *The Beauty* will have legions of delighted readers."— Kurt Andersen, author of *Turn of the Century*

"Nagy imagines the present as a burning building which her characters must make their way out of. The Beauty is a terrific fable about the futility of escape, the inevitability of evil, and the power of redemption."—John Hockenberry, author of *A River Out of Eden*

"*The Beauty* starts fast and speeds up. Gloria Nagy is a skilled driver on a very scenic road, and keeps her passenger guessing what's waiting around each new turn. It's well worth the trip."—Forrest Sawyer, NBC News

Marriage

"Many people claim to know what marriage is or is not. But few write about it's familiar yet mysterious realm as Gloria Nagy does in this sensitive, humorous, and compassionate novel."— Elie Wiesel, Nobel Laureate

"Gloria Nagy's *Marriage* is brimful of domestic wisdom. Wonderfully and easily readable."— Fay Weldon author of *The Lives and Souls of a She-Devil*

"*Marriage* is a modern masterpiece. A giant, lusty, hilarious, heart-wrenching saga of midlife marriage. Every page holds a nugget of human tmth. You cannot put it down."— Patricia Auburdene author of *Megatrends for Women*

Looking For Leo

"Hip, hilarious, heartbreaking."—*Cosmopolitan*

"A Story of female bonding...imaginatively drawn characters and wickedly witty scenarios."—*Publisher's Weekly*

"Delightful!"—*Los Angeles Times*

"Nagy has been compared to Tom Wolfe and Nora Ephron ... She's as much a social critic as a novelist. Her insights are scalpel-sharp.—*Chicago Tribune*

TITLES BY GLORIA NAGY:

Virgin Kisses, Warner Books/Penguin International, 1978, 2013
Unapparent Wounds, William Morrow & Company, Inc., 1981, 2019
Natural Selections, Villard Books, 1985, 2015
Radio Blues, St. Martin's Press, 1988, 2019
A House in the Hamptons, Dell Publishing, 1990, 2013
Looking for Leo, Delacorte Press, 1992
Marriage, Little, Brown and Company, 1995, 2013
The Wizard Who Wanted To Be Santa,
Sheer Bliss Communications LLC, 2000
The Beauty, Peter Mayer/Overlook Press, 2001, 2014
SeaSick, Jorge Pinto Books, June, 2009
Remain Calm, Sheer Bliss Communications LLC, 2012

UNAPPARENT WOUNDS

A Novel by NYT Best-Selling Author

GLORIA NAGY

UNAPPARENT WOUNDS

Copyright © 1981, 2019 by Gloria Nagy

Published 2019 in the United States by
Sheer Bliss Communications, LLC.

First published 1981 in the United States by William Morrow and Company, Inc,
New York.

All characters in this publication are fictitious and any resemblance to real persons, living or dead, is purely coincidental.

All rights reserved. This Book may not be reproduced in whole or in part, in any form (beyond copying permitted by Sections 107 and 108 of the United States Copyright Law, and except limited excerpts by reviewer for the public press), without written permission from Gloria Nagy.

Author services including cover design, interior design, and layout provided by Pedernales Publishing, LLC.

Library of Congress Control Number: 2019914214

ISBN 978-0-9679436-7-1 Paperback Edition
ISBN 978-0-9679436-5-7 Digital Edition

Printed in the United States of America

To my mother and father.

My thanks to Stephane Philippe, my hand in the dark. Her superb skill sets and calm expertise made this possible. And to Jose and Barbara Ramirez, for making this a joyful creative journey.

What though Cimmerian anarchs dare blaspheme
Freedom and thee? A new Actoeon's error
Shall theirs have been, devoured by their own hounds!
Be thou like the imperial Basilisk,
Killing thy foe with unapparent wounds!

 —*Ode to Naples*, Percy Bysshe Shelley

PROLOGUE
A Beverly Hills Fable

Once there was a candy-counter City of Limitless Options, where it was possible (if one was driven and romantic enough) to synthetically sweeten all values indefinitely. One day, a nice, sturdy midwestern couple arrived in this land unprepared, and disturbing things began to happen.

They were young and snug. Married since high school and without experience in the world of Mercedes and Movie Stars; she with her short basic brown perm, harlequin glasses, touch of pearlized pink lipstick and sensible shoes. He, about the same, with the absence of lipstick and the addition of horn-rims. He wanted to be a writer. She wanted to have children.

They did not smoke, and drank (only on special occasions) things concocted of tropical punch and rye with whipping cream. A nice, normal, ground-footed young couple.

Time passes. He becomes a writer for a major talk show, his lack of discernible talent and mildly carnivorous personality serving him well. Hair begins to grow. She is seen drinking bourbon on ice.

Cyclamate City is beginning to weave its web.

A year passes. The wife is now several sizes smaller (except for her breasts, which seem to have swollen in some sort of macabre redistribution of the wealth), and her hair is now a long striped rainbow of blonds. Her face is painted in various reds, greens and blacks, and thickened eyelashes fight bravely to open and close behind her aviator glasses. The glasses, like a lifeline to her past.

The husband is now, snappy. His hair shaggy and lightly permed, and a moustache grows as if planted by a bonsai artist; he bounces on the metal-tapped heels of his Rodeo Drive cowboy boots, clenching a Cuban cigar between his newly capped teeth.

Then one night at a party high above the city, filled with people who reek of beauty and money as if it were drugstore cologne, they faltered.

She sat drinking vodka with a twist, sniffing back cocaine and passing a perfectly rolled stick of Maui Wowee. He sat drinking Chivas and water, talking show business and resting his hand under the buttocks of a very young model. As she spoke to some faceless drug-hazed man beside her, many drinks, many sniffs and puffs, loosening the terror of their transformation, the knifeless gender change, the lifting of one's sense of balance, of proportion, something happened.

Her husband and the handled young girl went to the bar for more drinks, and she sat forward suddenly, hissing into the insouciant stranger's ear with fierce whispers. "If he leaves, he'll be sorry. I'll take those babies and leave this stinking town and he'll never see them again! I'll show that bastard. I've got his best friend so hot for me...he thinks he can screw around, well, I'll show him! I'm taking my babies where he'll never find us."

They had no babies.

The night terrors had escaped, flooding her new candlelit world and releasing hidden, viscous fantasies into her unreal real life.

The moral of the tale is this. Beware of the singularly peculiar traps of Candy Land, where what is inside is outside and outside is inside and people strut about like demented contortionists trying to become whatever it is that will make them wanted. The Candy Lovers march along, dispensing sugar drops from Gucci satchels and turning your brain to make-believe. But they are not your friends and they will never tell you that the candy is poison and too much will make you sick like the girl with the striped hair and the thrashing, close-sighted eyes, lashing out at her childhood sweetheart, using imaginary babies as her only weapon.

Some things one must learn for oneself.

CHAPTER 1
Beginnings

When Hannah Oberman Nicoli's father, Norman, came to Los Angeles, it was 1942 and everyone else was away at war. He had driven west from the poverty and disappointment of his first twenty-two years in Indiana in search of power and opportunity. A skinny, young, close-sighted, acne-scarred Jewish pioneer at the gates of Hollywood, and they opened and let him in.

It was a good time to be in Los Angeles. The war had turned the local economy into a hustler's heaven, and land was plentiful and laid out before the young explorer like a cheap whore, having no sense of its value or potential, and the air was clean and clear and smelled like orange honey, and rents were low, and of course, you could wear a sweater in the winter, which was terrific for a poor boy who was desperate to make something of himself and had to think of every cent, so that the thought of not needing a winter coat was a jackpot from God.

And he worked very hard. He drove trucks and he serviced vending machines, hauling cigarettes and candy and colas from bar to bar until he dropped in exhaustion. And he saved every dime. Soon he had saved enough to buy his own vending machine route, hustling against the black market and the shadow of the big money just beginning to nose around his customers, and soon he was able to sell his route and start a mail-order business, "Norman's of California," sitting in a small, hot room wrapping boxes of authentic Indian moccasins and gold plastic slippers for war brides in Ohio.

He was lonely and stuffed with guilt over having been rejected by the Army and being glad and about his sisters and his parents, waiting in Indiana for Norman the Conqueror to send a golden Packard and whisk them all west to meet Joan Crawford and lie by a swimming pool. He did not want them to come. Did not want his broken-down, Jew-drunk, junk-peddling father, and his nagging, despair-ridden mother, and his possessive, clutching sisters here. He had finally escaped the shame and anguish of his beginnings and he did not want to remount the cross, walk back inside the herring-stinking cell of his neurosis. He wanted them to take their bloodied claws from his back and disappear. He thought about changing his name and having his nose fixed, and so he was stuffed with guilt.

They came. Only instead of blue lagoons and movie stars they entered a run-down house in Boyle Heights (the joke of the rich Jews being that everyone went from one B.H. to the other—Boyle Heights to Beverly Hills)— and all they saw were others like themselves and poor Mexicans who shared the neighborhood.

He supported them all. His two dour sisters, Ethel and Sophie, jealous of his freedom and their loss of control of their baby brother's life. Two serious, bitter young women who held grudges and waited for Prince Moses.

Sophie's prince was a big, curly-haired sergeant with an ear-touching smile and little ambition. Ethel's was a small, compatibly bitter chiropractor with some unresolved mother conflicts. Two down, thought Norman.

Norman Oberman came from a time when people still knew what they were supposed to do, and so he was free to live without doubt. He was doing the right things. And to continue in this acceptable path, a wife was necessary.

By now Norman knew the ropes in his particular part of Los

Angeles. He had an almost-new Chrysler convertible, a fashionably wide-shouldered blue suit, curly red hair, money in his pocket and an open invitation to all the respectable Jewish dancing events on the East Side of the city. On a summer night in July 1946, he walked into the East Side Jewish Community Center dance and spotted a blonde in a bright red dress sitting across the room. Because Norman was vain about wearing his glasses, the blonde in the red dress waved before his weak, watery green eyes like a flag before a Brahma bull, and he self-consciously strutted across the polished wood floor, hands already dripping with cold, wet fear, to ask her to dance. When he was close enough to focus on her face, she stood up suddenly and walked away, leaving him dangling before an empty chair and a shy-faced, rather plain brunette who looked up at him, thinking he had come for her, and smiled. The brunette's name was Leah Bodkin and she was considered an old maid. She was at the time pushing twenty-seven years and still living with her parents and remaining siblings in a run-down old house behind her father's grocery store, working long hours as a secretary and turning all her money over to her mother. She had beautiful teeth, nice features, a weak stomach, and she was a virgin.

A conventional courtship followed. Leah was fascinated and frightened by Norman. She had never been in the world, hiding behind her parents' pickle barrels, daydreaming in an olive tree, while her two beauteous sisters, Estelle (later to be changed to Candy to fit her Rosie-the-Riveter image and her short-lived career as Miss Most Perfect Back of East Los Angeles) and Louise (a raven-haired artist given to bouts of fervent delusiveness), and her pretty-faced and hysterical baby brother, Morley, dominated the family and the world around her. She lived in everyone's shadow, holding her perpetually knotted stomach and being a good girl. She had fantasies of men (usually her sisters' boyfriends) and she tried in her own extremely subtle and brilliantly manipulative way to cause trouble for them, but her fear of men was greater even than her power as the seemingly weakest member, and so her yearnings went unanswered. The techniques of survival that she developed during this childhood and young womanhood would be transformed neatly and completely into her life with Norman and her relationships with her children.

Norman would bring to this union his anxiety, his dripping-handed fear of life, and Leah would bring her martyrdom and her inability to operate without the games of a passive child-girl.

Also, Leah would bring $1,000 which she had saved from her wages (and from what her parents had given her). Her own money. All that she had. The only viable symbol of her independence. She gave this symbol to Norman reluctantly, and for the rest of her life she would chart the end of herself as the day she gave her new husband the $1,000. Twenty-five years later when she had died an agonizing, merciless death from cancer, the only thing she had of her own was a bank account with $1,000, saved from her household money. She had so carefully hidden the book that it was never found, and the money is somewhere still.

With the help of Leah's secretarial skills and the $1,000, Norman began his rise. He sniffed out land deals with the nose of a bloodhound, seeing Los Angeles as one enormous, ripening oasis with endless potential. Land. Property. Power. He worked painfully hard. He studied construction, real estate law, drafting, architecture, finance. And he did everything himself. Fear of the world fueling his native paranoia, fanning it from a tiny, hot ember until it would one day consume his being. Until there would be no one, including his own children, who was not suspect, not possibly part of the omniscient army of enemies who had no purpose but to try to take from Norman Oberman what he had worked his life to achieve.

Two years pass, and Leah Bodkin, who had never thought she would marry or live on her own, is the wife of a wealthy young man, co-owner of a shiny new home (designed by Norman) and the mother of a chubby, redheaded baby girl named Hannah and firmly planted on the path to her destiny.

And so Hannah Oberman appears. A first-generation native Angeleno born to good circumstance and surrounded by an adoring (but disconcertingly unstable) assortment of relatives and grandparents.

Norman Oberman had his first affair when Hannah was still in her mother's womb, and so she began in an atmosphere of guilt and tension, for though her mother was not to know the terrible truth for fifteen years, the effect of such an aberration in the life of this privileged young family was pungent.

And Hannah grew healthy and fat. And Norman grew testy and richer. And Leah grew sad and weepy and pregnant with a second heir.

During this time, Norman's mother and father died of heart attacks six months apart, and the guilt which he had continued stuffing down inside himself like homemade sausage began to strain against its casing and push upward in his consciousness. He began to develop the symptoms of anxiety. He grew phobic and believed that his heart was going to stop, that he would die at any moment. He cried and moaned in fear. Soon he could not leave the house without Leah or sleep in his own bed.

Leah carried her husband and small daughter and her growing belly around with her, outwardly martyred and distressed, but also, somewhere very deep and far back inside, pleased at her power, her importance. It was the first time Norman had not been in charge, leading her life, making the rules. She wanted him to be her father, but she also wanted to be his mother (the perfect fifties relationship). His panic allowed her such an opportunity. The litany of her life became a martyred reminder of how she had nursed him, and of his helplessness. It worked well; it cemented his dependence for the rest of their life together.

When Hannah Oberman was three years old, her father's nerves broke completely and he was sent to a hospital. Leah went to another hospital (to give birth to Hannah's brother). Hannah was left with a huge black lady (it was still the time of black maids with switches to snap at naughty little shins and white uniforms and smelling of Cream of Wheat with raisins and brown sugar and of liniment, singing of Jesus while they wrapped tired, swollen feet in Ace bandages).

It was also the time of the influenza epidemic and Hannah's mother and the baby became ill and could not come home. And Hannah fell ill, vomiting up chocolate-flavored sulfur medicine and aching with abandonment. She had been smothered by attention for three full years, and then suddenly everyone was gone and she was all alone.

Her aunt Estelle came to stay and taught her the shimmy and polished her tiny baby toenails, and necked with a tall, slick-haired man in the living room, and made her march around the den naked to admire her body. ("Oh, Hanny, what a sweet little body you've got. You're going to drive the fellas crazy!") And her aunt Louise came and drew her picture and sighed deeply (a trait that would persist and grow into piercing inhalations for maximum effect as the years passed), and Sophie and Ethel would come, bringing her baby cousins and their jealousy at her mother's good fortune (if only the truth be known).

Sophie's husband was now a policeman, and she held against her heart the rage of Norman's betrayal. He had married someone else and become rich. Leah got the maid and the new house and Norman, and she got to iron a lot of black shirts. Ethel did not have such fantasies, being as earth-footed as an Indian scout and about as passionate. Her jealousies were more complicated. She had wanted a daughter and had drawn two surly sons, who hated Hannah for the attention she got and once tried to kill her by cutting her stomach with a rusty nail.

For one month Hannah lived in this strange new way, dazed with fever and change, her aunts zooming in and out motivated by something that Hannah sensed in her child-wisdom but could not understand, knowing only, somehow, that what they offered did not fill the hole of longing, the nightmare, sobbing need for her mother. Her father came once, driven by Sophie to sit by her bed and cry to himself.

And then one day she was well enough to swallow orange juice and play with her toys, and the next day her mother returned, carrying a small thing wrapped in blue blankets and quickly hidden away behind sliding glass doors with instructions that Hannah was not to go near him, and her father came home and life went on. Only things had changed, trusts had been ruptured, sanctity torn and nothing would be quite the same again.

And the Obermans moved on into their lives and up into the world. When Hannah was six and her brother Allan three, Norman built his dream house in Beverly Hills and closed the circle of his escape from his beginnings.

Geographically and financially, the Obermans moved, that is, but their cores were sealed in the past. They were never comfortable in this new world, where *everyone* was successful and played cards and golf and had groceries delivered. Norman had nothing to say to these people. The money protected him from having to cater to them, but it did not protect him from his insecurity and sense of inferiority. They were they and he was an outsider.

Leah was a nice, nonthreatening woman, and so, though she would never be a leader or a sought-after bridge partner, she made friends, mostly with others somewhat like herself, and created for them what social life they had.

And Hannah grew up in this sheltered world, where it was easy to believe that all Mexican, Oriental and black people were given white uniforms by God, and dirty laundry went into a magic chute and returned to your closets unaided, and there were more Jewish people than any other kind, and not having a swimming pool or living below Santa Monica Boulevard was something so sad and peculiar that you must pray every night for that poor person's happiness.

Beverly Hills in the fifties was a loving cup, which those poor, hard-working Jews like Norman Oberman, who had wanted a sip badly enough and had paid enough dues, could hold in their grizzled fists and drink from. It was a symbol *and* it was a community. Ninety-five percent of the inhabitants of the Flats of Beverly Hills were families that resembled (at least to the eye) the Obermans, and it seemed to the grown-ups and children who lived there to be the safest and best place on earth. The driveways filled with Cadillacs and station wagons and the trucks of Japanese gardeners were as much a part of every family's life as the telephone and *I Love Lucy*. Beneath the surface of manicured lawns, there was agony and rot, and by the time Hannah was grown and had fled the Venus flytrap embrace of her childhood place, she would learn this and know that it had not been safe at all, had been done with antique gold mirrors and breakaway walls, but then it looked perfect. Except, that is, inside the Oberman house.

Inside Hannah's house, things were not perfect. Norman and Leah Oberman were bonded in the way of that generation. And the resoluteness of the bonding together of two people filled with resentment and anger for one another creates a kind of dead-ended despair that the children inhale like the smoke of tainted cigarettes.

The Obermans fought. Endless screeching, hysterical fighting that left Hannah and her brother holding on to one another in self-protection and terror. After such a fight, Hannah's mother would take to her bed, sobbing hysterically behind the gold-handled doors to her room, punishing them all for her pain. And her father would skulk around the house, filled with remorse and stubborn ego, waiting for her mother to come out and make the first move back to the off-key harmony that they had settled for instead of love. Hannah and Allan would hate to come home, afraid to bring friends inside the tension, comparing their friends' families to their own and hating their parents with passionate intensity.

Leah Oberman lived without affection or warmth or the caressing of her spirit from the one allowable source, from this husband, for whom she had given up her child-world and her independence. He did not know how to show love and he did not need to learn. Getting him to give it to her consumed Leah's life and rotted her will and turned her into the worst parts of herself. A complaining, empty woman, pitting her children and husband against one another, trying to divide and conquer this family as she had done with the Bodkins as a little girl. She chose to believe that she had no power, that she was helpless before the might of her husband, and so her life depended on his will and his love and he could not give her life. She had no interests, no hobbies, and though she cared deeply about her children and loved them and tried, she was not interested in them, being too obsessed with her own unfilled needs to focus on theirs.

The years passed. Norman continued taking risks, mortgaging the houses that he kept moving the family into, upward, upward, driving for more, afraid to stop, to be there. They never traveled farther than Palm Springs and entertained rarely, and did not collect butterflies or play tennis or fill their lives with anything but the quest for more. And because to make more, more must be used, they were always on the verge of bankruptcy, and so Hannah and Allan thought that they must be poor, the really rich kids being the ones who always had new tennis shoes and their own credit cards at Saks Fifth Avenue and never heard their parents fighting about money.

By this time Norman Oberman had had many affairs, and this fact was most likely a propellant behind many of the increasingly vicious fights about what bananas cost or the dent in the fender of the new Coupe de Ville, but none of them knew this then.

Hannah Oberman did all right in her world. She grew into adolescence with her father's red hair and weak green eyes and a sense of humor. She had scars from the past and enough self-loathing and doubt to be concerned about and a nervous system as highly tuned as a Stradivarius, but she did all right.

She was sensitive and independent and romantic, and

hated math and the restrictions of school and peer approval, and suffered from unrequited crushes and lost friendships and the shame of her parents' outsideness. (She longed for a mother with a New York accent who belonged to Hillcrest Country Club and wore red fingernail polish.) She suffered from sibling rivalry and psychosomatic bouts of bronchitis and too much insight and sensitivity for her age. Leah called her the "Little Old Lady," and in a way it was true. She was poised and wise for her years, and wrote poetry and dreamed of eastern colleges and a career in the theater and marrying Frank Sinatra, who was far more appealing to her than Elvis Presley and that sort.

She had grown up in a home that did not have time to think about higher values, with two emotionally immature parents without much character or bravery, and so these qualities were inordinately important to her. She passed her values, made in reaction against rather than imitation of her parents' behavior, on to her brother and so in many ways, she raised him and they raised themselves. She was unique-looking and popular in an outsider's way, and had the lead in most of the plays at Beverly Hills High School, and wrote for the newspaper and the poetry magazine. She dated college boys when she was only fifteen, and wanted to be too old, too fast. She could not wait to be out of school and free to rush forth, open-armed, far away from the stifling certainty of the life she knew and into the romance of the future.

She was a strong person, liking control and the center of the stage, and she was motivated by a fierce desire not to be like her own mother, whom she needed too much but did not respect. "I will never be like that. No man will ever do that to me" was the rosary of her puberty, and she would pay for it as a woman and have to learn from scratch that life was not black and white and men were not gods or monsters.

She was a good girl, setting impossibly high standards for herself and her friends. ("If you let him feel you up, I can never be your friend again!") But it kept her from wavering like some of her peers who ended up pregnant and married before graduation or into drug troubles long before it was fashionable.

Then, when she was in her last year of high school, the lid of acceptability bounced off her life and ended her childhood.

In the middle of a winter night shortly before Christmas vacation, something woke Hannah. A feeling of something, more than a sound, a feeling that she would have again fifteen years later which would again end a part of her life. This feeling moved her from her bed, heart thumping against her throat, to her bathroom window, which faced the front door and allowed her to watch blind dates approach without witness. Something stopped her from looking out. She was afraid to look out and she did not know why. There was someone there, she was certain. She heard heavy foot sounds on the terrazzo-floored entry and loud breathing masking her own frightened gasps for air. And then a finger pushed against the doorbell, sending crescendos of clean firm music down the silent darkened hallways. She heard her parents in the background, robes being wrapped, hands groping for lights, doors opening, her name being called. She was motionless, frozen before this intruder like an icicle, caught before it could drop to safety. Blood pounding in her forehead, she climbed up onto her pink-crocheted toilet seat and looked out. A woman's shadow, a tall, dark woman in a nightgown, leaned against the doorbell of her father's palace, grunting drunkenly into the cool, still night.

She heard her mother's voice, shrill and hysterical in the hallway, calling her name. She went to her and together they approached the safe side of the massive white doors, tiptoeing in tension. The woman kept her hand on the bell. She was yelling now.

"Norman, you son of a bitch, if you won't tell that old hag of yours about me, I'll tell her myself. Your husband hasn't wanted to fuck you since your wedding night, you stupid old bitch! You're a laughingstock. Everyone knows about Norman and me! He's just afraid you'll take his money, he loves me! Ask him, he'll tell you!"

On and on it went. Hannah and her mother stood holding

hands, faces locked in disbelief, reality suspended, reason thwarted. Lights went on in the maid's room and across the street.

"Oh, God, Mother, call the police!"

Her mother began to cry, tears running down her face, mucus dripping from her nose. "I can't. I just can't. Your father said not to!"

"I don't care what he said. Call them! I'll talk to him!"

Down the hall she marched, the passenger taking over for the stricken pilot, fear displaced by duty. Her father, a stranger now more than ever. More than just the absence of a sense of closeness that she had accepted all her life, the separateness of never holding his hand or going anywhere with him alone or feeling his arms around her or being told who she was. This was different. She, with the high, impossible standards. ("My father would never be unfaithful, that's the worst thing *anyone* can do.") Now it was her turn and it was too hard for her to accept. She opened the door to his dressing room and called his name. There was no answer.

She saw him reflected in the gold-rimmed mirror over the marble sink, standing in his closet quivering in fear.

The bell pounded on, sending the sweet happy music through them in nerve-racking cacophony. "I told Mother to call the police. You come out and help us. This is your mess. You clean it up."

She had never dared speak to him in such a way, but for the first time in her life she was not afraid of him. She was the grown-up now and he was the naughty child, and she sensed that he would not fight and would accept her authority. His face was flushed red with misery. "Okay. Okay."

It was a long night. Police coming, the intruder, the cracker of the Oberman family skull, dragged away handcuffed and ranting in the fresh air of her father's betrayal; the witch from *Macbeth* wandering the bougainvillea-covered landscape, peeling the lies like thick purple grapes.

Her brother never woke up and was spared, for the moment, the horror of what had happened to their childhood. For though

Unapparent Wounds

Hannah would deny it and push it away for years and years to come, that night was the beginning of her mother's end and the last time that she would ever not be the shoulder, rather than the head on the breast, again.

CHAPTER 2
The Present

▰▱▰▱▰▱▰▱▰

Hannah Oberman Nicoli sat at her desk working on her family history. She had decided to record the most personally impressive details of her rapidly disappearing assortment of relatives as the reality of her thirty-second birthday took hold. She was getting it now. That feeling of time passing. It had not been real to her at thirty, but it was very real now. Her goals unreached and the itching restlessness of empty places irritating her mind and shortening her temper.

Her dreams were filled with her childhood and her mother, who reappeared before her so vividly that she would awake, convinced that it had all been a joke and her mother was still alive. And so she had begun exorcising the itch in the only available way. Typing out her thoughts, filling pages with her doubts.

SELF-DESTRUCT NOTEBOOK (VOLUME I)

I am Hannah Nicoli. I am thirty-two years old. I have one husband, Nicholas, who loves me very much and who, after nine years of marriage, I still have not begun to trust for a valid or invalid assortment of reasons.

Unapparent Wounds

I have two small children whom I love more than my life, but have very little patience with. There, I said it. I do not like storytelling, art projects, cannot sew or teach a five-year-old to tell time for all hell. It was almost over my head to instruct in the art of shoe-tying.

I live much too close to my father.

My mother is dead. A fact, which, though I was present at the very moment of the occurrence, I cannot fully comprehend. My dreams indicate that I do not really believe that it could happen to me (or, less selfishly, to her).

My father sleeps with a lot of fairly revolting women. My brother, the doctor, married before exploring such possibilities. That is my only real family.

Others include an assortment of aunts and uncles and cousins so screamingly ill that they provide few of the common requirements of family members.

Coming from bad emotional stock is really lousy for your self-image. If my aunt Estelle, for example, were Golda Meir or Margaret Mead, somehow all those comparisons my mother used to make between me and her would not have left such doubts as to my worth.

Likewise, if my father were Harry Truman or Norman Vincent Peale (or even Al Pacino), all of my mother's shrieks of "You're just like your father" would have not been so disturbing.

Aunt Estelle is fifty-seven years old. She dresses in matched mini-outfits. She had not changed her hairstyle, makeup or approach to life since she won the title of Most Perfect Back of East Los Angeles in 1943. The first impulse you have on seeing her is to give her your drink order and send her back into the darkness.

Her life is as rigid as an overfilled ice tray. Mondays she rises early (2 p.m., she is an insomniac). She cleans the apartment, left to her by my grandparents with whom she lived until they passed onward at age eighty-six.

At 4 p.m., Estelle (who affects the nickname "Candy" for social occasions) prepares her one meal of the day, which she will eat promptly at 5 p.m., puts on her makeup, which occupies the next hour and one half of her day, and relacquers her hair. (Her hair is never combed or moved in any way between beauty shop visits and is stuffed nightly with wads of tissue before retiring.)

When Estelle is dressed, she waters the lawn. Then she watches TV and cleans her dishes. At exactly 7:30, she leaves her house for the "show," a movie theater nearby. Every single Monday she does this. She buys popcorn and she sits in the same seat. If someone, by some odd, uncontrollable chance, should be occupying "her" seat, she will ask him to move.

Once my parents happened to be in this same theater on Aunt Estelle's movie night. My mother asked her to sit with them. She refused, saying she could not possibly sit in another seat.

When she returns home, she will read her two newspapers, *The National Enquirer* and the *Star*. (When my mother was dying, Estelle was fond of sending her clips from *The National Enquirer* about miracle cancer cures being developed in remote mountain regions of Nepal, extracted from the tissue of leprous pygmies.) Then, at about 2 a.m., she eats exactly one-half pint of peppermint ice cream and goes in to prepare her face and head for the nocturnal hours.

The ritual is repeated daily with one change each day: Tuesday she markets and stays home at night. Wednesday she goes to the beauty shop in the evening. Thursday night she polishes furniture and does her mud pack treatment. Friday night I don't know what the hell she does. Saturday she closes herself up to rest and prepare for Sunday.

SUNDAY is THE DAY she DANCES. For the last twenty years or so, every Sunday my aunt decks herself out from hair bows to turquoise stockings and gold lame cincher (her pride and joy is her twenty-two-inch waist), gets on a crosstown bus and rides into the seamier part of Hollywood to her "club." A helluva club that anyone who is ambulatory and has five bucks in his pocket can join merely by falling across the threshold. My aunt is a "LIFER" at the club, so she only pays half. She orders herself an orange juice (she does not drink) and waits for someone to ask her to dance. Now, as to men…

My aunt, I learned while eavesdropping before I knew what it was, is something of an easy lay.

Considering the fact that she is fifty-seven (admits to thirty-six) and will not accept a date or even a dance offer from anyone who is over thirty, short, balding or with even a trace of a paunch, well, you can see why she probably has to spread 'em without too much elasticity. And so she dances away. A Rumba-Rumba that's her numba.

Once in a while she has a boyfriend for a couple of weeks. One guy, she told me, "was a little old. Thirty-three." And he had the beginnings of a bald spot, which he swore to her (probably just as the ol' rubber bands were stretching) he would cover with a wig if she would go steady with him. However, she said (even given these failings), he was a "terrific dipper."

My uncle Morley was diagnosed as a borderline schizophrenic during his adolescence. At the time, he aspired to be a Shakespearean actor, following in my grandfather's footprints.

My mother's father, Zada Bodkin, had enjoyed brief fame as a silent-film actor after being accidentally discovered by two talent scouts as he hit at a stray dog with his cap in front of his grocery store. They told my grandmother (who made most of the decisions) that they were overwhelmed with his naturalness and had been looking for someone who could chase a dog with his hat to play a butcher in a major film. He did several. One day my grandmother bundled Morley, Estelle, my mother and my aunt Louise in all their potato-sack finery, got on the streetcar and rode from East Los Angeles to Hollywood to watch my grandfather make a movie. She sat there all day without saying a word. When she got him home, she told him in no uncertain terms that a grocery store was a lot better way to support a family than running around all day wearing makeup on his face, with a bunch of floozies and Gentiles, and to stop it immediately. The studio pleaded and offered him a contract. He went back to the pickle barrels. A fate sealed.

Anyway, Uncle Morley had been bitten by the acting bug. However, after losing a part in some local theatrical production, Uncle Morley took to sitting under the kitchen table eating pounds of butter with his hands and crying hysterically.

After this episode, Uncle Morley gave up the theater and settled down as a supervisor in a nuts and bolts company. He married a fragile young woman with bad lungs who died one Mother's Day, leaving him with unquenchable guilt (they did not get on) and a highly disturbed three-year-old son.

Nuts and bolts do not allow one much outlet for crushing panic, loss and guilt. And since Uncle Morley no longer had Shakespeare, he found something else (something my shrink told me later saves a lot of borderline schizos from the screw box). He found RELIGION.

Now, my uncle Morley found religion the way Hitler found politics. Lightning flashing. Lights exploding. I mean HE *found* religion. He eventually remarried, a terrific woman who gave up a maiden life as a hosiery buyer for Bergdorf Goodman to keep house for Uncle Morley and his kid, and is now reduced to sneaking cigarettes in the bathroom and cheating on dairy products with salami. Uncle Morley has taken to greeting you as if his smile and touch were THE WORD. "Bless you my children and you shall be free." Morley even drives his *rabbi* crazy. Morley celebrates holidays the rabbi never heard of. And his rabbi is straight out of the sixteenth century and so horny from his ten-year search for a woman ill enough to marry him that he looks like a guy whose right hand has abused its best friend beyond the rehabilitation stage.

One of the most disconcerting life experiences was going to Uncle Morley's house after my mother's funeral. He crawled to the door, all of his clothes torn, no shoes on and ashes smeared on his face.

He opened it on his knees and then crawled away. "Hello, Uncle Morley," we said.

The Horny Rabbi explained that Uncle Morley was performing

ancient Jewish mourning rituals and was not allowed to be higher than the mourners or acknowledge greetings and a lot of other similar bullshit. I headed for the whiskey.

Uncle Morley spends one year in deep mourning for every relative or close friend. During this year, he rises before dawn, goes to temple, then to work and cannot accept any social engagement or do anything (even eat) just for pleasure. No movies. No restaurants. Probably no nooky. The thing about it is, that first my grandmother died and when the year of mourning was up, my grandfather died and when that was up, my mother died. The only way out for my poor aunt is to strangle him with one of her old hosiery samples before someone else goes.

And one thing beyond the way he chooses to play out his own trip around the planet. Something I did not like at all. He told me that the reason my mother died so hideously was that she must have broken one of God's commandments. Not one of the BIG TEN, too simple and she hadn't broken any of them anyway, but one of the "thousands that God has devised." Somewhere along the way she broke some of those. Without even knowing it. I said, "Gee, I wonder what commandments stillborn babies break" and stuff like that. He merely beamed at me. And then I said, "What about my father? He's broken some of the BIGGIES like LYING and ADULTERY and GREED," and he beamed further (the shmuck) and he said, "The Lord works in strange ways." You said it, Uncle Morley.

My aunt Louise, my mother was fond of saying, had been a really exceptional girl. "Looking at her now I know it's hard to believe, but Louise was something. All the men were crazy about her even though Estelle was prettier. And she was so independent and so smart. She left high school, moved out of Papa's house and got a job as a sketch artist in a nightclub! And she had millionaires after her and she was so intelligent. I know it's hard to believe to see her now, but it's true."

Yes, it's a little hard. Aunt Louise, the former Holly Golightly of the Depression years, lives next door to Aunt Estelle. However, they fight, then they sulk, so they are always either not speaking or fighting and consequently see little of one another. Aunt Louise has been married for almost forty years (she is sixty-one years old) to my uncle Marvin, who, legend has it, was the least desirable, smart or promising of her suitors, but did have lots of curly hair, a good build and made her feel sorry for him. Didn't last long. He went bald and started feeling sorry for her.

They had one child. A boy, who Aunt Louise, in the sighing, hand-wringing way of hers that somewhere along the years replaced her former spunk, blames for her loss of health. "I almost died having HIM, and I've never been the same." She says this a lot. He grew up with that. Now two ex-wives and four kids later, he has a reported affinity for tying girls to chairs and beating them with whips. Recently he abandoned a transitory career as a draftsman to become, probably, the first middle-class Jewish cowboy in the world and now lives on a ranch, which is really a tract house in the San Fernando Valley, where he keeps an assortment of stringy animals and a horse.

Louise is also an insomniac. Louise, however, unlike Estelle, has made insomnia a life-style and a cult. It is the only thing she cares about. It consumes her waking hours. She practices meditation, sees fortune-tellers, psychics, performs self-hypnosis, communicates with the other world. And she *talks* about it. Continually. Punctuated by long, penetrating sighs and hand wringings. No one has ever suffered like Louise with her insomnia. As poor Marvin (whose only aim in life at this point is to live until his retirement, when I believe he will ditch Louise and fly to Mexico) stumbles out at 4:30 in the morning to go to work at the beer factory, Aunt Louise, full of sleeping pills and mysticism, stumbles past him to go to bed.

And that is the other thing she talks about. Besides her insomnia, you see, she talks about what happens when she tries to sleep.

People plot against her getting any. The tenants upstairs flush the toilet, on purpose. The lady next door hired a carpenter to fix her roof just to keep her awake.

One time, my uncle, who had gone to his beloved Mexico to get away from Louise and sample (I have heard tell) some of the local Haciendas de la Noche, returned a day early to surprise her. She accused him of coming home unexpectedly just to wake her up.

Because she spends all of her time either sleeping or trying to sleep, Louise doesn't get out much. In fact, she has been known to go for two or three months at a time without ever putting on real shoes (slippers are her passion).

When she does go out, it is often just to stand on her porch with a hand mirror and search for wrinkles. And sigh.

"If I could only get some sleep, I could stop all these wrinkles!" The worst part about it is that Aunt Louise is almost sixty-two years old and doesn't *have* any wrinkles.

Aunt Louise is always starting art projects. They are scattered or laid out on tables, floors, wherever she happens to have put them down before trying to get some more sleep. But she never finishes them. "I want to do a nude soap sculpture of John Travolta, but my eyes are just too tired all the time," she told me the last time I saw her.

My father does not get on with my mother's side of the family. (He also does not get on with his side of the family.) And I sympathize with him. It is only recently that I have been able to look at my father with enough burgeoning maturity to sympathize with him about much of anything, and that causes many lumps in my throat and is probably long overdue and good for me.

I grew up seeing my father as my mother saw him, an overpowering monster on whom our very existence depended. I believed that if we displeased him, he would leave us all penniless and, thus, helpless. (My mother was not one of feminism's leaders.) It's only been since she died that I have been able to look at him realistically. My father is a weak, selfish, frightened man who did the best he could with us. He has little character and lives for his money, though he would not admit it. He can be very sweet and charming, though it is almost unbearable for him to accept or express affection to anyone over ten. My children get the love. I probably did, too, when I was five, but he's already afraid of how fast they're growing, how soon he'll be unable to kiss, to hug, to be vulnerable to them. Right now, I am trying to sort out my father.

Sometimes I feel bitter and very old because I lost my mother before I was grown up enough to accept it (if anyone ever really is). But it was bloody hard to accept her maiming and disintegration and my father's blind panic. Maybe it wasn't the panic that was so hard; it was his defense against it, the other women calling while she lay innocent of anything but her fight to stay here. The inequity got me. I overidentified. I saw her as myself and all women as victims, and I saw the end of all hope that there was still a saucer of family life under me.

Now I can see that my father acted out of fear and weakness and loneliness. But I am still haunted by the unfairness of life. The survival of the fittest often being only the survival of those most able to live out a monster-child's existence. Fueled by selfishness and the ability to live with clouded conscience and thus capable of any act that leads to the satisfaction of their needs at anyone's expense. My parents played out a thirty-year Monopoly game that I am just beginning to decipher the rules of, but one thing is certain. He won. He's alive and he's doing fine. Still attractive. Rich. Sought after. His kids still scared to displease him. He found a woman with a lack of self-esteem similar to my mother to take the shit and hold his hand when he needs it, and other kinds of women when he doesn't. He's doing fine.

Me and my kind, the Joan of Arcs, the people who believe that integrity is essential and lies and cruelty cannot be tolerated in oneself; the civilizers, who give up jobs and inheritances and marriages rather than lose their lives' value; we noble bitches and bastards often don't come out so well. Better people, perhaps, but not necessarily better survivors, or happier.

I know that my mother is *not* going to miraculously reappear in the hat department of Saks Fifth Avenue for all my nightmares. My aunts will continue. Uncle Morley will keep the faith. My brother will never be ten years old and my best friend again.

And my father will never, ever be Uncle Wiggily. And me? I am way behind on my ten-year plan. Writing for magazines without a novel in sight and not keeping up with the Schwartzes, no swimming pool and no paddle-tennis court.

I am not a weak person but I am a scared person. I will probably never like the way I look or the sound of my voice on a tape recorder. I am trying to tell the truth and grow up.

There it is. I don't know what the hell I'm really accomplishing with my children. I don't even know right now if I want to be married. I'm scared to death about that. My sexuality is on hold. I think about affairs and changing my life before the mold sets. I daydream about being married to my psychiatrist, who would be, of course, that miraculous Father in the sky, who would protect me and guide me and make me seem less aggressive to myself. I have a lot of things that other women envy. I am loved. I have a "career." I have material comforts. I seem to be wise and stable. I am considered by some to be beautiful (if they only knew).

Looking for answers. Looking for peace. I would very much like to reach out for my husband and know that I have accepted all of him, as is, and can relax and stay awhile. I would really like that.

And now, before my husband or one of my relatives shows up, I will hide this and resist all temptation to place it in a coffee can and bury it for future generations.

"Rats." Hannah stopped typing and reached for the phone. "Hello."

"Hannah," a hesitant voice, the caller, waiting to be rejected. "This is Patsy."

Hannah sat back. "Hello, Patsy, how are you?"

"Oh, fine. Um, my boss gave me some tickets to the Ice Follies, and, uh, your father said that he'd like to take Neilie, and, uh, so I was calling to ask if she can go with us Friday night."

Bribery, Hannah thought, smiling to herself. The way to an old cocker's heart is through his granddaughter.

"Sure, I guess it's all right. I'm sure Neilie will be delighted. She's never been."

"Oh, good. Um, my boss, you know, he gets tickets all the time. I've taken your dad to lots of things and next time something comes up, I'll get more. Maybe you and, um, Nick and your father and I could go to Las Vegas or something. Sometimes my boss gets free weekends. I've been wanting to go when Sergio Franchi is there. You get a free drink and a brunch and your room."

Hannah was shifting between her dislike of and pity for this woman.

"Well, that's very sweet, Patsy. Listen, I'm working on an article right now and I really can't talk. I'll have Neilie ready about six-thirty on Friday, okay?"

"Yeah, I guess, we'll go eat first. Your father will probably just want to get a hot dog at the show, but I know you don't like Neilie to eat too much of that stuff."

What you mean is that my father is a cheap son of a bitch and you want a steak.

"Well, a hot dog's okay. She doesn't have them often." Hannah grinned.

"Well, I'll ask your dad."

"Okay, Patsy, see you Friday, bye."

Hannah replaced the phone and sat back suddenly exhausted. The phone had disconnected her, cutting into her concentration and pulling her deeper into memories.

She closed her eyes.

But the images were flashing. "Why Grandma got dead?" Her daughter's sweet-skinned face, looking at her with clear blue X-ray eyes blinking against things unknown. "If I grow up and be a mommy, will you get dead?"

"Did someone shoot her, like TV?" "Is heaven further than Chicago?" "Can I get dead if I eat a lot of junk? Did Grandma eat a lot of junk? When you gets dead can you watch TV?"

The thought of her mother as an emaciated cancer-riddled ghost watching a tiny TV set in her coffin shot through Hannah's mind.

Momma.

Lately, she found herself whispering the word inside her head, a word not said since childhood, not even as she died. "Mother," never Momma, but now, often, the word -MOMMA.

Two weeks after her mother's death, trying to restart the wheels of her grief-suspended daily life, she had gone to an exercise class. As she sat on the sweat-stinking floor, exhausted from the exertion, the teacher's voice moved over her.

"All right, ladies! One for those throat muscles! Remember, we never get-old-think-young! We *Will Not Get Old*, ladies! Think good thoughts and like yourself! All right now, chins back, open your mouth and make the Ma sound. All together now, MA MA MAMAMAMA!" Hannah had started and with the word, the unspoken word more painful in the chirpy degeneracy of this place, a flush of pain had filled her, and she had run from the room, weaving between the swollen old ladies and the pudgy teenagers sent by their mothers and the young matrons like herself, she ran, tears and sweat looping together as the sagging chins popped up and down in tuneless chorus, "MA MA MA MA MA MA."

Hannah stood up quickly and stretched, the restlessness returning. She climbed the stairs, unbuttoning her shirt as she went, and threw on jogging clothes and tennis shoes as if the house were on fire or the baby had swallowed something lethal. She called to the slow Mexican girl, the latest in the chain of border-smuggled maids who made motherhood possible for women of Hannah's lifestyle. Working mothers and restless mothers who had had babies before they could comprehend the reality of such responsibility or the loss of freedom that accompanied it. And so they lived with this dependency and the conflict and self-hate it periodically produced. It was to her part of the package of motherhood and she had never been without it. "Tina, *voy para caminar.*"

And she was out. Walking was her therapy. Her meditation. And she walked today, surrendering to the splatter of threatening thoughts against her head, breathing in the courage to consider. She saw herself at nineteen alone in New York City chasing rainbows. She had fled college as she had fled Beverly Hills, looking for the magic promised her in fairy stories. She had met her husband then and finally relinquished her virginity. She knew now that she had chosen him to perform the sacred task because he was safe. He had seemed to be perfect but unattainable, and so if rejection followed her long-fantasized surrender, it would not crush her.

She had met him at a young playwright's audition, walking into an empty theater and seeing this rough-edged sexy man, hunched over a piano alone on a true-life New York stage, playing jazz and dangling a cigarette between his downturned, sullen lips. He was creative and he was a Director, and she could tell from his expensive clothes and briefcase that he was not poor, and of course (because to her everyone was) he must be Jewish.

And by the end of the audition she was madly and obsessively in love. It would be weeks before she would learn that he was married to a very rich and pregnant girl, and the pain of this would fill her like a violent sickness and consume her young life. And so she would give him her most precious prize, her virginity, being still of a time when such a thing was true and nineteen not insanely late to lose it, and they would plunge deeply into the black, stagnant waters of adultery, where everyone swims blind and reason is no longer a word.

It went on for a long time. From coast to coast and year to year, draining Hannah's innocence and clarity. She ended it often and went home to finish school, but somehow it was never over, and finally he left his wife and his little girl and followed her.

Then it was real. And this man, who was now on dry land, out of the mystery and the black, blinding romance of the night waters, frightened her. He was a stranger to everything she knew. An Italian-Catholic kid from the South Side of Chicago who had never finished high school, but worked his way up through the Navy and city college, denying his past and the grossness of his brutal alcoholic father and dry, cold mother. He was handsome and he was smart, and he longed to be a film director and travel in a world of fancy people. But more than any of that, he wanted to be part of a family. To play golf with a father-in-law and belong to a private country club and be taken care of in a way he had never known, but had watched from the kitchens and caddy jobs that took his childhood.

She fell in love with a myth who had cared enough about her to come down to earth and reveal himself as a man. But the man he revealed frightened and disappointed her, and so she pushed him back into fantasy and began the lie with which so many such unions begin, seeing what you want, because to see what is might force you to tell the truth and the truth is often the end.

Hannah walked faster, pushing her body uphill through the small winding streets of West Hollywood, Beverly Hills' poor cousin, living in its reflected glory. It was a nice neighborhood, filled with trees and pretty houses, and mixed with children and elegant fags, and Hannah loved it. It was her first house and even though it had been her father's money that helped buy and furnish it, it felt like her own. But today she cringed at the reality of the fact. "My father gave it to us."

When Nick Nicoli came to California, he gave his child away out of guilt and because it was easier than the price he would pay for continuing to perform in the lives of two similar women who both wanted him to be more than he was. Hannah *was* similar. Younger and considerably less spoiled, but having been born into a world that promised to Nick the family and security that he had sought all of his life. They loved each other deeply. They had been romantic and tragic and passionate together and creative and vulnerable. But he knew that she did not see him clearly, did not see the self-doubt, the tears in the lining of the cashmere coat, and so he withheld the parts of himself that would have helped her love him honestly and hid from her, as he had from the woman she replaced, inside his wide-set blue eyes and behind the mask of affability that he wore with the same easy fit as his tennis clothes.

Her parents were violently against the affair, saw the differences between them. "An out-of-work piano player! A divorced man with a child. What kind of husband is that for a girl like you, with your intelligence and beauty? A goddamn Catholic!"

She wavered and began having headaches and waking in the morning with the stomach-heaving sickness of anxiety, and he went to San Francisco to look for work, and she lay in the sun and swam and felt cared for and young like a normal, well-bred twenty-two-year-old girl-woman. She allowed the separation from him for the first time to reconsider and try to tell the truth.

But while he was away, her mother began to bleed. Gushing black blood and diarrhea, filling the toilet and her father's being with dread. Norman told Hannah about her mother the night before her last midterm, and she had listened and been positive that it was nothing, so inconceivable was it to her that anything could happen to Leah.

Not her mother. Her mother was always there; waiting in the kitchen, waiting in the car pool, waiting at the ballet class, waiting at the airport. It could not possibly be anything.

Her mother had raised her to believe that she could not really exist without her, and even as she performed the role of grown-up and cradled her mother and kept her going through the years of shrill despair following that long-ago night of which they never spoke, she believed in her gut that she was three years old and her mother might leave her again, and if so she would die.

But it was not nothing. It was cancer. She followed her mother down the green-walled hospital hall, holding her dry warm hands that were to Hannah safety, and they wheeled her away and cut out her rectum and pushed a hole through her stomach to shit from without control like an infant. And Hannah sat by her bed twelve hours a day, seven days a week, and missed her finals and took care of Leah, her mother, who was now someone else. She was now a woman dealing with maiming and mortality and a child wanting her own mother, and Hannah was pushed away by her suffering and could not get back in.

And so she got married. Much later Hannah would admit that if her mother had not gotten sick, she probably would not have married Nick. But the threat to her security with the impossible possibility of her mother's leaving her had been too much, and so she fled from facing the reasons for this and hid in the only waiting arms.

They were married in her parents' home, the Bodkins on one side and the Obermans on the other, all sitting with unspoken horror and disapproval at this goy in the woodpile. Her mother stood beside her, thin and pale, being kept alive by the force of their will, hiding the truth from her family and friends and from herself.

Her father had found a house for them and offered Nick a job, which he accepted because he was afraid of Hannah's expectations and of his own failure to achieve his dreams. And so their marriage began with self-deception and betrayal, and they both stepped backward from the truth.

Hannah stalked the streets, sweat mingling with tears at the thoughts filling her. Talking to herself to calm the fear. "What are you doing? That's all yesterday. It's all done. You have a good marriage, two beautiful children, interesting work, a lovely home. Stop all of that old stuff. Stop it!"

She reached Sunset Boulevard and turned west, heading home.

But something was wrong. "I shouldn't be doing those notebooks." A rush of grief filled her. Loss so strong that it stopped her legs and doubled her over with sadness. She leaned against a tree, oblivious to the traffic and the well-dressed pedestrians strolling around her, and sobbed into her hands.

When it was over, she felt better. "Must be ready for the rag or something." And she sprinted the rest of the way home as if it had never happened.

CHAPTER 3

T he phone woke her. Hannah jumped, every nerve alerted. "Goddamn telephone. Hello." She stretched, trying to wake up and calm down simultaneously.

"Are you still alive?" Her friend Agatha's Australian richness warmed her ear.

"I'm not sure. How was your weekend?" Hannah relaxed.

"Oh, God. Shocking. Don't ask."

"I'm asking. Listen, you should have seen *me* Saturday. There I was, in my dressing room, getting ready to go to dinner with my father and I'm trying to decide what to wear and I'm saying things to myself like 'I wore the red dress twice last month and I haven't worn the black one in a year, I look better in the red one, but the black one will feel bad, so I'd better wear the black one."

They laughed.

Hannah sat up. "So how *was* your weekend? Didn't you see that gorgeous antique dealer?"

"Yes, darling. Very gorgeous, he hit me in the eye and I've got a shiner and my shock therapist told me that I'm the *only* patient that his 'treatment' hasn't worked on and that I'm potentially suicidal and he won't even charge me and good-bye."

"He deduced all that from watching you eat Hershey bars?"

"Oh, God knows."

"Agatha, now, seriously, what do you mean he hit you in the eye, you mean he slapped you? Was he drunk?"

"Well, I took him to a very In Bel Air dinner thing, all terribly chic fags and exiled Arab princes, and he seemed to really enjoy himself and then we left and he said something about someone putting their hand on his knee and I was teasing him and I said, 'Well, darling, if you didn't like it you could have removed it' and splat, he socked me. *Closed* fist, with a ring on, and I made him get out of the car. You should see me! Then I went home and I kept thinking about what my shock doctor said and I was afraid I might be 'overcome' and jump out the window."

"Now, listen to me. That doctor doesn't have a Chinese clue about you. Forget it. You are an ace survivor."

"Oh, yes, darling, I know. Actually it was hilarious. There I was with these wires hooked all over my chest and this Snickers bar in front of me and he'd electrocute me or whatever you call it and then I'd leave, hit the nearest market and buy twenty Snickers bars. And the next day I'd go in very upset and tell him that it was not working and he'd say, 'You think you've got troubles,' and he'd tell me the boring story of his misspent life. I had *my* pen and paper out, my dear."

They laughed a long time, building strength, laughing in shots of oxygen and courage and self, their ritual beginning to each new week.

"Agatha, now, really are you okay?"

"I'm fine, darling."

"Are you sure?"

"I'm sure."

"Really?"

"Yes. Really. Enough of that, what did you do, besides placate your party clothes?"

Hannah smiled, filled with love and compassion for this woman. They had been friends for a long time, building a nest of companionship out of forgiveness and acceptance. They lived lives that had nothing in common but their mutual dissatisfaction with the routes they had chosen.

Hannah had been attracted to Agatha's freedom. No children, no husband, living in a world of martini lunches, summers in Italy and fancy French dinners. But as the years had passed, Hannah saw more of the emptiness and tension, the invisible trap that held her friend and prevented her from growing up and letting go of the illusion that she was free. Agatha performed for the buyers of the French dinners and airplane tickets much as Hannah performed for the approval of her father and husband. And she saw this about her friend and was afraid to tell her, so she pretended not to know it and in so doing, weakened their bond.

"*Now*, one last time, are you really okay?"

Agatha sighed. "Oh, yes, darling. A bit of the old panic. I had one of those awful spells. My head was floating above me, I was at a cocktail party and I had to put my head between my legs to keep from fainting."

"That's all anxiety."

"Oh, I guess. I just want to run away from this whole mess of a life. I haven't got a dime and everyone thinks I'm still a marquesa. I am over-imaged, my dear. I'm sitting here trying to figure out ways to do telephone sales for the blind or embezzle some more from my ex, and people are asking me for funding to start motion picture companies! And I refuse to get a job. I cannot do it. Coffee and doughnuts, nine to five, water coolers, shocking! What I need is a fifty-year-old fag who has ten million dollars and wants to marry for friendship. I feel so trapped. I want to be free of all this hustling for a buck, trying to make deals for someone's movie, someone's book, someone's cock. I just want to get out."

Hannah sighed. She had heard Agatha's litany so many times and nothing ever changed. Because she did not truly want it to, because, like herself, Agatha had nothing to replace it with.

"Oh, God, it all just exhausts me," Agatha sighed. "I just want to go away, get out of this awful city and retire to a cottage in Ireland where I can be all alone. I don't want to talk to anyone. I just can't be bothered. All I want is enough money to live, my candy bars, lots of vodka and maybe my vibrator. No, maybe not even THAT." Hannah yawned, stretching her arms, releasing morning tension. "Sounds serious."

"Not to worry, darling. Let's have lunch Friday. I'll be better by then, as long as I don't take my glasses off. You won't believe my eye, it looks like the inside of an eggplant."

"Terrific. I'm making a mercy visit to my aunt Louise Friday morning, sort of a Halloween present. Lunch will give me something to look forward to. Take it easy today. Call if you need anything."

"I'll be fine, darling, see you then, bye."

Hannah put down the phone, sighed and went in to placate her bathrobes.

CHAPTER 4

If rain is a release, an eruption of the sky's emotion, then fear is a mist. A vapor clinging to our lives, and we half-consciously move through it, swatting out compulsively, waving it away, moving through perennial spider webs, searching for hideous creatures that live there and finding only angel hairs. Fear is a mist, all right. A taste in the mouth. A shadow making familiar forms ominous. A word.

Murder. Kidnapping. Mutilation. These are not the words of the enlightened classes. In the world of $400,000 homes, border-smuggled maids, Jacuzzis, one foreign sports and one family car, private nursery schools, tennis lessons, classes in wok cookery, these words do not exist.

Cancer. That word comes in. Not a person *with* it, not a formed fear, "*You* have IT," but the word is permitted.

Adultery; that one comes in floating free, misting the air, hazing the happy-couple eyes, moistening the hands, "Does he?... would she?"...then neatly, seeing only angel hairs, it disappears back into the mist with the other spiders.

But the word is in. It is an okay word in the dinner party world. Auto accident is allowed. But acid in the face is unthinkable. Neurotic and depressed are even chic. Schizophrenia and suicide, however, do not happen here.

A statement such as "I was so tense about the party I took two Valium," is perfectly all right. But "I was so strung out I fixed twice before the caterer came" isn't.

Colds, flus, cystitis, hepatitis, hysterectomy, vasectomy are all perfectly fine health problems.

Paralysis, amputation, syphilis, blindness, deformed child, however, cannot occur.

People are allowed to die. If they are very old. They are also allowed heart attacks, preferably if they fully recover.' They cannot, however, expect to be treated as before; eyes will ever wander toward the poor chest muscle as if they can see inside, as if while watching, it may just suddenly—stop. People never forget other people's wounds.

The Let's Pretend people do not die violently. No fratricide. No child beating. No crimes of passion. There is no drunken raging between adults, no punching of one's love object; no evil blue-collar things.

Not long ago in a very exclusive area of Los Angeles at approximately 1 a.m. on a summer night, a gunshot crashed through the air above the weatherproofed rooftops. People woke up, looked around, saw they were not affected and returned to bed.

Soon the police came. Low-flying helicopters streaking through the anemones, screeching wheels and motorcycles, all landed like night creatures on the freshly tarred driveway of an American dream house.

The family that had lived so comfortably within consisted of two healthy teenage daughters, one tweedy, tennis-playing mother and a successful, appropriately authoritative dad.

They were envied. They were considered totally acceptable. On the night in question, Dad, the *real* Dad, the black poisonous Dad that lived inside the angel hairs, had entered his daughters' room while they were at the movies. He had gone through their drawers, pushing moist hands between baby-doll nighties, his hairy fingers crawling through their most private places, and he had found things.

A funny cigarette. His oldest daughter's diary. Baby-elimination pills. Having found his weapons, he crawled out of the drawer and, sitting down between their Princess telephone and Snoopy pillows, he began to read. And as he read, the poison, stored for so long in self-protection, began to move upward.

He read about the boys they had "screwed," and the joints they had smoked, and the pills they had popped. He read his daughter's soul thoughts, her hatred of him, her fears, her sex growing within her and coming forth in dreams and bathrooms, and about the boys. The boy parts he re-read. And the poison moved and the pressure grew and then he waited.

At eleven o'clock his girls came home. Flushed, jeans clinging, blond hair flapping. Two pretty, unwinding young girls of fourteen and fifteen. And the poison came.

The mother, not unloving but caught too long ago in the froth of her own fears, cowered, sobbing her helplessness, as he stripped his girls, ripping the hand-embroidered T-shirts, humiliating their new body pride with words and fists. He blackened their eyes and slashed their breasts with his elegant belt buckle. And he tore up the diary and took the pills, and then he locked them in their room.

And, the poison released, he went to bed.

At 12:43 a.m., his firstborn child crawled out of her pink-curtained window and made her way around to where the spare key was hidden in the tulips. She entered her home, a stranger now, and crept down the hall to the room where her parents lived their night lives. Without a sound she opened the door and entered. Hanging in the room, heavy with the breathing of middle-aged slumber, was something shapeless, cooling the child into a new being, icy and exquisite and beyond fear. She took his gun, rested it between his hooded eyes and pulled the trigger.

They took her that night. Out past the basketball hoop and the bicycle rack and the agony noises within, into the black-creatured night, leaving everything changed there forever.

The neighbors shook their heads and, seeing they were not affected, went back to bed, and the myth returned with morning coffee.

At four o'clock in the afternoon on the Monday before Halloween, the phone rang and Hannah, dripping from the bath, ran to answer.

A voice light and girlishly high, yet not a young voice, asked for her husband.

"He isn't in right now, if you leave your number I'll have him call you back." Hannah was polite, but something tightened in her throat.

The voice was teasing, playing with the communication as if the telephone, providing total intimacy and the protection of distance, were fueling the caller with some luscious sense of power. "Oh, wellll, thaat's a shame. You just tell *Nick* that Maria called, sweetie, he knows the number."

The phone closed on Hannah. The voice, a presence now, the sound of a demented child—hung.

Hannah realized her heart was pounding. There was something in that voice cruder than anything she had ever heard.

She stood, beads of sweat popping across her forehead like dime-store pearls, her chest tight and her heart pounding in her throat, holding the phone for a long time.

One hour later, it happened again.

"Hello," Hannah answered the phone, off guard.

The voice, even slower and more babyish. "Hello, *Hannah*, this is Maria. Please have Nick call me."

"Listen, I don't know who you are or how you know our names, but I'm sure my husband doesn't have your number."

The voice cut in excitedly, like a child teasing, wanting to hurt, to say forbidden things. "OH, he do, he do, he do know."

Hannah hung up quickly as if listening longer could do her some terrible harm.

The thought that Nick was having an affair flew in half-wishful fantasies through her mind.

Then I could leave.

The words hit and bounced at her in quickly repressed panic.

When her husband came home, they discussed it, thought it strange and watched the phone. But no calls came. And Hannah forgot the voice. But the voice didn't forget.

The calls began around Halloween. A ghost, a misty ghost was taking shape now over Hannah's world. Over the family car; over the rose bushes and under the beds, all the ghosts inside the lies of all the unaffected lives, all the wood-knockings and "Let's not even think about it" 's, a ghost sat down for a rest on Hannah's life.

CHAPTER 5

▰◣▱◣▰◣▱◣▰

Donna Summer swung out, swung out, full and bright, filling the lights and whirling digits of the mechanized miracle; sexy Summer at 7 a.m. more of an intruder than the alarm bell. "Oh, shit." Hannah's first thought was the same every weekday morning.

No more sleep, no more hiding in my electric womb.

Arms stretching, husbands and wives groping toward consciousness to digital timepieces and the blues, groping their way out of cozy places, separated, awake as in sleep, the way only most intimately acquainted people can separate. Stumbling over slippers to separate sinks, separate toothbrushes, separate rituals. Washing or creaming. Shaving or eye dropping, deodorizing, deep breathing, showering, peeing, gas escaping, separate morning worlds, connected by barely focused eyes and habit.

Hannah rolled over and touched her husband's broad, pillow-clutching shoulders.

"Honey, the alarm went off." He remained motionless. Waking up was not one of Nick's favorite experiences. It worried Hannah because she knew him so well and the more he resisted facing the day, the more unhappy he was with his lot.

He had deserted his dream and lost himself, and now he worked in the shadow of her father, carrying the burden of three dependents like a cement-filled briefcase he could not set down. They pretended that it was temporary and that as soon as he put some money together again, he would produce a film and they would be off. But there had been too many deals and too much of other people's money lost, wasted (including her father's, though of this they never, ever spoke), and he had lost his faith in himself and he was afraid to risk anymore. And there was jealousy. Because she worked at what she loved and he didn't.

Hannah lay beside him, yawning and wanting to zip them up in the lazy, warm, king-sized escape machine and sleep away all the unsettling thoughts. But she was afraid to do that, too.

"Nick, come on, honey. You promised you'd drive Neilie to school."

"Okay, okay." He sat up quickly, swinging his heavily muscled legs over the side of the bed and rubbing his eyes with his hands.

If I'd been coached early enough I could have played pro football. She swallowed hard, watching him, feeling guilty for expecting him to meet the requirements of their life, longing for him to be happy, to come home whistling, like he had in the beginning, full of ideas and energy for the future. It was gone now. He did what he had to and she did what she had to, but the energy was dead in it.

She hid in the children and yoga classes and her work, and he hid at the piano and on the tennis court, and sometimes he hid in depression and liquor and she could not reach him or help them at all.

Anger flooded her. She was still the good girl, getting up on time, paying the bills on time, never missing a deadline or a dinnertime or a storytime. He missed lots of things, but then he wasn't trying to be perfect. She knew that somewhere deep inside he blamed her for the turns his life had taken, and so she spent her faltering energy, trying to make it up to him and asking for as little as possible. But lately she felt bullied and angry and so it wasn't working.

Nick stood up without speaking and made his way wearily to the bathroom. Hannah followed behind, feeling anger and sadness pushing at her heart.

"Oh, damn, Nick, you flushed the toilet."

"Sorry, I forgot." Her husband stumbled into the shower.

Private joke. Neilie had been trained in a moment of sheer parental brilliance to listen for the toilet flush as a sign Mommy and Daddy were receiving. She had obeyed impeccably, passing the knowledge on to little Charlie, who wandered now about the kitchen, toast and bananas squeezed in his fat little fingers, muttering, "Mommy flush, Daddy flush," his eyes wandering up to the ceiling as if waiting for a visitation.

They had heard.

Two blue-eyed, jam-smeared faces peeked around the door.

"Mommy! Daddy!" Neilie burst in. "We was watching 'The Brady Bunch' and Charlie spilled his milk all over the place! I told Tina to spank him, but she didn't understand. He's a big pain in the ass."

"It runs in the family." Hannah laughed, always loving the first moment of their morning meetings so full of a new day, *all* of them in wonder that they had been allowed to wake up one more time, all the anxieties of the night, the fears of unconsciousness, chair shadows, witches in the bathroom, fire, burglars, maniacs, heart attacks, blanket electrocution, all the fleeting night thoughts of child and adult had been conquered. HEY GUYS, WE MADE IT! WE DID IT AGAIN! The feeling came with the fresh, day-greeting baby faces.

They sat on the bath stool watching as Hannah sucked in air, raising her arms in yoga breathing and inhaling her never quite sufficient breath and the oxygen releasing her from the night memories and freeing her to face the new day.

"I can do that, we do that stuff at school." Neilie was down, her tiny muscles reaching in imitation. Charlie followed, crashing headfirst in a heap. "Mommy, wash dis, dis, Charlie dis." Neilie and Hannah laughed.

"He's a cute little bugger, isn't he?" Neilie, picking up the big world words, allowing herself respite from the ever-present indignity of Charlie's birth.

"I want a penis! I want to be a big, mean boy! I want a different baby! Mommy, can I wear a Pampers?" Baby talk returning and bed accidents. A child fighting with her anger, her displacement; lashing out in overburdened moments. "I hate Charlie! Even when I *like* him I hate him. I wish he was dead. Can't he live outside? Can't you just sell him and I hate you! You are the most horrible Mommy in the earth and you don't love me at all; nobody loves me!"

Hannah, feeling her pain, remembering her own, now covered in humor. Words that made people laugh. "Listen," she had said to a psychiatrist and his wife at dinner one night, "what the hell can I say to Neilie about being nice to a little brother and sharing and we love you both equally, but in different ways and all that crap? I mean, I'm thirty-two years old, been in therapy, the whole potato, and every time my brother walks into a room, I think, what did they need *him* for."

Love for her daughter flooded her. "Give me kisses! I want some kisses, quick! quick!" Neilie hugged her and they kissed, noisy wet lips smacking. Hannah sniffed in the lovely jelly smells of her child. "Charlie, kiss...kiss me, Mommy!" She embraced him, feeling Neilie stiffen slightly, trying to juggle both, equal but separate, like husbands and wives and toothbrushes.

In the morning paper that Friday was a small story that Hannah clipped for her idea file. Throughout the morning the article moved up into her thoughts will-lessly, fueling the uneasiness that had shadowed her all week.

The story was one of those emotional recaps. A fresh look at dead gossip. A pain-welled tidbit. This one churned up the "accidental death" years before of Christina Onassis's mother. The elegant wife of a Greek shipping hotshot, former wife of THE Greek shipping hotshot, had died in Paris at age unstated "Due to edema in the lungs." The woman, still young, stunning, moneyed beyond meaning, had (between the lines) ended herself. The fact being, rich, fortyish lungs do not swell to extinction unaided.

The year before, her only son had died hideously, his brain

destroyed, leaving only a puppet's body jerking at life for a few soul-screaming days. And then, some two months before her own, mysterious "death," her only living child, the heiress, the plump, unproud Greek girl who had surgically re-created herself in the image of a nubile jet starling, had taken a massive overdose of sleeping potions. She recovered, but Mother did not. No more sable coats. No more Patino Balls. No more Rothschild weddings. No more skiing in Gstaad. No more summer nights in the Mediterranean. No more Dior. No more offspring to watch pushing forth toward perfectly planned lives. No more baby boy. No more shining-eyed daughter. No more Mother. Mother had had enough. She chose to swell. To surrender to the obesity of panic begun in the astonishing smack of the world on their gilded lives. Begun with the overwhelming knowledge that there was no place to hide. Helpless as a Mexican peasant squatting in the mud before a raging hurricane, the Lady had watched the gilding flake and fall off. Money, beauty, power, HA, HA, HA, life said. YOK, YOK, YOK. Ghosts form anywhere.

The story chilled her, pushing at the edge of consciousness, making her feel vulnerable, wood-knocking against the possibilities of the dark side of life and praying silently for protection, for her children.

And the memory of the caller came back.

She put on her makeup and pulled her car out into the late October sunshine.

She drove too fast, swishing down Melrose Avenue past the Blue Whale, bastion of overpriced furniture and Italian bath fixtures, and the two famous restaurants with unlisted phone numbers, and the continually changing rows of overpriced boutiques featuring punk-rock chic and intimidating saleswomen, and the antique shops spilling their aging wares onto the sidewalks, and whirled right on Fairfax Avenue, almost hitting a tiny old lady lugging a weather-beaten wooden shopping cart and causing her heart to jump. "Your nerves are definitely shot, dear girl," she said aloud to soothe herself as she parked her shiny white Mercedes behind her uncle's respectable powder-blue Chevrolet and braced herself for whatever awaited her.

Her aunt was standing on the porch, her dyed jet-black hair hidden under curlers and sleeping cap, revealing only perfectly waved bangs, her face carefully made up. She was wearing what Hannah called "the uniform," a flower-blossomed housecoat, seamed nylons and gold slippers, and she stood with her back to Hannah intently gazing at herself in a hand-held mirror.

"Hi, Louise."

Her aunt gasped, almost dropping her looking glass. "Oh, my, Hannah, you frightened me. I didn't sleep all night and I'm very nervous this morning. Look at all these new wrinkles! Every night of sleep lost is right here on my face."

"Louise, your skin is perfect, I've got more wrinkles than you do, for godsakes."

"Oh, Hannah, don't be silly. You have beautiful skin. Just like Momma's. Your grandmother had the most wonderful skin in the world. At eighty-six she did not have one line on her face. I used to have the same skin, but this insomnia just destroys your complexion. You know the European women have much better skin because they sleep more. Sophia Loren sleeps ten to twelve hours a night. I read all about it in the *Enquirer*, Estelle gave me the article. And now, on top of everything, two punkers moved in across the street and they play that horrible music all night long." Her aunt sighed deeply several times. Hannah sighed with her.

"Well, as long as you're up, why don't we go inside and have a cup of coffee? I brought some new pictures of the children and one of my stories. It's in a magazine."

"Oh, Hannah, that's so nice. I invited Estelle over to see you. You know how sensitive she is. If she woke up and saw your car here and I didn't invite her, she'd be sick for a week."

"I thought you weren't speaking."

"Oh, we made up. She's got a new boyfriend, so she's not so touchy these days."

Hannah followed her aunt inside; she blinked, her eyes fighting to adjust to the perennial twilight of her aunt's heavily draped living room.

Everything in sight was shrouded in plastic, giving the room the feeling of a department-store storage vault. Hannah's heels dug into the plastic floor runner as she made her way awkwardly across the sacredly protected lime-wool shag carpet to the plastic-slipcovered, mauve-nylon couch. The walls were filled with her aunt's memories. Nude women with hair flowing backward from their idealized brows into the wind, curving into tree branches. Voluptuous nymphets chased stags across black-velvet backgrounds.

The paintings were part of Louise's "other" life. The brazen life of her young womanhood that Hannah had never seen. The days of Louise's vitality and independence. A raven-tressed, ivory-skinned temptress, painting black-velvet beauties in the nightclubs of Los Angeles. Everything in the room was the past. Fifties moderne furniture with sexual limbs, and lamps with forties ruffled shades and half-nude warriors supporting the sixty-watt headdresses. Pictures of Louise and Marvin and Hannah's grandparents in their prime filled the mantel. The only concessions to the march of time were the overlarge floor-model color TV that served as Louise's only connection to the outside world, and her massive white freezer (which she kept in the bedroom—stocked for famine or nuclear war).

"Everything's such a mess, I just don't have time to clean up anymore." Her aunt picked knitting needles and water-color brushes off the dining room table, sighing more deeply still, making Hannah light-headed with empathy.

"How's Uncle Marvin?"

"Tired."

"How's Lance?"

"He's putting on a Wild West beauty contest. He was such a creative little boy. I lost my health trying to teach him about art and he won't touch it now. My psychic says that in a past life he was a famous painter, maybe even Correggio. I don't know. He's in this show business thing. I never see his kids unless he wants something. He's going with two beauty contest winners. Shiksas." Louise sighed a perfect, oxygenated, resonating sigh. Hannah resisted doing the same.

The doorbell saved her.

"That's Estelle."

"I'll get it." Hannah jumped up to open the door. The light seared her eyes, causing her to squint.

"Hanny, baby, don't do that, it makes wrinkles! I always told your momma that, and she never listened and she had more little lines than any woman in the history of our family! Let me look at you! Look at that cute body. I wouldn't believe you had two children. Look at those beautiful breasts. Come in the bathroom and let me see them. You wear a bra don't you? You'll sag to your belly knot if you don't." Estelle ran her smooth, white, hand-buffed nails down Hannah's chest.

"Estelle! Stop that! You're embarrassing me."

"Don't be so silly! I've been watching you shake your little tushy and touch your little love button since you were two days old. Come on, let me look at you."

"I'll send you a Polaroid. Now stop it! Uncle Marvin's here!" Hannah trudged backward, toward the safety of Louise's perking coffeepot, her cheeks flushed.

Estelle followed, wiggling her pedal-pushered legs and ballet-slippered feet across the runner like a hula dancer on the sand. Her lacquered orange hair stood high over her delicate face, allowing no movement or connection with the rest of her. Her face smiled, her hips waddled, her tiny belted waist twisted, her halter-topped breasts jiggled, but her hair sat, frozen above her like a judge of the remains, unforgiving and unyielding.

Louise was a brilliant cook. It always astonished Hannah that somehow, in the middle of all the fey dialogue and apathy, absolutely succulent and thoughtful food would appear. The coffee was brought steaming in chicory and cinnamon harmony, and three exquisite coffee cakes that somehow in the middle of one mystical insomniac night she had managed to throw together.

Her aunts made no sense to her. They were always one step beyond her reach, flying above her, layered in endless yards of gauze, always one roll away from discovery. She knew only that they were truly eccentric, truly selfish and truly harmless. Manipulative and childish, but basically well-meaning, not negative and resentful like Sophie and Ethel, but also not in touch with any known landing gear either.

The three white-skinned women sat in shadows, sipping coffee and nibbling sweets.

"How's that gorgeous Nick?"

"Fine, Estelle."

"And Neilie and Charlie-Cake? I haven't seen them in so long."

"I know. I'm sorry. We've all been so busy and mornings are really best for them to visit..."

"Oh, Hanny, you know I'm not up mornings. Today is special because my hair lady is going away and she can't take me tonight, so I made myself get up, but I'll pay for it tomorrow."

"Maybe you could take a nap this afternoon." Hannah shifted effortlessly into their reality. She did it with all of her relatives, suspending herself to make things work. There was no other way to be there.

"No! Not right after I have my hair done! It flattens it."

Louise sighed. "No one's eating the prune cake."

"Louise, if I eat the prune cake my tummy will run all day and besides it's too fattening. You know I only eat one meal, I shouldn't be here at all, I'm never even up yet."

Hannah cut in, sonar instinct sensing trouble between these two high-strung siblings. "Louise told me that you're seeing someone. What's he like?"

"Oh, he's real cute." Estelle grinned, poking her red tongue over her lips like a happy kitty. "He's about six-two and he's got a real good build, his hair's thinning out a little, but he's a great dancer. I met him at my club. He's a taxi driver, but he's going to night school and studying real estate. He thinks I'm thirty."

Hannah choked on her coffee. "How old is *he?*"

"Twenty-six. But he looks older." Estelle wiggled back and forth in her seat, pleased with her confession. "He asked me to go steady, but I don't know. Next thing he'll want to move in or something, and I could never do that! Already he wants to come over when it's my newspaper time. I told him that I have my routine and I'm a very nervous person and it upsets me to have my schedule mixed up, but you know how men are. They all think with their thingies."

Hannah blushed. Louise did not respond. Louise never paid any attention to Estelle. "I should have used peaches. But it takes so long to peel them, I'm just too tired to peel them."

"How's your daddy, Hanny?"

"Fine."

"Does he have a girl friend? You know he's Scorpio like me and we need our...you know."

"I know." Hannah sighed on her own. Time to go, Hannah, they're rubbing off.

"Oh, dear. I didn't realize how late it was. I have someone coming for lunch, I've really got to go."

"But you haven't seen Uncle Marvin yet. I'll wake him up."

"Oh, Louise, please don't. He's worked all night. Just tell him I sent my love. I'll see him next time."

She was on her feet before they could resist. Just move toward the door in a straight line, leaving no options.

"I left the pictures and things on the coffee table." Her aunts followed behind her like two pet Poodles, leaping about her, waiting for a pat, a biscuit, a breath of life.

She gave it by being their only niece and a memory of themselves, and because she knew this, she was gentle with them. "You both look so gorgeous. I love you." She kissed their upturned cheeks and moved out of their white-armed grasp back into the sunlight.

"The trouble with Gordon is simply that his cock is always getting in his way." Agatha passed Hannah a large breast of chicken and deftly picked up a menacing kitchen knife, whacking away at huge juicy tomatoes with calculated relish.

"For chrissake, Agatha, he's sixty-five years old, you'd think he'd put it back in his pants already." Hannah offered a bowl.

"Darling, at his age, it hardly matters where he puts it."

They giggled, biting on chicken legs in Hannah's kitchen like two teenage girls sneaking a smoke.

"Is someone writing this down? Someone should be writing this down!" Hannah put the plates on a tray and carried it to the breakfast room table.

"I tell you, I hate them all, I really do. They're all horrors. Remember that psychiatrist I told you about that I thought was so marvelous?"

"You mean the one who whines about his children not loving him all the time, the one who's taken you out for three months and never tried to screw you...THAT marvelous one?"

"THAT is what I liked about him." They giggled again, stuffing chicken in their mouths.

"Anyway, he called last week and invited me to a lecture he was giving and then to dinner. So there I was, you know me, with everything I own on my back. I dragged out the sables, the emerald ring (which I most likely will have to hock next week), and he shows up in black tie looking *very* nice. We get into his car and in the back seat is a huge wicker basket with strange things sticking out. Some rabbity, furry-looking thing, gloves, hats and rubber balls. I thought, maybe they belong to his children.

"No, my dear, they were magic tricks! *His* magic tricks! We ended up in El Segundo at the Holiday Inn. I wouldn't go to El Segundo to pick up a check from Bernard Baruch, and there I was, sitting with a bunch of little old ladies, watching him do magic tricks. And badly! None of them worked, none of them!

"And all the way home he kept asking me over and over,

'Was I good? Was I really good? How did you like the one with the balls?' Of course I was furious. And he *knew* I was angry. We finally got home, no dinner, no drink, no apology, and he says to me, 'Aren't you going to ask me up? You don't want to sleep alone, do you, cupcake?' This horror had never even *kissed* me, and all of a sudden, when it's safe, when he KNOWS damn well I'll say no, he's Virgil the Virile. Then he can depart with his poor, faggy prick intact and say to himself, 'She's frigid!' I tell you I hate them all!"

Hannah smiled. "Gee, I should have invited my aunt Estelle, she *loves* them all. It would have made an interesting debate."

The phone rang.

"I'll grab it, Hannah, don't get up." Agatha reached behind her and picked up the receiver.

"Good afternoon."

Hannah reached for the phone, but Agatha waved her hand away. "Who is this?" Her eyes, stretched from laughter, relaxed inward. "Just a moment."

Agatha put her hand over the mouthpiece and leaned toward her. "There's a woman on the line. She sounds drunk or high or something. She said she wanted Nick or 'that bitch he's married to."

Hannah stiffened. The forgotten day lurching at her with breathless speed. "Agatha, quick, go pick up the extension." Hannah's throat felt tight with fear. "Hello." The laugh was high and forced like a mechanized doll. "Hello, bitch. Bet you forgot all about me. This is Mariiaa. Is Nicky home?"

"No, he is not, and he said if you ever called here again to call the police, which I fully intend to do."

The laugh again, filled with demented power, feeding on the fear, the impotence of its victim.

"Oh, you are a stupid cunt. The police!" The words spat back at Hannah, cutting her control. "The police! You don't even know who I am. I'm the one who's screwing your husband. Don't you know that? Are you so dumb? Don't you know he only stays with you because of your father's money? You dumb bitch. Don't you know he was with me last night? What a fuck."

Something was fighting for reason, something clicking, fighting for clarity, battling the fear, the horror of the words, yet drawn to the voice like a stone-headed bird to the earth and unable to pull away from the pain it was causing.

"My husband and I were together all day and *all* night, yesterday. I don't know why you are doing this, but you're obviously sick and you're a liar."

"Oh, you think so? You're just like your mother."

Hannah froze. Anger and apprehension, chilled suddenly by the word. "What did you say?"

The voice, knowing with rapacious animal instinct that it had revealed too much, moved away. "Oh, no, no, no, no, I'm not telling, you dumb dummy. You're in trouble now. Something terrible's going to happen to you and that STUD husband of yours." The laughter grew softer now, almost heavenly, almost sweet. And the phone went dead.

Firm footsteps came toward her. Agatha stopped in the doorway, her eyes wide, her mouth half-open in stunned acknowledgment of what they had shared.

"My God!"

They stood facing one another, not moving or speaking.

"She called before about a week ago. I just figured she was some drunk that Nick had done work for. I forgot about it."

"Oh, my God! That voice. And that laugh! That's the most frightening thing I've ever heard." Agatha sat straight down in a chair, her mouth still ajar, her eyes never leaving Hannah's face.

Hannah sat beside her, dazed and embarrassed, as if something unclean, something she was ashamed of, had been exposed. "It's so ugly. She sounds so crazy. Nick and I talked about it and he had no idea who it could be and GOD knows, I believe him. But this time..."

Then the impossible word, the crooked key unfitting, slid

quietly in. "Mother. She mentioned my *mother* like she knew her, Agatha."

"That's right. My God, that's right. How peculiar. How could she possibly have known your mother?"

"I don't know. I don't understand any of this. I'd better call Nick. We should do something, call the police, something."

"Darling, the police can't do a goddamn thing. You don't even know who it is. They probably get a thousand calls a day like this." Agatha reached for her hand, trying to bridge the helplessness of the moment.

"Call Nick. Maybe he can go over his client list, find a clue. Oh, God!" Agatha sat up straight. "Something else she said." She stopped, swallowing the discomfort of repeating the words. "She said Nick stayed with you for your father's money. How could she know anything about your father? And she said something was going to happen to you. Now that's a threat, that might bring the police!"

"I'd better call him."

Hannah rose and moved to the phone, dialing quickly with growing desperation, needing to make contact with someone who might bring her back to safety. She slammed down the receiver. "Dammit. Answering machine. No one's there."

"Do you want me to stay with you, in case she calls again?"

"No, no, I'll be all right. I'm sure she's harmless. I know you have a meeting. I'll be fine."

"My God." Agatha shook her head. "This is absolutely shocking."

"It's so ugly." Hannah repeated the word, deep embarrassment flooding her.

Agatha rose and kissed her cheek. "Take a Valium and go lie down, and for chrissake take the damn thing off the hook."

"I will. I'm sorry you had to hear that."

"Don't be silly. I'll phone you later. No, you phone me, keep it *off* the hook."

"I will."

She stood in the doorway waving away her friend, alone with something she did not understand floating around her like oil on water.

Hannah closed the door and went back to the kitchen, mechanically gathering greasy plates and glasses.

She looked at the phone, lifted it and placed the receiver on the sink. Then some undefined pulling, a scratching in her head, guided her back.

She recradled the phone and resumed her day.

CHAPTER 6

And in Miami today, a twenty-one-year-old college coed, deep in a coma for more than a year, has been sued for trespassing by a hospital seeking to evict her. The suit against the girl, who has been unable to hear, speak or see since a traffic accident last year produced extensive brain damage, is being brought by the hospital on the grounds that she has virtually no possibility of recovery or improvement, and therefore is wasting valuable space better utilized by other patients. The fact that her family's health insurance has expired and a debt of over $60,000 has accumulated is not a factor in their request that she be transferred to a nursing home, according to a spokesman for the hospital.

The spokesman went on to say, "With this kind of injury, if they don't wake up after a few months, that's it." Although two hospital committees have reached the same conclusion, Miss Freidman's mother refuses to accept the diagnosis. "At first her eyes were closed all the time. Now she opens them during the day and closes them at night. She certainly feels discomfort and pain. She can't tell you, but if you're in the room, you know," said Mrs. Freidman, "sometimes you can see tears in the corners of her eyes..." And in sports tonight...

"Mrs., Charlie no want eat y Neilie *tambien*." Hannah turned heavy-lidded eyes toward the voice moving through the darkness.

"That's okay. *Baños para dos, por favor, Tina. Yo no estoy buena. Por* favor. *Tengo dolor en mi cabeza, temperatura. Por favor."* Her voice wavered with the effort to talk, to reach unfamiliar words.

"Okay, Mrs."

The door closed.

Hannah tried to sit up, feeling numbed by the heat rising from her body like some alien presence. "Jesus, I'm so weak, I can't believe this." Her eyes, narrowed with fatigue, stared unconsciously at the powdered, pompous faces of the news team. The girl's face, looking like a picture from a college yearbook save for a small tube poking demurely from the entrance to her nose, faded from the screen. Hannah blinked slowly, as if all of her motions were being thwarted by the fever.

She's dead, only she feels pain. She's a huge, expensive, oxygenating vegetable. Can a vegetable trespass? Not a mark on her. Not a pimple. She cries and she can't blow her nose and she can't even die. And not a mark on her. Not a hair turned.

Hannah tried to sit up, stretching toward her pillows in defiance of her helplessness.

Bette Davis would sit up.

"Oh, Nick, please come home." She was crying now, all the tension and strangeness of the day surrounding her. "Please, come home."

She sobbed, tears turning hot and thick on her cheeks.

The phone rang.

She jumped now, like a battered fighter at the bell, reaching blindly, wanting only to still it.

"Hello."

"You said you were going to take the damn thing off the hook."

"I know. But I couldn't, just couldn't. I wanted to know who she was, couldn't help it, but now, oh, Agatha, now I'm getting scared."

"What's the matter? You sound awful. Did you take a sleeping pill?"

"Uh-huh. I...it was the strangest thing. I guess it's nerves, but she kept calling and I listened, and then she got really crazy and I couldn't listen anymore, and I took the phone off and I went to get Neilie at school, and while I was driving home, I started to get terribly ill, chills and everything, and when I got home I took my temperature and it was over a hundred and four from normal straight up, and I can't reach Nick, so I called the police and they said that someone will be out to take a statement, but I'm so weak. It's terrible." She was crying again, muffling the sounds with her hand.

"I'm coming over."

"No, no. Please! Nick will be home any minute. It's okay. It's just some of the things she said and I think I know who she is, not her name or anything, but why she's calling me." She stopped, suddenly cool. "I think she's someone my father was involved with. She's got to be." Hannah swallowed hard, the meaning of the words moving sluggishly through her aching, heavy head.

"Oh, my God, darling! It makes sense. That would *explain* how she knows about him and your mother and all that. How horrible."

"She said that I had destroyed her relationship with my father because I was jealous. Want to know *why* I was jealous? Because my father and I commit *incest* and *she* was a threat to our relationship!"

"I don't believe it. Was she drunk?"

"Hard to tell. She slurs some words, but she sounds so schitzy, that's what scared me." Hannah's stomach tumbled, nausea threatening to consume her. "She said she was going to throw acid in my face."

"Oh, my God! She's insane."

"And she said that she was going to kidnap Neilie. That she had hired someone to do it. I can't even talk about it anymore. I'm going to be sick."

"Hannah, please, darling. She's probably harmless. People who make threats like that never do anything. And the police are coming."

Agatha stopped, knowing that Hannah would not any more

than she herself find comfort in the comforting words. "Just what you needed, now. Those bastards! I told you, they're all bastards! Your father's cunt putting her sleazy little paws on your life."

The fever, fueled by rage at her father, made Hannah's head whirl, the room, the TV, Agatha's voice all flashing by and she, in dazed, apathetic confusion, like the comatose college girl, opening her eyes in the morning, waiting for someone to do something.

"What's so horrible, more horrible than my father knowing someone like that," she paused, fighting for control, "is that he would tell her about his family, about his *grandchildren*, our names, everything! And she wouldn't listen to me. She wouldn't believe that I hadn't done anything to her, that I didn't even know about her!"

"Now, listen to me. If Nick isn't home in fifteen minutes, you call immediately and I'll be over. Now, I mean it."

"I will, I promise. I just want to rest. I'm so woozy. If my fever gets any higher, I'm going to call the doctor. I'll call you later. Don't worry. Please don't."

Her voice trailed off, sleep grabbing at her will-lessly.

Hannah slept, dreaming of sleep. Sleep's beautiful, all curled up, not supposed to sleep with pillows, bad for your posture. Not supposed to sleep on your stomach, makes wrinkles. Bunch of crap, lots of pillows, smash your cheeks into lots of pillows, curl your legs in a ball. Only way to sleep. "Sleep on your back without a pillow. See how much better your posture is, see how much better your skin looks!" Takes all the pleasure out of sleeping, no place to crash. Then sleep's another fucking discipline. No place to curl up and give in. "Too much sleep isn't good for you!" People brag about not doing it. "Hardly ever sleep, never touch the stuff." I want to just sleep and sleep and sleep.

"What in the hell is going on here!"

Light clicking. Presence in the room. Someone from the other world cutting through the palladium.

"I called you a dozen times! First the line was busy, then it was off the hook. What are you doing in bed? Tina said you were sick, Neilie said you were crying. What in hell is going on?"

"Thank God you're home. I forgot about the phone. I was furious with you. I needed you and you didn't come and you never called me back. I forgot about the phone."

Hannah struggled to sit up, her head pounding with fever and the loss of her shield.

"Nick, that crazy lady, remember the one that called and asked for you? She called again today. Agatha was here. She called all day. She said she was going to throw acid on me, she said she was screwing you and that she was going to have Neilie kidnapped. She's someone my father knows, I'm sure of it. She talked about my mother and she said, you won't believe it, she said I destroyed her relationship with my father because we sleep together. MY FATHER AND I SLEEP TOGETHER! And she wouldn't listen to me, and then I got sick and I couldn't get you and I was so scared. I called the police and I took the phone off the hook and then I fell asleep and you weren't here and..."

"Okay, okay, Hannah, calm down. Stop a minute. Give me a minute to get hold of all of this." Nick sat down on the bed, not touching her or looking at her, staring ahead as if waiting for an answer to drop down before him.

"That son of a bitch."

"Who?"

"Your father. I knew it. I had a feeling when you got that first call that it was someone he knew. That son of a bitch. Now *we've* got it, his shit and *we've* got to clean it up."

"Nick, please, I can't handle that now. I'll break apart. If I think about him, I'll come apart. Let's just try to figure out what's happening, what to tell the police. They didn't want to come, they know it's a waste of time."

"But they *did* say they'd send someone. After all, she made *threats*. They threaten the Kennedy kids and the whole fucking Secret Service shows up!"

"Excuse me, Mrs., someone at the door, *para listed*." Tina stood awkwardly in the doorway, sensing trouble. Trouble that could affect her by touching the house, the walls, the air. Trouble that settled on every spoon and every chair, making the dog twitch, the children cry, the "help" tiptoe about, trying not to see anything, trying not to notice.

"Oh, God, Nick! Maybe it's her!"

"Just relax. Don't move." He rose and went to the window, pulling back the shutters, his face rigid. "Hannah, it's a deliveryman, it's okay. I'll be right back." Hannah sat forward. The need to feel strong, to be in control, mixed with the mystic, euphoric power of physical illness, making her almost godly and regal in the cloak of her drama. She stood up, bracing herself with her hands, and moved cautiously toward the bathroom. Cold water slapped at her face, entering her mouth, sweetening her. She combed her hair and put on lipstick; rituals of the normal, everyday world. She put on a fresh gown, splashing perfume and feeling sickened by the smell. Then she made her way back, holding on to closets and tables for support, fluffing pillows and straightening sheets, changing this place that had let her curl, let her mess and roll and rest. She made it neat and impersonal. Like lovers leaving a motel room, discarding their intimacy in the doorway.

Her husband walked toward her, holding a paper in his hand, his face tense with anger.

"What is it? Who was that?"

"It was a telegram."

"Who is it from?"

"Hannah, it's from 'your father's friend.' I don't think you should read it now. Wait till the police come."

"Nick, I've been listening to her all day. I'm not a child. I want to know what it says."

"Okay, honey." He stopped, not knowing what to do, afraid of her reaction, of what she might expect from him.

Hannah reached out and took the telegram, trying to stay calm.

She had spent so many years soft-shoeing between her husband and father, trying to make them friends, fighting her own truth to keep peace and terrified of confrontation between them, and now a phone call and a slip of paper threatened her entire structure; waves lapping against her sand castle wall:

> You have destroyed my life. You have destroyed your father's life. You are evil. You have killed our relationship. You are going to learn what that feels like. You think you have everything. But I'm going to change that. You just wait. You'll see.

"Oh, God, Nick, she really does want to hurt me. You see! It's not just some drunk. She wants me. She wants to hurt *me*\"

"Hannah, please! She probably just gets her rocks off this way. Just wait, let's talk to the police first. Let me get you some aspirin. You're sick and you're getting all worked up. Try to relax until we know something more."

She tried, knowing that her emotion was dangerous, knowing she should turn this conversation around away from inflammation.

He got up, sighing deeply, sighing not in surrender, but in acceptance of this new weight, this new pressure, pounding into their lives.

"This is all we need now. Things were just starting to settle down. Your mother, all that finally over, and our bills paid off, and now this. Shit." He turned from her and left the room.

Hannah was silent, relieved that the fire had not spread, deep sadness replacing the fear. And a shame. A sense of shame, harbored all day, harbored secretly all her life. A blot on her character, left by her makers. Bad stock. Crazy relatives. Diseased mother. Father who hid in closets, had hidden literally and otherwise in closets as long as she could remember. Hiding away behind his Italian suits, while the grown-ups took care of the mess. And she felt shamed. Hours passed in darkness. Sounds echoing upward, sliding under the door. Voices, soft sounds, drifting under like smoke through a needle's eye. Children laughing, music playing, plates being filled, lights clicking on and off. The sounds of day becoming night. The sounds of a family, peculiar to units of large and small people living together. Sounds that are missed. Sounds that grow up and leave; a well going dry. Sounds evaporating, bellwethers of change. Time passing. Growing old.

Family sounds hummed around Hannah, lying in darkness, sweating in the cold November night, buzzing in her ears. Lulling. Whispering, everything is fine, these are fine, safe family noises, not to worry. No ghosts here.

"Mommy, Mommy! There's two pleecemens here, great big pleecemens! And they got guns! Mommy, wake up. There's pleecemens in our living room. Daddy said to wake you up. Mommy, did you hit somebody? Are they going to take you at jail? Mommy! Mommy!"

Hannah woke. Head snapping up. Arms grabbing in the darkness for clothing, heart pounding in her chest. Neilie was holding her arm, eyes wide, tears starting to fall.

"Mommy, I don't want you to go in jail. Mommy, did you shoot someone?"

Hannah enclosed her, comfort passing simultaneously from one to the other. "No, sweetheart, the police are not going to take me to jail. I called them because someone was bothering us. They're here to help. There's nothing to be afraid of, bunny." Hannah kissed her daughter's cheeks. Baby tears, tastes of hot cream on her lips. She held her child, sniffing in her hair and the crease of her neck, like a sculptor gone blind, touching marble.

"Come on, baby, it's bedtime. Mommy and Daddy have to talk to the policemen and I'll tell you all about it in the morning. Let's go, you help Mommy, Mommy doesn't feel very well. Let's go down and get Tina."

"Okay, Mommy. Mommy, is that the whole truth? The pleecemens aren't going to take you away?"

"The whole truth."

The child and the woman moved slowly toward the door, leaning on one another.

"Hannah, this is Officer Williams and Officer Adams. I told them what I could, but since you're the only one that's talked to her, they need your statement."

Hannah sat down. The presence of these two figures, like visitors from another world, unsettling her. She felt very small and, she thought, guilty.

"I'll tell you all I can. I'm not feeling very well, I'm a bit woozy."

Shouldn't have said that, they'll think I'm drunk.

The two massive men sat across from her. Legs almost meeting chins. Two faces coated with indifference. One black man and one white man. A team. Lips set, guns and clubs hanging like sepulchral ornaments. Pads and pencils rigidly positioned on huge, angular thighs.

"Your husband says that you've been getting some threatening phone calls." The black officer spoke, pinning his eyes to Hannah without hesitation.

Fred MacMurray did it! I'm innocent. Innocent I tell you!

"Yes. I have. And I'm sure that I can find out who is doing it. I think it's an old girl friend of my father's, but he's out of town and I haven't been able to contact him."

"Well, until then, there isn't much we can do."

"But this isn't just an anonymous threat. She knows all about me and my family. She said she was going to throw acid in my face and she said that she had hired someone to kidnap my daughter. And she sounds very sick. And drunk or high or something. God knows what she can do. Look, look."

Hannah fumbled in the pocket of her robe, searching for the telegram. "Look! She sent this! Read this! How can we sit back and do nothing? She knows where we live, everything."

The black officer reached forward, avoiding her eyes.

Don't panic. Barbara Stanwyck wouldn't panic.

Nick watched her. All of them sat in diffident silence, waiting for the wrinkled yellow paper to be assessed. Hannah leaned forward, beginning to feel for the first time the full weight of the situation, sensing, before they spoke, that these paladins of the public good, this convoy roaming the night, allowing all the families to sleep snug in their department-store beds, were a lie. Knowing in her gut that this surety, this unwritten guarantee of impregnability that we create like some mythical black-shawled duenna, does not exist.

"Like I said before, ma'am, not much we can do, even if you know who she is. Well, you *can* file a report." He sighed at the numbing sameness of the speech, repeated countless times, while avoiding endless pairs of frightened eyes. "And she'll have to appear, but it will take weeks and then, to be perfectly frank, the judge will just slap her on the hands a little and tell her to stop. It really isn't worth your time."

She was all alone. Nick sat still, looking at his hands.

I am all alone.

She thought of her notebook.

No one is going to help me. No one can. No one.

"Of course, if she does anything, why, we can pull her right in."

Anger flooded her. "Oh, I see. You mean if she mutilates me or kidnaps my child or comes here drunk and shoots somebody, then something can be done."

The two heavy heads lowered, looking at their pads with distracting intensity.

"I'm afraid that's about it. But, like I said, if you can find out her name, why, you could file a report, but they'll probably just give her a warning and it will take a lot of your time. Why don't you just have your phone number changed?"

"That's fine. Except that she knows our address and if she is *not* just a nut, if she's dangerous, changing our number won't really eliminate the problem." She was starting to cry. Fever and frustration making her too vulnerable to perform properly.

Nick stood up, wanting, now that there was nothing to hope for from these men, to empty their lives of them.

"Okay, thank you, officers. If we get her name, we'll call you. There might be a warrant out on her or something. But we do want you to be aware of this situation. Just because we're not the Kennedys doesn't mean things like this can't happen and it is your job, after all, to try and prevent it."

The officers stiffened. Years of training working against their instinct to reply.

Hannah stood up, bracing herself with the arm of the chair, sensing his anger, knowing he would act out his helplessness on these safe victims, who would not strike back or lose control. "I thought that a kidnap threat was a criminal offense. My father has a lot of money. Someone could try to kidnap his grandchild, it's not at all unlikely that someone would do that."

"Well, you let us know if you find out who it is." The officers moved past them and out the door, relieved to be released from the emotions of strangers experiencing something they were not a part of.

Nick closed the door behind them and took her arm.

"Come upstairs, Hannah."

"Nick, they can't do anything. Nick."

"Come on now, get into bed, we'll talk about it in the morning. If she tries to come here I'll knock her down and sit on her till those jokers come back. Don't worry, we'll find out who it is and then we'll see. Your father may know, she's probably just a lonely old nut."

Her husband guided her up, and for the first time in years, she let him, trusted him, leaned on him without tension, step by step, back to the dark thrashing place she had lived this day in. He brought her three aspirin, watched her swallow; turned off her light and left her alone.

Sometime later, long after the murmurs of life below had ceased, as her husband lay sleeping beside her, she woke. She was ice cold, as if the fever had possessed and then rejected her. She lay there for several moments thinking about the voice and this thing, this untenable possibility that had entered the sanctity of her mind, loosening the moisture of fear she kept hidden there. She rose, stumbling over cast-off clothing, icy cold and sweating, eyes closed against the darkness, and made her way to the bathroom to be violently, uncontrollably sick.

CHAPTER 7

"Dad?"

"Yeah, hi, honey. I was going to stop by and see the kids yesterday, but we got back too late."

"How was the desert?"

"Good, good. Found a great little restaurant, if you get there before seven, you get a steak and a salad and a baked potato for five ninety-five, and it's more than you can eat. How are the kids?"

"Okay. Listen, I want to talk to you about something. We've, well, me, really, I've been getting some terrible phone calls and threats against me and the kids, and the lady that's calling, she seems to know all about you, and we had the police here last night and they weren't very encouraging. But they did say if we could find out who it was, they could try to do something. And I have a feeling it's someone you know."

"What kind of threats? What do you mean, *threats?*"

"Threats. What difference does it make? THREATS. Kidnap threats against the kids, threats against me, and she keeps saying that I destroyed her relationship with you. I think it's someone you know and if it is, I want the name, so we can call the police back. It's been a nightmare. I'm afraid to leave the house."

"Uh-huh, yeah, well, it's probably just some kooky broad, some drunk, I meet all kinds of broads. I wouldn't pay any attention to it."

Father of the bride.

"Well, I'm sorry to disagree, but it's my life and my children and I cannot afford to ignore it. So will you please try to think about it?"

"Yeah, yeah, okay, but I don't think it's anyone I know."

"Dad?"

"Yeah."

"Remember when I was in high school and you were involved with that woman, and she used to call Mother and she came to the house and we had her arrested? I was thinking about that today and I wondered if it could be her. She mentioned Mother, too."

Hannah felt her father's discomfort, could see his face through the phone, white-lipped and afraid. Her head swam with memories of his face at her bedside when she had the mumps and almost died, at her mother's funeral, hiding in the closet, in the hospital when Neilie was born.

"Nah, don't think so, she left the state. I haven't heard from her. Listen, you're getting upset over nothing. I said I'll think about it. I'll think about it. Tell Neilie I'll pick her up Saturday and take her to the ponies."

"Okay, Dad. Good-bye."

Small little bits and taps of feelings touched her. Moving here and there, up and down, in and out of her mind and body like dust in the wind, thrown confetti. Pricks and stabs of feeling, mild precursors, gentle tappings of pain, depression, despair, falling softly like petals from a ripening tree. Settling easily. Nothing chopped. Nothing jagged, nothing uncontrollable or sweeping. Still-functional annoyances. Angel hairs, those damn angel hairs. Pings and thumps and whispers of feelings dropping here and there, causing no permanent damage. Weightless tugs at the heart. Visible only if one was blessed, or cursed, with the tiny light, a sonar for the soul, charting endlessly the drops of pain, the burdens of consciousness. The trepidations of growth. Ping, flutter, pitter-pat. Hannah sat in silence listening to the street sounds, eyes edged with thought.

"Dad?"

"Yeah, hi, honey."

"I've had three more phone calls. She says she talked to you yesterday and she said that you told her not to call me because I was mentally ill. Is that true?"

"She's full of shit! I never said anything about you being mentally ill."

Spencer Tracy just died.

"Then, you *do* know who it is. You knew yesterday! You knew and you didn't tell me! You lied to me! It's that woman, isn't it? You knew and you wouldn't tell me! What kind of a father would do that! How could you do that?"

Hannah's heart hurt. She had never felt so betrayed or abandoned. Not even by her mother's death. Her mother had not left on purpose, not exploded the cocoon of her child-trust as if it were a passing balloon before a careless pin.

"She's harmless. She's harmless. Listen, now, listen! I appease her. She gets loaded and she calls me, and so I talk to her, to keep her quiet, so she doesn't bother anybody. If you call the police, she might get mad. If you let her talk, she's okay. I'm sorry about it. What do you want me to do? I haven't had anything to do with her in years, but when she gets on these jags, I talk to her so she doesn't bother anyone."

"Well, it isn't working anymore, is it? She's bothering *me*. You were trying to protect scum like that? She threatened your *granddaughter* and you wouldn't tell me her *name*! Do you know how that makes me feel about you? I can't believe it. I just can *not* believe it!"

"Okay, okay. I said I was sorry." Norman paused, his voice lowering defensively. "I thought I could get her to leave you alone, but she won't listen. She's harmless. She's just a lush."

"Give me her phone number and her name and her address."

"Uh, I don't remember her address, I have it somewhere."

"Give me her name." She was in charge again, like that long-ago night, and he did not fight her.

"Well, uh, she uses two or three names. I don't know which one she's using now."

"Give me all of them."

"Uh, let's see, Wanda Miller is her maiden name, and then sometimes she uses, uh, Mary Smith. I can't remember the other one."

"Phone number."

"Uh, I'm not sure. I think it's, uh, 545-2304."

"I'll hold on, while you get the address."

Hannah's hands were cold with sweat. The risk she was taking with the matchstick village inside which she and her husband had lived for so long overwhelming her.

"Okay, okay. Just a minute. Okay, here it is. Now, I don't know, she probably doesn't live there anymore, there was a bench warrant out for her and she's probably moved, but the only one here is one-five-four West Second."

"Los Angeles?"

"Yeah, yeah."

"Thank you."

"Listen, Hannah, you're just getting excited, she's just a drunken broad. She won't do anything."

"She already has, Dad."

CHAPTER 8

Control to Monorail I, "You are now leaving Fantasy-land, next stop Tomorrowland." Hannah and Nick gathered sweaters and tickets and anxious children and waited to enter the Magic Kingdom. A family. An impulsive outing. Pack up the children and flee from the trouble. No telephone. No forwarding address. Hot dogs and root beer and brass bands marching. Father and mother smiling, children laughing, they had raced away, seeking relief, a Walt Disney ending to their anxiety. A day in the Enchanted Kingdom, thick-scooped ice cream, Tom Sawyer's tree house, eyes pleading "Everything's gonna be fine."

When the Nicolis left Disneyland, it was after midnight and they drove home heavy-eyed with fatigue and depression. They had stayed long past pleasure, held by the escape and not wanting to return to the uneasiness of their overstressed daily life. Hannah sat beside her husband, solemn-faced and quiet. The children lay curled together, filling the leather-lined chariot with sweet, soft breathing.

The streets were quiet. Several teenage hookers lounged against the graffiti-decorated walls on Sunset Boulevard, night animals covered in sequins and Lastex shorts and face paint. Lately, Hannah had noticed that there were more and more young male hustlers working the East Sunset scene. Rosy-cheeked teenagers in skin-tight jeans and sleeveless T-shirts, thrusting their groins toward the late-night traffic. Hannah glanced at Nick, hoping he had seen, wanting to share the mood that held them but not having the energy to speak of it.

"Did you see those hustlers?"

"No."

"Strange times."

"Yeah."

They drove on in silence, lost in private places. When they pulled into their driveway, Hannah's stomach tightened. Something felt wrong. She got out of the car quickly, catching her sleeve on the door and pulling the door against her ankle.

"Ow." Tears formed in the corners of her eyes. "The nerves are definitely not good, Hannah," she whispered to herself. Neilie and Charlie allowed themselves to be lifted, carried off, sure of protection. Hannah and Nick walked together up their driveway, a child held by each of them, the parents processional. Nick opened the door, hoisting Neilie over his shoulder. Hannah followed behind, limping on her bruised ankle, her stomach still quivering with the sense of something out of order. They carried the sleeping babies upstairs, untying little shoes, unbuttoning small sweaters, and then it was done and they were free of responsibility till morning.

"Want some hot tea, honey?" Hannah moved toward the stairs, still restless.

"Good idea."

"I'll make a deal. If you'll run a bath for me, I'll make tea and toast and get the mail?"

"You've got it."

Hannah put on her robe and limped downstairs barefoot to the kitchen. She filled the kettle, carefully measured out cupfuls of fresh herb tea, popped two English muffins in the toaster and turned on the porch light. She opened the door and limped across the grass to the mailbox, fighting the anxiety still squeezing against her belly.

A neatly wrapped box with a carefully typed label addressed to her sat on top of a pile of advertisements for brush clearance and Books-of-the-Month and utility bills and a letter from her aunt Sophie and a reminder that she was due for a tooth-cleaning and an invitation to a gallery opening. There was no return address, and Hannah carried it back across the lawn, her knuckles clenched, holding too tightly to the unsolicited gift. She closed and locked the front door, turned off the light, turned off the kettle, took out the muffins, buttered them, put everything on a tray and carried it slowly upstairs. The bathroom door was closed and she could hear the bath water and the shower going at the same time. "What a waste of hot water," she mumbled to herself. She poured some tea and picked up the package, using the side of her fingernails to break through the tape. It took a long time. Beneath the brown postal wrapping sat an old fabric-covered box, smelling of mothballs and nicotine and filling Hannah's throat with apprehension. She was afraid to open this midnight surprise and yet she could not stop. She took the lid off carefully. Maybe it's a bomb. It could be a bomb, what was that movie? Someone got it, a letter bomb, terrorists use them all the time.

A small black bottle rested between two dime-store dolls. The dolls had seamstress pins stuck in the eyes and the hearts. The label on the bottle read LYE. Poison. Keep away from eyes and mouths. Fatal if swallowed. Keep out of reach of children.

Hannah screamed, knocking over her cup, spilling hot tea over her thighs.

"Nick!"

The shower ran on and her screams ran on. Screams of pain of body and spirit filling the cozy, well-decorated bedroom.

She ran down the hall, banging on the door, sobbing in terror. "Nick! Nick!"

Finally, it opened. Hannah collapsed against her naked, dripping husband, incoherent with pain and panic. "I burned my legs! I burned my legs! Nick, go look. On the bed. Go look!" She collapsed on the floor, holding her red, throbbing legs with her arms, sobbing uncontrollably.

Nick Nicoli crossed the beige-carpeted floor, leaving wet footprints like a Nordic explorer in the Arctic snow. He picked up the pieces of the box and stood, face blank, blue eyes blinking away the unacceptable reality, not moving. He walked back to Hannah without a word and helped her stand up. "Let me see your legs."

She obeyed, letting him sit her down on the toilet seat, opening her robe over the red flesh. He cared for her. Packing her legs with bags of ice, feeding her aspirin, calling the doctor.

She was calm now, teeth chattering with shock, but free of panic. Watching her husband, without a word, following his movements, trying to see what he was feeling, like a chastised child, not risking a question, wanting to apologize to him and not knowing how or for what, seeing him beside her the night Charlie was born, her nails digging into his forearms for twelve endless hours, sobbing on his shoulder the day her mother died. It seemed all to be her fault everything hard that happened. He was not happy and there was more mess and it was hers once again.

"The robe saved you. I don't think they'll blister, honey. The doctor said to keep the ice on and call him in the morning. Let's go to bed."

She nodded and let him carry her. Nothing remained of the surprise package and she did not ask any questions. He piled pillows neatly under her legs and wrapped the ice bags in towels and covered her up and kissed her good night. She was asleep instantly, but inside her sleep she heard muffled sobs escaping beneath the locked bathroom door. He never cries, she thought, finding the answer to her unasked question.

She awakened to find him gone. "Need some time alone," said the note he had left on his pillow. And so they had passed that awful night separated from one another, rather than wound together in comfort. She unwrapped her frozen legs, wincing in memory. The redness was fading. She was okay. "Sure I am," she whispered to herself. The package was nowhere in sight. She was no longer afraid of it, seeing it now in the clarity of morning light as a tool, a bargaining instrument to show the police and Norman that she was not just a hysterical woman, but had acceptable reasons for her emotion.

"See! See! Hear! Hear!" She wanted to leap into her car and race with her evidence into the police station, over to her father's palace. "Your honors, gentlemen of the jury, I am here to prove beyond a shadow of a doubt that Hannah Nicoli is not overreacting! Let the record show that she is not the recipient of bad genes or a DNA deficiency, but an innocent victim of circumstance." But she could not find the box anywhere. She took a cool bath, called the doctor, drove Neilie to school in her robe, came home, made coffee, fed Charlie and sat at the kitchen table, sorting the harmless mail abandoned in the panic of the night.

She opened her aunt's letter. "Mea culpa, mea culpa. What have I done now?" The only time her aunt Sophie wrote to her was when some infraction of her rules had occurred.

Hannah,

I hope you are not sick. We did not hear from you on Rosh Hashanah. Or Yom Kippur or your cousin Howard's birthday. We know that you and your father have busy lives, but families must stick together. If we don't have each other, what do we have? I know your mother was not religious, but your father knows better. Your uncle and I had your brother and you and your parents over every Passover for ten years. God knows we don't want to interfere in your lives, but a phone call or a note once in a while couldn't hurt.

Aunt Sophie

Hannah sighed. "Why me? She wouldn't dare send Allan a note like that or my father." She took a deep breath, let it out and picked up the phone, dialing slowly.

"Hello, Aunt Sophie, it's Hannah."

"Well, hello, stranger."

"I just got your note and I called to apologize. We've been under a lot of pressure and time has just run away from us. I haven't seen anyone in months, we totally forgot the holidays."

"You saw Estelle and Louise. I bumped into Estelle at the fish market last week."

"I just happened to be in the neighborhood, they do live much closer than you and Ethel, you know. Anyway, I am sorry. Why don't you and Ethel come for lunch next week? Maybe Estelle and Louise can come, too."

"Ethel and Estelle don't get along."

"For one lunch they can."

"I'm not one to tell others what to do. It will be nice to see you, either way. How are the children?"

"Just fine. How is Uncle Eddie?"

"His back is bothering him."

"Sorry to hear that. How are you?"

"Still having headaches."

"Sorry to hear that. How are Ethel and Simon?"

"We're not speaking, but I heard that he has bursitis in his shoulder."

"Sorry to hear that. If you're not speaking, how can you come to lunch?"

"By then we should be speaking."

"All right. Why don't we do it next Wednesday?"

"Wednesday's my needlepoint day. What's wrong with Tuesday?"

"Absolutely nothing. Tuesday at twelve?"

"Eleven-thirty. I'm making pot roast Tuesday."

"Eleven-thirty it is."

"Maybe your father could find time to join us. Tell him his sister, the one that raised him and wiped his runny nose and gave him all her candy, would like to see him."

"I'll see if I can reach him. He's been out of town." Hannah crossed her fingers with the white lie, fantasizing her aunt's reaction to the truth. You see Sophie, baby, Norman's old mistress sent me lye in the mail. So we ain't communicatin' so good nowadays...

"Don't put yourself out. But if you should happen to speak to him, you might just tell him I said, 'Hello, stranger.'"

"I will. I'll see you next week."

Hannah was late. She ran upstairs, wincing at the soreness of her legs, and got dressed. "Got to go to the office and finish that story, meet Agatha at twelve. Why do I put up with that? Family, shmamily, I must be nuts." She moved faster than her thoughts, blocking out the empty pillow beside her and the memory of her agonizing night.

CHAPTER 9

Hannah stood in the darkened doorway, trying to readjust her eyes to the Day-for-Night atmosphere. She was early. She liked to be early. Sit for a moment, alone, watching the parade of lunching ladies, listening to the din of high-pitched overstimulated flattery.

"You look fabulous! I love your hair!"
"I love that hat!"
"You look so THIN!"
"You look so rested!"
"You look taller!"

Ladies in their early thirties. Big-city women. Wives of doctors and lawyers. Mothers of small children. Volvos and Mercedes. Blow-dried hair. Tennis lessons. Weekends in "the Springs." The St. Tropez look. Dinner parties for eight or ten. Overpriced Italian "bistros." Digital orgasms. Transcendental Meditation. *Ms. Women's Wear Daily. Vogue.* All liberal causes. Husbands with the Dry Look and wandering eyes. Going back to teaching.

Two ladies moved down the aisle toward Hannah, glasses of white wine in hand, smug chins turned upward, resisting the gravity of their lives, eyes clicking back and forth, comparing Guccis and nose bobs without turning their heads.

Hannah watched. The "Death to the Enemies March," she called this ritual walk to the table. The "Eat Your Hearts Out, Women over Forty; Women with Mushy Tushies; Women with

Bad Haircuts. Eat Your Little Under-$ 100,000-a-Year Hearts Out" walk.

Hannah smiled, sipping her drink. The women, so like herself and yet so utterly strange to her, created a loneliness that disturbed her deeply. "You know, Hannah," Nick had said to her one night, "what's wrong is that you still really believe that deep inside every human being, no matter how paltry the evidence, is some brilliant and special spark, and that's just bullshit. A whole lot of people are just here, taking up space, contributing to charity and overpopulation, and then are just not here anymore. Human fillers."

The fear was back. Hannah felt her chest tighten and her breath stop.

The marching ladies, chins strained upward and radiating victory, goose-stepped past Hannah and sat down at the next table.

May you both have gas attacks from your spinach salads.

Hannah was feeling bad. Her chest felt constricted in the now familiar panic.

Someone wants to hurt me. Someone wants to hurt my children.

The noise from the bar was moving in and out, like the roar of the sea when you sleep. Louder then softer, lulling, separating, pulling you to consciousness and then away, somewhere smoother.

"Is the other lady coming, madam?" Hannah jumped. Madam. Thirty-two seemed a little soon for "madam."

"Yes, she should be here any minute."

The waiter was not pleased.

She wasn't feeling well.

My father's filth is stuck to me. Nick ran away from me. Pinned a note on the pillow and disappeared. Her guilt had cut her off from the rightful rage of his desertion. "He gets to run, I get to stay." He had done it before and always with drama. The "Garbo Maneuver," Hannah called it. And he always went to the same place, driving too fast up the coast to Santa Barbara, not telling anyone and never calling home. Tears filled her eyes, she felt sick with anger and disappointment.

The ladies at the next table were talking about their children. "I've pulled Joshua out of three nursery schools in the last six months. You know, I spend a lot of time at school observing. Very few mothers do that and I'm appalled at how little the schools respond to what he *needs*. At one school, the teacher *actually* FINISHED an art project FOR him! Why, that just kills personal initiative. But now he's in a very good, very progressive school. Only organic foods, unisex clothes and NO structure. I have my 'credential,' you know, so I'm probably more critical, but I react very strongly when I feel his needs are being suppressed."

"Does Joshua have an art room?"

"No, but he has a specially designed free-form play structure in the garden, which, frankly, I feel is more stimulating."

"Well, Sasha and Jennifer have a handmade sandbox and slide set, and we've made an art room in the pool house and all of their little school projects are hung there.

It gives them a feeling of importance. I think their little egos are so fragile, they need a special creative place. And, of course, it keeps them from messing up the house."

"I think children should be free to explore their total environment."

Hannah felt better, inhaling the lady lunch conversation.

A tall, dark-haired woman of middle age, looking trapped inside a pair of strangling French jeans, was moving toward her. Hannah stiffened.

God, maybe it's her; don't be crazy, Hannah. Why is that woman staring? Jesus, I'm getting so paranoid.

"I know you!" The woman grabbed her shoulder and leaned over her, breath mints and perfume smells covering Hannah's fear. "You're Hannah Oberman."

"It's Nicoli now."

"I'm Ruth Gold! I was a friend of your mother's, darling. I hardly recognized you, you've lost sooo much weight!"

"Maybe five pounds." Hannah winced as she remembered how much she disliked this smothering perfumed woman, but felt her heart throbbing in relief.

"Well, Hannah, you are really soo skinny, you're not ill are you?"

"No, I'm just fine, thank you."

"I can't get over how different you look, you've, well how can I say it, you've matured well."

This bean-brain is standing here telling me that I look old and sick and I'm smiling at her. I wonder how she'd look with a Bloody Mary on her head.

"I heard about poor Momma. I called your daddy several times, but he was always busy."

I bet you did, sweetheart.

"Are you eating *here*? No one *eats* here. It's fine for a drink, but the food is ghastly. Why don't you come with me, dear? There's a fabulous new little Italian bistro on Canon, you wouldn't believe how chic it is! They won't even speak to you in English. Isn't that marvelous! It's just like being in a *ristorante* in Roma. All the Saudi princesses eat there when they're in town shopping. Last week one of them came in with twenty bodyguards!"

"I'm sorry, but I'm expecting a friend."

"Oh, well, dear, some other time. Why don't you call me? I'm selling real estate now, if you ever need something, I have the best listings in the city. I was the one who really sold that Arab sheikh's mansion. I didn't get credit, you know how competitive this business is, but *I* showed it to his uncle, first. It burned down, you know. It's a bargain now, probably could pick it up for three million, needs work now, of course. Maybe your father might be interested?"

"No, I don't think so, he's kind of superstitious about Arabs."

"Well, maybe we can all have dinner some night, he must be so lonely without Momma."

The call girls and teenyboppers keep him pretty busy. "Yes, I'll call you, Mrs. Gold."

"Ruth, dear. You're a grown-up now!"

That's right. I went directly from being a frightened child to being an aging, sick grown-up without even passing go, whaddayaknow.

The woman patted her cheek, leaving red marks, and stomped off, buttocks rolling behind her.

Hannah smiled to herself. Hugging herself invisibly, she mothered her fear.

Italian restaurants where they won't speak English and a three-million-dollar Arab burnout for my father. I remember when Beverly Hills had family drugstores with homemade malts and Suzie Q french fries and a mom-and-pop delicatessen, and a real record store with booths and they let you play Johnny Mathis, and the mailman knew your first name. Twenty bodyguards! Never heard such stuff.

"Hello, darling, sorry I'm late."

A whisper of perfume, a smile, Agatha, with her sables flying, the perennial hat jauntily set, small, perfect features peeking out like a tiny child in her mother's clothes, the mischievous eyes intense and twinkling.

"It was 'Bank Day' and I had to steam open the statements. There I was hiding in the washroom with my letter opener and the hot water wilting my sables, looking for that bloody check I forged. I'm in an absolute panic! Gordon's accountant is coming in today, and I know they're going to go over the books. I took two tranquilizers. Oh, God, I am mad, totally mad! And I've got two root canals being done. Three hundred and seventy-five dollars *apiece*\ (Why God gave us teeth, I will never understand.) And my car's quit dead away again and Gordon's going over the *bank* statements! I wish someone would just shut the hatch and let me go quietly insane."

"Agatha, you have got to get out of there. Gordon's no dummy. He gave you nothing in the divorce settlement, he pays you shit, and he's still in love with you. He knows you don't have enough for a moth to live on, and he damn well knows you're supplementing. He *likes* that. He WANTS you right where he's got you. He knows you still need him, and he's playing you like a viola."

"Oh, God, I know, I know, but I'm such a coward, I just can't leave. I'll end up selling cosmetics at Saks or something. No, I couldn't even do that, they'd make me take my hat off."

Hannah sipped her drink. Knowing Agatha did not want advice and not really having any to give, she felt alienated from her for the first time in all the years of their friendship by the changes exploding inside her life.

There was no room now for platitudes and performance, for pretending that she did not see into her friend's problems; for withholding the truth.

Agatha watched her, feeling the breach. She leaned back and lit a cigarette with quick, nervous motions. "How was Disneyland?"

"Marvelous. Charlie and Neilie got diarrhea from an overdose of chocolate-chip ice cream. I nearly broke my ankle getting out of a whirling tea cup, and it cost enough to pay for your root canal. Really, we had fun, but it was only a momentary escape. Something awful happened last night."

Hannah stopped and took a sip of water. She laughed in spite of herself. "Oh, Christ, Agatha, we sound like something from daytime television. This is so unreal! There was a package in the mailbox with no address or anything and it was all gift wrapped. I opened it and inside was a little bottle of lye. And two little dolls with pins stuck in them, and I spilled hot tea all over my legs. They hurt like hell."

Their eyes locked across the table, holding one another up.

"Oh, no. No. No. NO!"

"Open the hatch, I'm coming with you." Agatha inhaled deeply. "I need a martini."

They were silent, waiting for the waiter, ordering, impatiently arranging plates and napkins.

"Oh, and I haven't told you the best part. We know who it is. Ready? It's an old friend of my father's. And he *lied* to me about it. He *knew* who it was and he was so scared that she might do something to *him* if he told me, or that he might have to talk to the police or some other grown-up thing, that he *lied* to me!

"I guess what I just cannot bear is that this is happening to us because of the way *he* lives his life and he's snug as a bug. I'm getting the lye in the mail. Cheers."

"Agatha, sweetheart, what a surprise!" Hannah looked up. Two elegantly dressed men were leaning into their table.

Agatha turned, seeming relieved to escape the tension of Hannah's battle and the possibility that what was happening to her friend might change the tightly knit fabric of their pampered and delicately woven relationship, ripping into some forbidden area, treading on some unspoken hurt.

"Alphonse, darling, how good to see you. This is my friend, Hannah Nicoli. Alphonse Guttierez."

"Charmed. And this is my friend from Italy, Count DiMezzo."

Hannah watched Agatha, smiling to herself, knowing her so well. The glimmer of possibility rocketing her off like a shooting star. This could be the one, my prince at last, to carry me off in his private jet away from the necessities of survival.

"*Buona sera, signore.*" Agatha flashed her most beguiling smile, opening her bright blue eyes wide and cocking her head slightly, provocatively to the side.

Hannah watched this game she had never played. The game of the alone, the unmarried. It frightened her and it fascinated her. I'd never be good at it, she thought, I'd end up playing solitaire for the rest of my life.

Agatha and the California Count flirted in Italian, and Hannah sat quietly, relieved to be released from the effort at conversation, not being able to forget the burden burning into her life like the sting on her legs, reminding her that things were not as they were.

"Why don't you and your friend join us for drinks and dinner tomorrow night? I'm hosting a small party in Malibu for the Count."

"That's very kind of you, but I can't." Hannah resisted the urge to accept, to put on her sexiest dress and flee into Agatha's papier-mâché world. Dance on the beach like the Barefoot Contessa and drink champagne from Baccarat crystal.

"I'd adore it, Alphonse." Agatha smiled, her face rosy with excitement, and nodded to him as he and the Count turned to go. *Maybe him, or maybe tomorrow I'll open the mail and find that someone has died and left me a million dollars...*

Hannah watched her, knowing what she was thinking.

"What's an Alphonse?"

Agatha laughed. "Fag, darling. Rich, darling. The Count looks interesting. Very attractive."

"Yes, but is he fag, darling, rich, darling? He may be hustling Alphonse." She was sorry she had said it, thinking out loud, not wanting to disappoint Agatha or cut into the adrenalin of new possibilities.

Agatha's smile faded. She lit another cigarette and finished her drink in one fast gulp. "Probably not, darling. But, at least he's under seventy and the food will be good."

Hannah leaned forward and took her hand. "He's awfully handsome, it could be fate."

And they finished their lunch, covering the sore spots and the space between them, and left one another to their own uncertainty.

Hannah swung into her driveway, almost knocking over her uncle Morley, who stood beside the Jacaranda tree, arms folded before him like a patient angel recently floated to earth.

"Someone died," Hannah whispered to herself, pulse throbbing, unable to see any other reason for this visitation. She got out of the car quickly, leaving her purse and the dry cleaning and the plump chicken she would roast for the children, and walked toward him, her face pale.

"Uncle Morley. What a surprise! Is everything all right?"

Her uncle beamed down upon her, smelling of sweat and onions, and extended one long, white, hairless hand, resting it on her forehead like a street corner Christ.

"Yes, Hannah, child, everything is fine, but I've been concerned about you. Louise and Estelle said that you seemed nervous and tired, and I've been praying for you."

"Louise and Estelle say that about everyone, it's called projection. I'm fine. Really. It's kind of you to worry about me, but you really didn't have to, we're all fine."

He beamed on. Not speaking, looking into her eyes with angelic glee.

Maybe he'll fly away. Hannah relaxed.

"Why don't you come in and have a cup of tea? We're going to a party tonight, but I've got a little time to visit."

Hannah stood at the sink, filling the kettle, unwrapping the chicken.

"Is it kosher, Hannah?"

"No, it's a fryer."

Her uncle shook his head before the heathen, free of conflict, a believer, certain of his road, not affected by the cynicism of heretics.

Hannah poured tea for herself and hesitated before him.

"Morley, I don't have any kosher dishes, what do I do?"

He was serene. "Do you have a paper cup?"

She watched her uncle sip his holy tea from a Styrofoam cup, a being surrounded by calm, and for the first time, she did not see him as silly and fanatical. A fierce desire to lean on his shoulder covered her. Some great angel's shoulder, strong and sure, caressing her, softening her body, taking charge, protecting. The need for someone to have an answer she could not reach, to surrender, to trust, moving beyond the walk-in closet of reality in which she and everyone she knew lived their overly structured lives. She remembered herself, wearing a big silver cross, a child of five or six wanting to belong to some great mystery. "Suzie wears one, Mommy, and everyone in her house goes to church, and a big man with a black suit holds her hand. I want to be what she is."

"How's Aunt Mildred?"

"God bless her, she's fine. She sends her love."

"I'm sorry I haven't called in so long, we've been so busy."

"We understand. We know how hard it's been for you since Mother's leaving. It's God's will, Hannah. She's in a better place now."

Hannah put down her cup, moving away from him back to the safety of her disbelief. "I'm really fine, Uncle Morley. It's been over two years now."

Her uncle sighed, exhaling garlic odors, and patted her hand. Sighing is definitely hereditary, Hannah thought. She stood up, taking cups and spoons to the sink, not knowing what else to say.

"Sorry Neilie isn't home yet, and Charlie is taking his nap or you could see him. I really wasn't expecting anyone."

The phone rang.

"I'll answer it, Hannah."

She stiffened. "No, Morley, please, I'm expecting a long-distance call." She grabbed the phone from his hand, envisioning his beatific, ever-beaming face in conversation with their Caller. "Hello?"

"Hi, Hanny, it's Candy. Is Uncle Morley there? He said he was coming by, I wanted to ask him if he could pick me up. Mildred invited me for dinner. I'm bringing my boyfriend to meet them."

"Oh, that's great. Yes, he's right here, Estelle, Candy. I'll see you next week."

"Oh, by the way, Hanny, dear, I'm sending you an article from the *Star* about health, because of Momma. It says that all sickness can be cured by eating the organ of the part of your body that's sick, like hearts for heart trouble, liver for liver trouble, brains for brain trouble."

"Momma had bowel trouble."

"Oh, Hanny, that's not funny."

She handed the phone back to her uncle, blushing at her behavior, feeling uncomfortable before his patronizing presence, not wanting him to see beyond her pose.

I'm fine, everything's fine. I have a perfect life. She demanded that the world believe what she was fighting fiercely to believe herself.

Her uncle hung up and walked toward her, arms outstretched, covering her with sour smells. He put his white, bony hands on her shoulders and beamed brightly down at her, forcing her to meet his glance.

"You are in my prayers, child. You must have faith. Read the Bible. Go to synagogue. God will hear you." She resisted the urge to say something funny, choosing to play in his court. "Thank you, Uncle Morley. I will." She walked him down the driveway and waved him away. I wonder if I could get him a TV show. Morley Bodkin, the first Jewish evangelist. He always wanted to be an actor. The idea has possibilities. Hannah watched him disappear, feeling lonely and unsettled.

CHAPTER 10

Hannah and Nick had accepted the invitation weeks before the calls began. And, almost reckless in their need to carry on as usual, neutralizing this thing forming over their lives, they decided to go.

It was to be a big party, given by two of their more ambitious friends in honor of a visiting Literary Lord.

"Oooo, Mommy, you look gorgeous." Neilie pounced in, eyes wide in little-girl pleasure over the glitters and colors and smells of a mommy getting dressed.

"You're prettier than me." Neilie watched, intent. "When I get six, can I wear makeup?"

"You don't need makeup."

"Uh-huh. I want to be gorgee-us, too."

"You're gorgeous without makeup." Hannah squinted into the mirror, concentrating on the mascara miracle she was performing on her white-blond lashes.

"Hannah." Nick poked his head around the dressing room door. "I'm all ready and you aren't even dressed yet. Come on."

"Sorry, honey."

Hannah rushed, hurt by his abruptness. She gathered shoes, dress, stockings, feeling excitement, tension. Leaving her hiding place to face unknown situations. People who could hurt, ignore, reject, expect. A tension she always felt approaching a party and now increased by her new fear, *What if she comes here while we're gone?*

"Hannah."

She jumped, went to the bathroom, took out the tranquilizers, decided against it, grabbed her purse and headed for the stairs; her daughter, somber now that the moment of actual departure was real, trailing behind.

"Nick, did you leave the number? Did you tell Tina about calling my father if she calls, and the police number?"

"I did everything. Relax." Nick reached for her, wanting to reassure. "It'll be fine, we deserve it."

"Okay." She relaxed and untensed her body, sucking in her apprehension and swallowing.

Charlie came waddling down the hall in Neilie's shoes, a battered pink headband poking through his curls and one of Hannah's old bracelets around his neck.

"Mommy bye-bye, Daddy bye-bye, Charlie bye-bye."

"Charlie no bye-bye, Charlie home."

Tears falling from Charlie to Neilie, two moaning little people suffering the gravest injustice.

"What time will you come back?" Neilie forced more tears and waited for hearts to melt and treats to be proffered.

"At about twelve o'clock, and you and Charlie can both stay up for fifteen minutes"—time meaning nothing in their world except when it ran out—"and you can each have a cookie."

Tears shut off like windows slamming.

"Cookie," Charlie bounced.

And they fled in a big foreign car from the crushing needs of children toward the pressure of their own.

> Everyone goes to cocktail parties out of some compulsion toward inclusion, to compare, maneuver, flaunt, endear, make out, what have you. A choreographed desperation. A reach toward some nonexistent level of acceptance from humanity. Most people loathe them or fear them or both. And most people go. (Of course we don't

really know how crazy the Trobrianders were about canoe-building either.)

> —Hannah Nicoli Sociology I
> Comparison of Primitive and
> Modern Social Ritual

Fourteen years and a thousand cocktail wieners later, Hannah crossed the Persian-shrouded threshold, feeling like an antebellum relic returning to a desecrated village.

The party was humming. Voices celebrating the end of the arriving stoniness of alienation and sobriety. Faces turned to take in the newest entry. Some eyes lingered, others returning to half-developed conversations. "Holy Christ, there must be five hundred people here!" Hannah let Nick guide her through the throng toward the bar.

Their hosts beamed at them from the receiving line, standing tall and regal as if waiting for the glory of their overcelebrated guest to pass over them.

"Oh, God," Nick moaned, pushing her forward quickly. "Let's stay away from that line. That I couldn't do, especially sober."

"Nick! Stop pushing me. I'm going to sit. Can you bring me some champagne or something, please?"

He left her and she wandered, glad to be alone for the moment. She was keenly aware of her separateness from her husband and how it was growing.

People watched her, confused by her apparent disinterest in making contact. She had always been ambivalent about parties. Excited to be invited, to break the routine of their overdisciplined daily life, wear something glamorous and make connections, and yet, once she was there she resisted, wanting to be alone and not having the energy to participate. She kept her eyes hazed, avoiding glances that might lead to conversations, wanting to wander in a group, cuddling against its warmth anonymously.

In the last year or so she had begun to see something at parties. At first, she did not understand what it was except that it made her uncomfortable and it became harder to look into people's eyes while she was talking to them. But since the calls, she had begun to understand it, to see her world from a different place.

I know something about all of us in this room.

It is clear enough. We are all like calves marching through the slaughterhouse door. Eyes blinking blindly at the death blow. The eyes. The poor, flashing, smiling, crinkling eyes. Tiny searchlights looking for a reality that could match their expectations. Hannah had recognized that it was an over-thirty malady. The bruising awareness that you were really the grown-ups and this was about it. You cannot turn around. You cannot go home. You will never be Miss America or Joe Namath. You will get old if you're lucky, and then, sometime, you know what. Dead.

Hannah watched, sipping the double scotch Nick had handed her. "Only thing I could get"—before he had been enveloped by a half-smashed tennis buddy. Hannah was content. The scotch worked a warm, welcome miracle in her head as voices buzzed above her.

"Did you read about those two sisters, just kids and both of them dropped dead of heart attacks just ten days apart?"

"Oh, don't tell me, I don't want to hear about it! What caused it?"

"Craziest damn thing. Some rare disease called cardio myopio or something, and they were healthy as hogs, never had a problem and pow! Fell over dead in their gym classes ten days apart!"

"Oh, I hate stories like that. I can't bear it. Did they do an autopsy?"

"Oh, sure. This is really unbelievable, the pathologist said that the seventeen-year-old had a heart like an overstressed old man and that the anxiety the twenty-year-old felt after her sister died probably pulled her trigger, too."

"Oh, I can't stand it, let's talk about movies or something."

Hannah had read the story. The doctors had said that it was a matter of genetics, "a running out of time, no matter where people are or what they are doing." The line had chilled her. And it was here. A part of what she had discovered about people's eyes at parties, as if they all were watching some sinister chronometer ticking away at their lives. Tick-tick—tick—click-click-click, some mad timekeeper twinkling venally. Tick-tick-tick, stop.

"I've found you!" Hannah started, looking up into a welcome face.

"Kathy! Sit quick! Before I have to talk to someone."

"*I'm* not someone?"

"Definitely not, anyone can be someone." Hannah was feeling happy, the tingling liquids rosying her face.

Kathy White lowered her full six feet, all glasses and blond hair and unfashionably short skirt, into the chair.

"So, how've ya been, kid?"

"Don't ask. It's like a B movie."

"I won't. I'm on such a bummer, I may get loaded and cry in my *petite quiche lorraine.*"

"What are you doing? I haven't seen you in ages."

"Seems longer than just ages. Let me see. I've been auditioning. I am becoming the Queen of the Audition World. I have been turned down by every floor wax, bathroom sweetener and dog biscuit company in the United States and Canada. I even offered to perform lurid acts on a freshly waxed floor... no soap. Oh, soap, that's another reject. I didn't have, are you listening? I didn't have a 'soap voice.' So I said, 'Maybe not, but I blow a fuckin' bubble."

Hannah roared. Loving this woman. Her first roommate at college. Loved her the first day she saw her. Red cape flying, horn-rim glasses sliding off her pug nose, stomping around campus like a malevolent Mary Pop-pins.

"Not fair. You should be Mary Tyler Moore by now. It's sickening."

"Speaking of sick, I also did a pain reliever audition, but I found I couldn't wince without wrinkling my forehead, which, I found out, is *de rigueur* in pain commercials. And I tried for a palsied housewife struggling to make instant coffee, but they said I didn't look 'fragile' enough. It's mad. I'm going back to the academic world, Pirandello, Garcia Lorca. Jesus, Chekhov never had anyone make 'fragile' coffee."

"Hi, you two," a small leather-suited man grinned down at them. "You don't know me, but I was standing across the room and I thought, those two girls are so foxy and they're digging each other so much, I've got to meet them."

"Oh, fuck off, teeny-weeny, can't you see we're gay?"

Hannah flushed, sputtering laughter. Lost in Kathy's overdefensive, purely vulnerable self, her humor—an iron face mask covering piercing hurts. "I'm sorry," she offered to the small, shocked leather body.

"Happens all the time, dolly, maybe later."

"Let's have another drink! I'll be right back." Kathy unfolded herself from the chair, ignoring the man's retreat, and bounded to the bar.

Hannah sat remembering that first year of school. Comparing fantasies and tentative love stories. Two vulnerable virgins hanging on to their dreams. The beautiful big dreams, the someday "I'll be on Broadway and I'll be starring in *your* play," tentative but shining dreamings. Kathy had lost her virginity to an overweight film student in the back of a borrowed camper, and Hannah had gone to New York and found Nick. For a while they wrote letters which grew too pretentious as the dreams ended. And so they began to use the telephone like everyone else and talked only of the present.

"Hi, there, baby doll, I was watching you from the john and decided to expose myself." Kathy slammed a huge, evil-looking glass into her hand and resettled.

"So, nothing's happening?"

"Shit is happening. I had a part on a soap. I played the frigid wife of an ex-convict who had, with the encouragement of the resident 'FINE FAMILY,' become a millionaire lawyer with a baby son. Somehow, in one year, the kid had gotten retarded and become *eight years old!* Anyway, I did two episodes and they decided I was too tall to 'Look Frigid.' I told them, you got it, God only makes short people frigid. I told this to the producer, who is a tiny little tight-ass broad. Anyway, they wrote me out of the script. I went to Tahiti to start a needlepoint boutique or something. It's all Coo-Coo City. This whole town is a regular type-casting tragedy."

Hannah sipped her drink, feeling happy for the first time in weeks, and laughed.

"I called you one night last week. I wanted you to watch this TV show, speaking of judgments of the flesh. It was about aging and what people do to try to stay young. And one segment was with a Beverly Hills Plastic Surgeon and his wife. They're in their 'Gym' and he's on this rowing machine and she is in a ballet costume doing leg lifts for the camera; and she says, 'Before we were married, Herb told me I needed my eyes done, and so he fixed my eyes. And then I said, well, I've always wanted a bigger bosom, you see I never thought of myself as an attractive person, I always felt masculine because of my chest; and so Herb said, well, I'll do your bosom on one condition, that you let me do your chin, your nose and pin back back your ears; and I said, it's a DEAL! And someday I hope to have my thighs done and my rear end lifted!"

"I wonder if he does forehead winces."

"Probably. And then, Herbie baby says about Frankensteina, 'She's very insecure, she thinks every woman is after me.' And on he goes about having his eye bags removed, about being scared of turning forty and how jealous ol' spare parts is, and they're both jogging and leg-lifting away. It was astonishing. I mean, what if a little kid saw that? Worse! Those two HAVE little kids! Can you see a five-year-old with a tushy-lift? And *they* never got turned down by a dog food company.

"Ya know, kid, I wander around sometimes and I think, I never get the right surface and so then I say, screw them, someone will want me for my Wrong Surface, and then the men I go out with are all like the auditions."

They sat. A bit woozy. Sounds swirling around them, being nice and liking each other. A rare safe island in the night sea.

"Kath?"

"Yes, Han?"

They laughed. They had been so good for one another. Knowing how to break through their own pomposity, teasing without hostility. Why can't it be that way with Nick? Hannah shivered.

"Is it anything like you thought it would be?"

"Life, my dear?"

She nodded.

"Well, let me put it this way. It's not what I *wanted* it to be, but it's what I thought it would be."

Hannah's heart filled. She thought of Agatha, of all of them, brave and cowardly all at once, wanting so much and not being able to risk having it. "It's not too late. I'm going to write you a perfectly happy ending."

"You must be kidding? How can anything that has death as the payoff have a happy ending?

"I've got to take a pee." Kathy unfurled and stretched, retreating from the danger of the conversation. She bent down and kissed Hannah's cheek. "Maybe tonight's the night I'll be discovered and fall madly in love. See you later."

Hannah watched her leave, feeling small and lost. "Come on, Hannah, let's get some food and some fresh air." She felt her husband's hand on her back. She stood up, feeling dizzy, and followed him through the crowd, conversation buzzing around her.

Nick and Hannah reached the buffet, standing, paper plates in hand, staring at a surreal montage of spreads and mixtures and dips and pick-skewered balls.

"I never know what I'm eating at these damn things," Nick whispered, grabbing meatball spears and slabs of nut-covered cheese. Hannah was caught between two longhaired, balding men reeking of French toilet water, making the collage of delicacies even more ominous.

"So, this kid comes in, black kid, real Jimi Hendrix type, try the shrimp puffs, they're out of sight, Sol. Anyway, I heard his shit and it's poetry, ya know, but no hot sound. So I told him, look, I really feel for ya. I know the slum scene is a drag, but nobody wants to hear music like that anymore, they want that Nashville shit."

"You're right, the shrimp's dynamite. I just signed a kid, good, real-nice sound, is that green stuff eggplant? I hate eggplant. Anyway, he's in a wheelchair, whaddya-callit?"

"It's grape leaves. Paraplegic."

"Yeah, yeah, that's it. Got it in Nam. Great gimmick." Hannah and Nick exchange glances, trying not to make their eavesdropping obvious.

"I'll find us a place outside to sit."

"Okay. I'll try to dig us up some wine." Nick handed her his plate and disappeared into the crowd.

Hannah maneuvered her way through the buffet gazers and toward the air.

She settled at a small table behind a sprawling, spider-branched tree.

"Wine, my dear." Her husband appeared, carrying a full red bottle and two highball glasses.

"How did you manage that?" Hannah laughed.

"I stole it from the rack. What the hell, we deserve it."

"Yeah, I know, we deserve everything, only problem is, all these other chickens feel the same way."

"True, true, only they didn't have the courage to act." Hannah took a sip, feeling silky tastes in her mouth. They were quiet, eating and sipping, relaxing from the pressure of being social. It was the first time they had been alone together in weeks. He had come home the night after their trauma, sullen and passive, and she, accepting the responsibility for what was happening, had backed away, allowing him his mood and hating him for having it.

Now, the wine had steamed open his shell and he was ready to come out.

"You okay? Want to call home?"

Hannah shuddered. "No—dammit, I don't want to call home. I want to forget we HAVE a HOME. It's the first night in weeks we've been unresponsible and I *don't* want to call home."

"Okay, I was just checking. You looked so unhappy."

"It's the meatballs, they're lousy, ruined my gaiety." She put down her fork. "I really look like that? Really? I didn't feel anything. I thought I felt fine. I don't even know what I feel anymore. I don't even know if I'm having a good time, it's absolutely ridiculous."

"I know. Want one of these tamales?"

She was embarrassed. She realized he was appeasing her, really needing, perhaps more than she did, the release from the heaviness that now surrounded their lives so completely.

"No, thank you. They look like they're decomposing."

"Excuse me, hate to interrupt, you look so content, but could you be so kind as to tell me where you found the wine? Vodka is just not bearable with whatever this plate of goodies is."

They looked up.

A small, overly perfected man, his disappearing hair parted at obtuse angles in geometrical, scalp-covering precision, stood stiffly over them.

"We stole it. They may be coming for us any minute, so grab a glass and join us." Hannah smiled, releasing them both from the canker of their conversation. Her enjoyment of this immaculate vision heightened by her friendship with Agatha ("My fate, darling, the youngest fag hag in Hollywood").

"Fab-u-lous, I'll be back in a flash."

The man made a touch of a bow and agilely, head held high, the conditioned response of one who has faced many doubling blows, moved away.

"Cute. Who the hell is that and why did you ask him to join us?"

"I think that's Bruno Valati, he's a friend of Agatha's. He works for some horror with a lot of money who fancies herself an author, sucks off his ideas and treats him like her personal lab experiment."

"Sounds fascinating. I think I'll leave you to the Flasher and see if I can get another in case Brutus has any friends."

"Bruno." Hannah stiffened. "Honey, we don't need any more." She knew his patterns. It was the kind of evening for him to drink too much, and then she would be shut out and alone, again.

"Are you leaving? Don't tell me I am chasing this charming man away. I am intruding."

"No, no, I'm just going on a wine hunt." Nick backed away from her, avoiding the disapproval in her eyes.

"Wonderful." He eased himself gracefully into her husband's seat, proffering his glass. "I know it's terribly unchic to drink wine from a vodka glass, but I was damned if I was going to face that mass of flesh in there to get a clean one."

"I think we have a very good friend in common, Agatha Howard?" Hannah smiled.

"Oh, my God, that's why you looked so familiar and so stunning, may I add! You're Hannah! I feel like such a fool. We only met once, but Agatha talks about you so often."

"I think I would have known you were Bruno even if we hadn't met."

"Yes, maybe so. I'm that peculiar, I suppose. You know Agatha is my dearest friend. She is just about the only person I have ever known who listens and really cares and, with a neurotic like me, you have *got* to CARE to bear it."

Hannah laughed, feeling almost overwhelming compassion for this delicate, cheated man. Knowing all the stories. The fierce bursts of self-destruction. The drinking. The seclusion. The terror of time moving, of the cage he lived in trapping him forever. His sex, not a curse so much as an added strain, making his self-victimization more resolute.

"Agatha has told me some wonderful stories about you."

"Oh, God, I bet. I am the only Italian in my family in a zillion generations to work for a woman and sleep with a boy, or boys, both of which I could probably accept if it wasn't for that big gray elephant that sits on me all the time. Every morning I wake up in a sack of depression, which is my *elephant*. And he's sitting on me! Worse, he won't even talk to me!

"Sometimes I get up and I think about shaving and dressing and going through the 'flower arranging' I have to do with my hair and eating and shitting and going out to face all THAT, and I can't bear it.

"You know what I do when that big gray Dumbo is on me like that? I take huge sheets of aluminum foil (I have a year's supply in case of a run on foil or something) and I cover all the windows in my bedroom with it, get back into bed, take three Valium, turn on the game shows, and I stay there—sometimes for days."

"When do you get up?"

"When the fucking elephant talks to me again."

Hannah laughed, hesitating a moment, pondering her own opening. How much to say; wanting to trust this stranger who was so suddenly important, so mothering in his honesty, bridging her loneliness.

"I know exactly what you mean. Whenever Agatha tells me about you, I feel very close to you. My mother died two years ago. She was sick for a very long time, and I really spent my twenties around sickness and hospitals, having babies and watching her die. You learn things other people don't know yet. It separates you."

Hearing herself, the admission she had avoided for so long, Hannah was frightened.

"You are so right, my dear. When you grow wise too soon and have seen life from the deep side, you can't lie anymore. When you try, you choke. You suffocate. It becomes literally impossible to deceive yourself for long and survive, and yet we're still scared to death to stand on our own little clay feet, but sooner or later we have to because we can't play the game."

He studied her, pausing for permission to continue the weave of the delicate web of communication, now half-woven and frightening to the rootless traveler, rupturable by a sharp glance or a shrug.

"I remember Agatha telling me about your mother; she had cancer, didn't she?"

"Cancer had her."

The old anger at the audacity of the insulated returned.

"People who don't know about life killed my mother." She looked up, hoping the words did not sound too bitter.

Bruno met her eyes.

"They did. Not symbolically or anything special. They really did. The arrogance of their ignorance. That's how. Doctors. Our pampered pussycats. And it's our own fault. We're all so scared of growing up, we need those omnipotent authority figures, so we create them and they thrive on it. Doctors and lawyers and CPA's and Robert Red-ford." Hannah smiled, tears clouding her eyes. "They practiced on my mother. She had cancer twice before and they still wouldn't listen to her. Any woman over forty that goes to a doctor, or at least before Betty Ford and her poor tit, forget it. They pumped her full of iron shots and hormones and tranquilizers, but no one listened. They *assumed*, 'We got it all,' 'It's something else,' they kept telling us, and God knows we wanted to believe it."

Hannah saw herself pregnant with Charlie, following her mother down another urine-stinking hallway—the last hallway, the baby kicking life against the death all around her. "And then, when the pain was unbearable, she went to another doctor, and he told her that it was psychosomatic and he sent her to a psychiatrist, and the psychiatrist sent her to my grandfather's grave and had her practicing 'reaching toward harmony with my father, who was not harmonizable,' and she walked around like that for a year, trusting them all.

"And then one night, it was my father's birthday, and I had them over for dinner, and my mother got up and went to the bathroom. But she didn't come back. No one paid any attention, which was easier, and when I finally went to find her, she was sitting on the toilet seat all dressed up with her hands in her lap and her legs crossed at the ankles, and the tears were oozing down her face, and she was just sitting there, all alone in the dark, and when I came in she didn't even turn her head. She just sat there, very dignified, and she said, 'Hannah, it hurts so bad. It hurts so bad."

Hannah stopped, a lump like a thumb pushing against her throat. She reached for her wine, trying to control the emotion, and needing, now that she had opened this wound, to swab it.

"And the next day I called the doctors and took her to the hospital. And four hours later, this GOD of healing came to me and told me that this 'imaginary pain' was a carcinoma the size of a cantaloupe in her pelvis.

"I'm sorry." She wiped her eyes. He took her moist hand and held it gently, not speaking or running from the awkwardness of this raw intimacy.

"There's more wine," her husband shouted at them from the patio. "I have found a stash."

Hannah stood, reluctantly letting go of Bruno's small strong hand. Then, someone was saying her name.

"Hannah, I've been looking all over for you, there's a call for you, take it in my bedroom." Her hostess embraced her, excitement and perfume smells filling the night air.

Hannah's body weakened. "Dear God."

She whirled around, searching for her husband.

He's never there when I need him. Why does he always get drunk when we need to be strong. I hate it. I hate it.

Then, the panic mounting, she turned away and pushed, almost bruising in her assault on the crowd, down the hall to the bedroom.

The phone lying harmlessly settled on a silk pillow like a mythical viper in cunning disguise. Her heart was throbbing in her head, her throat almost closed.

"Hello."

"You little idiot! Do you really think you can get away from me?" Laughter, baby giggles building in her ear. "Ya know, you really are dumb-dumb-dumb 'cause I know where you are, but you don't know where I am! No sirree! I'm going to your house, maybe I'm even there now and I'm going to do something bad!"—giggles of madness filling the room—"I'm going to take your children and do something bad!"

The voice was gone. Hannah stood, unable to move, like in so many nightmares—night terrors becoming shadows of reality.

"Hannah, what happened to you?" Nick stopped, weaving a bit. "What's the matter?" His face flushed as he sensed danger and Hannah's anger, which had always been in itself more danger than he could handle.

No tools, no voice, I need to scream to save myself in this dream, and I can't.

"She said she's going to come now and hurt the children."

He had her arm. They were running. Pushing past friends, strangers, eyes glanced quizzically over them, disapproving of the unacceptable behavior. Down the hall, over the elegant rugs, in a haze of disbelief and confusion, back to the big machine which delivered them so quickly and now seemed to creep along like an ant carrying rocks, back toward the presence they knew now, in gouging certainty, they could not escape.

Tires shrieked around the corner, and Hannah sat, hands clenched, not admonishing her husband for the drunken recklessness of their endless, agonizing return from coterie.

As if hallucinating, Hannah's eyes locked on blinking lights, fire trucks, police cars, gathered in front of her home, her asylum, denial causing her to blink and shake her head, trying to clear her vision, tipping the kaleidoscope, rearranging the images.

"Oh, my God! Oh, my God! Nick, Nick!"

The car screeched to a halt, and she was out, stumbling over the curb, her husband racing behind her.

Arms stopped her.

"You can't go in there, lady, we're checking things out. Are you Mrs. Nicoli?"

"Where are my children? Oh, God! Please tell me where are my babies!"

Nick took her arm and moved between her and the information of this City man, savior of small children, douser of fire, teller of tragedy.

"I'm her husband." His face was clouded with drink and helplessness.

"Yes, sir. Well, your children are okay, they're at your wife's father's house. We got a call from him. It seems your maid called him, can't speak English too good, but apparently you warned her about some threatening phone calls. Anyway, some woman called your maid and said she had planted explosives under your house. Your girl must have called your father, Mrs. Nicoli, and he called us. We're checking it out, haven't found anything. Did find a cigarette butt with some lipstick stains in the driveway near the street. Do you smoke or did you have any guests here tonight that smoke?"

"No, no, no one, no one." She was sobbing, trembling with immediate relief. One of life's reprieves, momentary dips on an airplane, brakes hit in a crosswalk.

"Well, we're checking everything out, but so far we haven't found anything. It may be just a crank call, the detective said you've had them before."

Nick held her tightly, and she could feel his heart, the only sign of his strain, throbbing against her ribs. "Where is the detective, is he here now?"

"He went over to your father's house to get a statement."

"We'll be over there. Can you send someone over or call and let us know if it's safe, when it's safe to come home?"

"Yes, sir, and don't worry, we do this all the time. We'll check the house inside and out."

"Thank you. Thank you very much."

She followed after him, stumbling in her high heels, dirtying her dress, wobbling down the hill in dazed, directionless disbelief.

And they were in the car again. Doors crashing. Tires grinding. Screaming around the corners into the land of the-new rich—minutes, but civilizations away. Houses whirled by in their determined silence.

Hannah sat like a bum at the movies, her eyes grazing in bovine stupor over huge gates and driveways filled with expensive cars and fountains cascading sewer water. Her head jerked suddenly, snapping back to consciousness as Nick slammed to a stop in her father's driveway.

"Nick, are you okay?" She watched him, trying to reach beyond herself, to see inside him, to understand what he was feeling. But she could not.

"Fine. I'm fine."

"Mommy, Mommy, Mommy, Daddy, Daddy, Daddy!" The massive wood doors opened, spilling forth their tiny, wide-eyed contents; pajama-clad freshness racing toward them, engulfing them in excitement and need for repair of the damaged night.

"Mommy, Charlie and me was sleeping and all of a sudden Tina grabbed us up in the dark and took us outside and there was firemens and pleecemens with big trucks like on TV, and we was so scared! Is our house blowed up? The firemens told Grandpa to take us away in case the house blowed up."

Nick and Hannah's eyes locked in focusless fury.

"No, darling, our house is just fine. It looks like it was all just a false alarm, darling." Hannah held her close, kneeling in the driveway, tearing her stocking, unable to rise or move between the giant portals.

"What's a false alarm, Mommy?"

"It means a mistake; something you think is going to happen and then it doesn't happen."

"Like staying up to see ghosts?"

"Well, kind of like that."

"Mommy, Mommy!"

Charlie pulled at her dress, squirming between them, irritated at his positioning. "Charlie no sleep, Charlie Bampa's house."

"Yes, Charlie and Neilie are having an adventure." Nick gently lifted Charlie. "Hannah, it's freezing out here. Take the kids in and put them down. I'll see what's going on."

Hannah stood, swallowing mouthfuls of frightened air. She dreaded entering that house. The house of her past. A house shrouded in resentment and sorrow. Feelings that now separated her from her father, the bestower of this new inheritance, like her green eyes and her red hair and the freckles on her shoulders. A bequest from her father. "Your father is killing me. He gave me cancer."

Words like ice picks in the flesh, never to leave, haunting her life forever. Flashes of her mother shriveled to a child's size, bald and boil-covered from the miracle drugs she could no longer swallow, could no longer have pumped into veins deflated and destroyed like stems of dead flowers. Her mother. Dragging herself along the floor of her lavender bedroom, using shreds of will; dragging herself along, clutching her savings account book and hiding it where no one ever found it. Hiding it from the father of her children; lover and husband for thirty-one years. Dragging her stick-figure body behind her to keep whatever of herself she had left. Her last grasp at power. At freedom. Keeping it at all costs. Denying her children and denying her disease to protect herself. Keeping her husband from the total and final control of her dying life. And Hannah had never told her father, so lost was he in his own grief. "I was supposed to die first," he had sobbed over and over. She had protected him from her mother's hate. Leah had died blaming him, never seeing her own motives or what she had done to herself. He had been her obsession but not her joy, and it was that that had killed her.

"Mommy, Grandpa said I can sleep over. Can I, please?" Neilie held tight to her hand as they passed through the doors, shutting them behind, making the walls twitch and the windows rattle and bend under their force.

"No, honey, not tonight. But you can rest here for a little bit while Daddy and I talk to Grandpa."

"Please, I want to! I like this house better than our house. Our house is little. We don't gots a swimming pool or nuthing. Please."

"I said no." Hannah took Charlie's hand from her husband, and they moved in opposite directions down the long, white-carpeted hallway.

Hannah opened the door to her room. It was the same pink-and-red womb of her childhood. Pictures painted by girl friends, poems she had written still tacked to the walls. Old sweaters and hair curlers abandoned and never reclaimed, still in the drawers. Wisps of the past, apparitions of herself. The room of her escape, of her private yearnings, her girl-dreams. Tears shed over lost friends and first loves. Body explored endlessly in closet mirrors. Secrets shared. Phone-call whispers in the middle of the night. "My parents are asleep, I've got the car keys." The web of inexperience hiding all dangers. Room of invincibility. Room of hope and future. Room of no consequences and no reality. Room where she was perfect, the smartest and the prettiest. The most special and secure. Room she had left eagerly to try the world, little knowing she could not go back. Little knowing that even if she had never left, it would still cast her out.

She entered it now with a daughter of her own; a son (like her brother), who had lived in the past behind her pink wall. A daughter of her own, who lived in a room, feeling protected and loving her life, sassy and happy in another trick room.

"Mommy, we're not sleepy, can't we watch TV? Please, Mommy?"

Restlessness moved over her, allowing appeasement, the mother's escape clause. Eat the cookie, have the chocolate, one more story, anything, anything, only let me be.

"Okay, okay, you can watch TV, but there's nothing for kids on.

Look, sweetheart, here's some of Mommy's old clothes from when I was little. You can play dress-up, and I'll have Tina bring some cookies and milk, but you stay in here. I have to talk to Grandpa. Understand?"

"Yes, Mommy, I'll keep the baby in here. Come on, Charlie, let's put Mommy's clothes on. You can be the father and I'll be the wife."

She closed the door behind them and moved quickly, holding her soiled skirt up off the heavy carpeting, electricity crackling under her feet.

Three men sat with solemn faces, speaking in low humming monotones. Her husband, her father and a stranger. A thickset, poorly dressed man. He rose when she entered. "Hello. I'm Detective Hudson, Mrs. Nicoli."

"Hello." Hannah sat in the corner.

Her father kept his head down, avoiding her eyes.

"Can somebody please tell me what happened?"

"Honey," Nick cleared his throat. "Basically, we know everything already. She got our number at the party from Tina. She disguised her voice and told Tina that she was your aunt and that your father was sick and she had to reach you. Then she called Tina back and told her about the bomb, and Tina called your father."

A low, defensive voice broke the heaviness.

"I told the detective all that! She's a kook. A drunken bitch! She gets her kicks this way. She's been calling me for years, but now she's getting crazy or something with these threats. You people haven't done a fucking thing! They've got tapes of her voice, you know her name. You've got to scare the shit out of her! She knows we've called the police! I thought she'd stop, dammit! She's been arrested before, I thought she'd be scared. She did stop for a few days. Why the hell can't you do anything? You shmucks waiting for a big bust or something, can't waste your time?" Her father lashed out, striking first.

The detective's voice was calm. "We can't locate her. We're

trying to trace her through car registration and the phone company. She hasn't worked recently that we know of, so we're trying to track her through the unemployment office. Got a description out on her, but, after all, she really hasn't done anything. Tonight is really the first serious infraction. So it's true that the whole department hasn't been on this. You wouldn't believe how many crank calls we get."

"Then there *still* isn't anything we can do, short of leaving town, and even so we have to come back! I don't want to go away and come back and have it start over. I want it to end! I can't take any more. She's scaring my children. We can't live in a cage! It's got to stop!" She shivered fiercely.

"When we talked to the police, they said to wait. Should we try that now?" Her husband leaned toward her.

"We can't afford it, Nick!"

Nick's face flushed in anger.

"I'm sorry," Hannah whispered.

"Well," the detective put his pen away, preparing to retreat, "it's awfully hard with no whereabouts. It's not like the movies. All we could really do is guard your house." He paused. "Do you have any means of self-protection?" He busied himself with his papers, the embarrassment of the need to ask, the buck-passing, making him uneasy.

"No. But we've been thinking about it." Nick avoided her eyes.

The detective rose. "Well, it might not be a bad idea. We don't usually recommend that, but since we don't quite know what we're dealing with here..."

"Why *can't* you assign an officer to protect us? Why do we have to do it ourselves?" Hannah's frustration propelled her. All three of them searching for someone to blame.

"We don't have the manpower, and so far there's still no real cause. Unless the fire department really finds a bomb, and I doubt if they will."

"Great. That's great." Hannah held her shaking body while the men rose in silence above her, clearing their throats in helplessness.

The door chimes startled them.

"That must be the fire guys." The detective moved past her.

She sat, stiff with rage, her teeth chattering uncontrollably, her father still ignoring her presence.

N ick watched her, his blue eyes watery with exhaustion and frustration.

"It's okay. They checked every corner. Nothing. We've got the cigarette. We'll send it to the lab. Could have been dropped by anyone, though. Well, good night, folks; keep making tapes and we'll go over them. Maybe we can find something. I'd hold off changing your number for a little while longer. The phone company's monitoring your calls. But chances are she's just a phone freak. Lot of them around."

"Yeah, yeah, that's what I kept telling them!" her father's arm shot out, circling their shadows. "But still, now she's threatening my grandchildren! That makes me mad! I'm going to stay on you bastards! I pay your goddamn salaries, all the property taxes on this place, I want that bitch in jail!"

The detective ignored him. Hannah and Nick rose and walked him to the door.

CHAPTER 11

EGOIST NOTEBOOK (VOLUME II)

Being an obsessive-compulsive person by nature, I feel driven to complete this work. I began with an overview of my family, but I find that that was just a warm-up; certain events of the last couple of months have made me realize that my relatives may form the body of my future work. Emily Bronte, eat your heart out. Also, in case this nightmare in which I am now a member in good standing should drive me into the loon room, I want my children to have *my* view of their ancestors.

There are two sides to every family. In mine there are the surviving Obermans, which consist of my father and his two dour sisters, Ethel and Sophie (see, see, such a fate, not a Gwendolyn or a Rosemary, not a Bitsey or a Corky, anywhere!). And, on the Bodkin side, you will remember, we have Morley and Estelle and Louise, the survivors, and my mother and maternal grandparents, the flower pushers.

If Louise, Morley and Estelle were the Scarletts and Rhett of Latvia, then Ethel and Sophie were the Cossacks. Serious. Acne-scarred. They hold grudges. Sophie was fond of writing letters, detailing all the sins my mother, father, baby brother and cuddly me had ever committed. And they were truly monstrous! For instance: When we moved into our first house, which featured wall-to-wall white carpets, my mother once during a rainstorm asked Sophie to come around to the kitchen door to avoid mud prints on the wondrous new rugs. Sophie wrote that she had been forced to use the "Maid's Entrance" because my mother didn't think she was fancy enough to use the front door.

In this same letter (which my mother kept for twenty years and would throw up to my father when he started on *her* family), she was also assailed for serving them hot dogs at a summer barbecue, indicating that the steaks were saved for more important visitors. There were also lists of all the things Sophie had ever done for them that went back thirty years and included: babysitting for me when my mother went to the hospital to have my brother. Driving my father to the psychiatrist, when he was having his nervous breakdown and my mother was in the hospital having my same brother. Having us to dinner fourteen times more than we had her and my uncle, the Jewish policeman, to dinner. Having Ethel to dinner five more times. Having Ethel's sons over ten more times. Turning cuddly me against her. And, especially for my mother, turning my father against her.

Sophie, you see, never got over the fact that my father, her darling little brother whom she, in her words, "raised from the time he was a baby, gave him everything, I was the *only friend he ever had*," anyway, she never recovered from the fact that he married my mother (instead of *her*, Doctah Freud) and became rich.

Sophie is the founding member of the "And after all I've done for you" school. Ethel is the treasurer. Ethel even says *that* to Sophie. But Ethel is so wrapped up in how rotten her sons are for growing up and getting married and not inviting her for dinner at least twenty-five times each (she counts by figuring out approximately when they might be having someone for dinner and then takes herself off the list, e.g., :"I bet they're having company after temple Friday night"). Also, even though her oldest, my cousin Louis, became a dentist ("took every rotten cent we had"), he still chose his *own* wife and then did not even produce a grandchild. And the younger son would not eat her famous matzo balls (the recipe was inscribed on the Dead Sea Scrolls) or come home by nine o'clock, no matter what she threatened. (He was, at the time, twenty-four.)

So, on the one side we have Estelle, Louise and Morley, all rose-petal skin, sighing, hand-wringing, romantic, hysterical, mystical, and on the other, we have Sophie and Ethel, smelling of witch hazel, stiff-lipped, practical, repressed. If you could mush them all together you'd probably have one relatively normal human being. One more thing Ethel and Sophie never forgave my father for. His legs. He got the good legs. They both have legs like Tupperware containers. "Look at that," Sophie would whisper, during summer poolside visits. "He got the legs and he's a man! He wears pants all the time, they're wasted on him!"

And now for the lurid adventures of my maternal grandma, Bubba Bodkin.

My mother's mother was my first negative role model for womanhood. It shaped me to have a grandmother who never stood upright. From my first memory she was sitting in a chair with her hands folded in her lap, dozing off. "Tell Bubba you're here, dear," my mother would whisper, and then in turn all my relatives would approach Grandma's good ear and shout into it, "Hannah's here, Momma!" Sometimes she would blink, open her eyes and take my hand. Sometimes she wouldn't. Since Aunt Estelle lived with her and my grandfather and took care of them, she was the least patient. "She does that on purpose, she hears everything."

Aunt Estelle's view of family history was all categorized as B.A. and A.A. (Before Arthritis and After Arthritis). My grandmother's arthritis was the turning point in Estelle's lustful life. "You know, Hanny, honey," she'd confide to me on those rare occasions when I was permitted to watch her make up (oh, Estelle, I miss your vanity table. I miss your hair lacquer in the atomizer with the bulb attached and your rat-handled combs and the Jergens lotion smelling of cherries and the eyelash curler, wonder of wonders, and the nail buffer and the lipstick brushes and the bright pink rouges from Woolworth's and the face powder with the purple duster, a work of art it was; truly, how I longed to be...you), "B.A., I could go dancing three nights a week and bring fellows home, but A.A., well, men don't like that, I mean Bubba looks so awful, sitting there like that with those black boots, spitting on herself. I had a lot more freedom B.A."

If ever a woman existed who should have proved to me that you don't have to be perfect to be loved, it was Bubba Bodkin. (Now, *that* would have been positive role modeling, so naturally I paddled right around it.) She did...nothing. Oh, before B.A. got too bad and senility was added to the list of her charms, she would soak lettuce in lemon juice and oil and leave it in a bowl on the table for my grandfather. "Crisp" was not a Yiddish word. But, mainly, since life turned sour and she gave up her independence, she just basically didn't give a damn about anything. And my grandfather worshiped her. He got her up every morning, and (A.A.) that was a feat in itself. He bathed her. He dressed her. He laced up her black boots. My grandmother only had one pair of shoes. She was wearing them in the family album in 1900, and she was wearing them the day she died. Black boots with 4,000 hooks and eyes. My grandfather took them off for her every night and laced them all the way back up every morning (which segued them right into soggy lettuce time). "Look at her, Hannah," he'd whisper to me. "Look how beautiful your Bubba is, as beautiful as the day I married her." I saw a toothless old dame with a little drool on her chin. If she raised her hand, my mother, Morley, Estelle and my grandfather leaped to their feet. "She's going to say something!" they would shout in glee. Usually she just lowered her hand again (probably testing the poor devils). Then one Mother's Day, when I was about fifteen, she called my name. Everyone went completely insane. "Hannah, Hannah, she wants you! Bubba wants you!" I was pushed forward like Salome to Herod and deposited at her feet. She raised her hand and opened her eyes. "She's going to say something! Shush, everyone! She's going to say something to Hannah!" She took my hand and stared at me for what seemed to be three hours. No one moved. My mother held her hand over my brother's mouth. Finally, she spoke. "Who are you?" she inquired. Not much to pass on to my grandchildren.

Well, notebook, just a bit more and I'll get you ready for the time capsule. I've been developing a theory called "People in Groups." Basically it is that everyone has some literal obsession, some object or person that is symbolic of their whole life. It involves their fear, hope and dream. Without it they would warp and wither (at least till it could be replaced). For my grandmother, it was arthritis and her boots; for my grandfather, it was my grandmother; for Estelle, it is her Vanity Table; for Agatha, it is her hat and her emerald ring; for me, it's my typewriter; for Nick, it's his... ? Funny. I don't know. For my father, it's his house. For Sophie, it's her letter writing. For Ethel, it's her matzo-ball recipe and her resentment. For Morley, it's the Old Testament; and for Aunt Louise, it's her freezer. The freezer is the most perfect symbolic obsession. Everything in her life is cluttered, unfocused and hysterical. But her freezer would bring Betty Crocker to her knees. She keeps it in her bedroom. It is very old. It is immaculate. It is always filled layer by layer with enough food to survive war with Russia. Whole sides of beef, cut and hand marked in red ink, twenty-pound turkeys, gallons of ice cream, stacks of frozen vegetables, endless containers of homemade tomato sauce, chicken soup, butter, bread, juices. It is as cool and orderly as she is hot and messy. I think she is in love with it. If Estelle had to choose between a man and her Vanity Table, she'd take the table. And if Louise had to choose between my uncle, my cousin and her deep freeze...may God never put her to the test. But why don't I know about my husband? Maybe because I've never seen the inside of his freezer.

I truly hope this notebook is not a regression. Somehow the madness that now surrounds me is pulling me back into the past, and all of these relatives who knew me first are banging on the door to my head, refusing to go away. I'm trying to open it.

Hannah's eyes hurt. She closed them, turning off her typewriter without looking, knowing every inch, every sound, putt-putt, creak and cranny.

She sat, hands held gently over her eyes, trying to unlatch the tension.

"I'm so tired. So damn tired. I shouldn't be this tired."

She opened her eyes and picked up her red pencil.

She worked steadily, face and body tensed in discipline. Do it. Just do it.

Tears. Appearing from some spastic part of her brain. Springing, without thought or access, washing her cheeks. "Oh, God, I'm so tired." Hannah put her head on her hands, then pressed her taut, throbbing eyes into her forearms. "Somebody help me, somebody make it go away." The fear was back, clutching her chest, reaching up at her from unconsciousness. "Momma," she started, the word, like the tears, uncontrollable, "somebody wants to hurt me."

The phone rang.

Hannah stiffened. Tears stopping as insensibly as they had started.

"Hello."

"Is this Mrs. Nicoli?"

"Yes, it is." Hannah wiped her eyes.

"This is Miss Robinson at the telephone company. I believe you called about changing your telephone number."

"Yes, I did, but we've changed our minds."

"My report says that you were receiving harassing and threatening calls, have they stopped?"

"No."

"I'm sorry, I'm afraid I don't understand."

"Yes, well, it's rather complicated. The police have requested that we do not change our number so that they can try and trace the calls. Well, not trace them exactly, but they want us to tape the messages." Hannah paused, fury choking her.

"That must be unpleasant."

"You might say that. Anyway, we will not be changing the number for a while. I'll call and re-place the order, when, um, when this is over."

"Well, good luck. I'll take your name off the list then."

"When *what?*" Hannah replaced the phone, holding it away from her body as if it were rotting. "When *what?*"

Hannah stood up, stacking sheets of paper carelessly together, fingers impatiently soiling words.

"Got to get this copied, got to hold on. Get home. Get some sleep."

The sun seared her eyes, still raw from their outburst. Hannah put on her huge dark glasses like an invisible shield protecting her from the light and the other eyes. She disappeared behind the glasses. "I can see them, but they can't see me." Covered, she marched, her step brisk, filled with forced energy, fighting her despair, down the street to her car.

She put the key in the ignition and turned it. Nothing happened. She tried it again and again. "Goddamn Germans, God's punishing me for buying a Nazi car." Hannah sat behind the wheel, feeling lame. She closed her eyes, trying to motivate herself back up the street to call for help.

In a moment she was asleep and dreaming; she was naked, flying across a black-velvet screen, being chased by a centaur with her father's face, her aunts and her mother flying above, flapping white arms through a black-velvet sky. A man appeared beside her who looked like her husband; she reached out her arms to pull him close, and he pushed her away, mocking her mistake and flying out of reach. Neilie was screaming and running toward her, hair flowing into branches, clutching her tiny face. Hannah pulled her hands away and her face was gone. "She burned me," the child cried.

A key was tapping loudly on her window. Someone was calling her name. Hannah jumped from sleep.

"Hannah! Hannah! Wake up." Nick stood outside her window, smiling in at her. See, it's okay. We're still okay. Nothing's wrong.

She opened the door. "Oh, honey, I fell asleep, how ridiculous. I was really tired and I got in and the damn battery is dead again and I just closed my eyes for a minute. What are you doing here, did God send you?"

He laughed. "No, Jesus called. I'm Catholic, remember, we use a middle man."

It felt good, better than for a very long while.

"I had a meeting with your father's stockbroker and I was just around the corner so I thought I'd walk over to your office, and I saw this little redhead snoring away."

"I was not snoring. Please tell me I wasn't snoring."

"Okay, you weren't snoring."

"Oh, God, I was. Was I? No!"

"Hannah, I am not going to have one of those conversations."

"Okay. Okay. I was *not* snoring. Do you happen to have a set of jumper cables in your efficient Japanese vehicle? I'll buy you a drink or let you sleep in the barn or whatever you want." Hannah stiffened, knowing how long it had been since the "whatever he wanted" had been good, been full of the lusty innocence with which it had started.

"Yep, I think so. Walk over to my car with me and I'll drive you back."

They walked up the quiet, late-afternoon city street, holding hands, looking like friends and lovers, looking happy. She stared up at him, feeling reassured. See, it's okay. Only a dream. Nothing's changed. Healthy children, nice house, a man who loves you. It's okay, baby. We're going to be fine.

CHAPTER 12

Hannah stood at the chopping board making chicken salad for her aunts and enjoying the early morning quiet. Charlie was at the park with Tina, Neilie was at nursery school, Nick was in the office and she was alone. She felt lulled by the silence, not thinking backward or forward, not analyzing or criticizing, just chopping celery and being alive.

It felt good. It was not usual. Usual was a mental slide show of memories and fantasies, clicking through her head, taking her from the present into a zone of unease. In the tension of the new pressure, Hannah's slide show had taken on Shakespearian proportions. She could blame it all on the madwoman, but when she was willing to be honest she knew that that was a lie. It had started before. That new dimension had simply accelerated it, pushing the pictures onto the screen at jet-stream pace. Now they were in remission. She and Nick were relaxed together, and she was not rerunning the past into this kinder new present.

Her father had called offering to take Neilie home from school, and they had spoken civilly with one another. Under her breath she kept reassuring herself, "See, see, you were just overreacting. Marriage is okay. Family is okay. Life is good." She had sold a story to a trendy new magazine, and Nick was talking about going into business for himself.

Hannah tightened. That subject was part of the slide show, part of the fantasies of loss and failure that had for the moment stopped clicking endlessly through her overworked brain. "Cut the onions, Hannah, just cut the onions."

By 11:30 everything was ready. The table was set and the house clean. Charlie was shiny, sitting on his plastic throne waiting to be admired. The doorbell rang and she took a long, deep breath, talking to herself as was her custom, preparing for the onslaught of this bizarre quartet. "Now, they cannot harm you, *or* manipulate you, you are guilty of nothing. Just referee and keep your mouth shut."

The Oberman sisters stood in the doorway unsmiling, holding their purses against their flat bellies as if constantly prepared for mugging. Two human bookends, standing side by side, wearing matching gray bobbed hair and brown orthopedic shoes and shirtwaist dresses with good wool sweaters jewelry-clipped to their shoulders, and bifocal lenses hanging on ribbons around their weathered necks.

"Hello, stranger."

"Hello, Aunt Sophie. Hello, Ethel. You both look well."

"Knock wood." Ethel tapped her small scrubbed hand on the front door.

"Why don't we sit in the living room and talk for a few minutes until Estelle and Louise get here?"

"Sit, shmit. Where's the baby?" Sophie and Ethel marched down the hall to the kitchen. Hannah followed, smiling to herself. Nice to see you, Hannah, you're looking wonderful, dear.

"He's in the kitchen."

Sophie and Ethel marched into the kitchen, forming a crisp critical wall around Charlie.

Come on, Charlie, one for the Gipper. Turn on the charm. Hannah stood behind her aunts trying to catch the baby's eye.

The baby looked up, taking in the new information, sizing up the intruders with the unerring intuition of the innocent. He giggled. He gurgled, he charmed. "Charlie eat tuney. Charlie go bye-bye. I lof vou. Charlie kiss. Charlie kiss."

It was an Academy Award performance. The Oberman sisters, sent by the Gestapo to wipe out the Nicolis, weakened before the secret weapon, smiles breaking into the hardened lines of their potato-blank faces. "What a doll. Sophie, he's a living doll. How he's grown! Look at those chunky arms. Look at those curls. He's a doll, Hannah. He looks just like your father did at that age. Doesn't he, Sophie? We'll send a picture. The same curls, what a doll."

Sophie and Ethel leaned into the baby, examining his soft pink body while Charlie beamed at them.

The doorbell rang. "That must be Estelle and Louise. I'll get it." Sophie and Ethel exchanged glances, which Hannah tried to ignore.

She opened the chiming door on the remainder of her family.

Perfume and powder smells engulfed her. Going out was such a unique and arduous ordeal for the Bodkin sisters that it required days of preparation and planning. The results were evident in the brightly painted and clothed visions before her. Louise sighed, turning her cheek for a makeup-protecting peck, her turquoise-rayon dress straining over her widening hips. "I baked you some fudge brownies, dear. I wanted to put fresh walnuts in them, but I haven't slept in days and I didn't have the strength to shell them."

"Oh, how nice, thank you, Louise. Hello, Estelle."

"*Candy*, Hanny. Call me *Candy* in public, you always forget." Her aunt wiggled forward caressing her cheeks, her hands moving over Hannah's shoulders and across her breasts and hips. "Such a gorgeous little body."

"Estelle—Candy—please!"

"Sorry, dear. I just can't help myself, such a pretty figure."

Louise sighed. "Are they here yet?"

"Yes, they're in the kitchen with the baby, come on in."

Hannah stood back, letting her fluorescent aunts wiggle down the hall before her.

"Sophie, Ethel, Estelle, um, Candy and Louise are here."

The Obermans stiffened, shutting off their smiles like windows slamming. Sophie handed Charlie to Ethel, territory claimed.

"So, who's Candy? I only see two people, Estelle and Louise."

Estelle blushed, Hannah moved forward. "Oh, remember, that's Estelle's nickname, remember, when she was an extra?"

"That was thirty years ago." Ethel's sharp, bifocaled eyes moved over Estelle, taking in the orange-haired pyramid, the bright purple jump suit with the pink Spring-Olator shoes exposing matching pink toenails. "Hello, *Estelle*. Hello, Louise. How've you been? Haven't seen you since Leah's funeral. How's Morley?"

"Tired. He's been running the Sunday school for his rabbi."

Louise unwrapped her luscious brownies and set them daintily on the sink.

Charlie began to cry, missing the limelight.

Estelle reached out her powdered bare arms. "Oh, Charlie-Cake, come to your aunt Candy! What a sweet handsome lamb chop! Gonna drive the girls crazy!" Ethel held him against her starched chest like her pocketbook, guarding against this unexpected attack.

"He's tired. He shouldn't be passed around like a salami."

"Oh, just a minute. He knows his auntie won't hurt him."

Ethel held on.

Estelle held on.

Charlie screamed.

"Now, now, Charlie." Hannah moved swiftly between them, gathering the baby like an intercepted pass.

"Why don't you all sit? I'll put him down for his nap."

Hannah slung Charlie over her shoulder and carried him, sobbing against her shoulder up to bed.

She could hear the phone ringing below and Sophie calling to her from the kitchen. She put Charlie in bed quickly, forgetting to change his diaper, so tense now from the referee's position, so filled with anger at her continual need to try to reach these people, to perform for the jaded troops, fighting the reality of her own aloneness and the emptiness inside that they could not fill.

Pretending that they had something she needed and that without them she did not exist.

If I have no mother, no father, no relatives, I will disappear.

Fantasy slides again, clicking behind her eyes.

She raced down the stairs two at a time and took the receiver from her aunt's cold hand.

"Please, everyone start without me, I'll only be a minute."

"Hello?"

"Having a party, slut?"

Hannah slammed down the receiver, her hand trembling.

Her aunts watched her, looking from one to another, silently.

"So, what kind of call was that?"

"Wrong number, Ethel."

It rang again.

"Better answer it, dear, they probably don't know they've made a mistake. My psychic says that all phone calls are the right number, that something in the person's higher consciousness causes them to dial a different number." Louise piled chicken salad into a neat, deep mound on her plate.

"Mumbo jumbo," Sophie muttered, buttering a hot croissant as if it were a concrete slab.

"Hanny, answer it, it's making me very nervous!" Estelle sipped ice tea, blinking at Hannah through thickly woven artificial lashes.

"I really don't want to. Someone's been annoying us. It's probably them. It's just a nuisance call. They'll stop soon."

But the phone rang on. Until she could not excuse it.

She picked it up, acting out the appropriate mood for the four sets of wary eyes watching her over their forks.

"Father fucker I"

She pressed down the button and put the receiver on the sink.

"Oh, Hanny! My boyfriend was going to call, maybe!"

"I'm sorry, Estelle. The calls are just too annoying. Let's leave it off for a while. You can call him later."

Estelle pouted. A child with a broken cookie.

"So, Hannah, how's Norman? I notice he's not here." Sophie picked the onions out of her salad.

Anger tightened her again. Reality breaking into her morning reverie.

Everything is not okay, Hannah. Face it.

"He's fine. He's been working very hard, buying a shopping center, and he had to be in Palm Springs early this morning. He sent his best."

Four Oberman eyebrows shot up. "Another shopping center? So, how much does a sixty-year-old widower need to be happy?"

Hannah did not respond, her attention diverted by the displaced receiver facing her across the table.

Finally, lunch was over. Estelle forgot her boyfriend, the baby slept late, taking their reason to linger. They had coffee and helped clear the table, Ethel and Sophie declining Louise's brownies as would be expected. She walked them to the door, promising to call, to visit, to send pictures of the children. She was drained, like a marathon swimmer pulled back into the boat, trailing her broken shark cage behind her. "So much for family life," Hannah sighed, grabbed her car keys and called to Tina, "*Voy para regalos por Navidad. Hasta luego,*" leaving the phone behind.

Christmas again. Impossible.

WALTER DOBINSKI'S GIFTS FROM AROUND THE WORLD—"HERE RETAIL IS A DIRTY WORD."

Hannah swung her car around and parked in front of the big red sign, not really thinking or caring what she would find inside.

I'll just take a peek, maybe something for the gardener.

The moment she opened the door, she knew she had made a mistake.

"What do you want, Charlie Brown?"

"I want to get in your pants, Lucy."

"Why, Charlie Brown?"

" 'Cause I just shit in mine, Lucy."

"Bring some love into the world—FUCK someone, TODAY."

An assortment of mangy party aprons strung along the walls stopped her.

Oh, Christ, Hannah, pick up a little towelette for the gardener.

"Hello, there, young lady. What can I do for you?" A skinny, tobacco-stained old man wearing a sequined string tie appeared out of nowhere.

"Oh, nothing, thank you. I really thought this was a different kind of gift store. I was just..."

"Don't be afraid. We've got something for everyone, one of a kind." He picked up a squirt gun with a huge pink rubber penis forming the barrel. "Great little gag, huh? Look at this!" He leaped across her, grabbed at a pair of spectacles with a big rubber nose shaped like the water-pistol penis and placed it on his face. "Open the door at a party like this and it'll kill 'um, just kill 'um."

Hannah stood mesmerized. "Yes, that's very cute, but it's not the kind of thing I had in mind. Thank you anyway."

But even as she spoke, she knew she didn't want to leave. Her eyes roamed the room over matching organ-shaped bride-and-groom lamps; vibrators in primary colors; a fried-chicken basket reading "BOX LUNCH" with a plastic vagina tufted with thick black hair set neatly between a knife and fork; dirty-joke books; floozy calendars adorned with thigh-expanded, mush-faced women; erected male puppets that thrust into naked female puppets with the flick of a switch.

"Look at this, young lady!" The skinny old man held two small plastic cylinders in his hand. "Watch this! When I turn on the batteries, these little dillies vibrate (drives a woman crazy, I don't have to tell you where, do I?)."

"No, I have two children, I think I know where."

I must be mad.

Hannah found herself standing in front of a little plastic man. He had a big gap-toothed grin and a large round nose. He was clad in a tiny Hawaiian-patterned terry-cloth towel from his waist down.

"Go on, push his head! That's a great one. Go on, young lady! You don't have to buy it 'cause you touch it!"

The urge to push the funny hobbling head was overwhelming. Her eyes glistened like a three-year-old forbidden Mommy's things. Despite her disdain and her discomfort, she could not keep her finger away. She quickly pushed the grinning head down. A bright red penis shot out from under the tiny terry-cloth swatch. And she did it again.

"You've got a great little sense of humor, young lady. Let me show you something really terrific. I've got a guy in Phoenix that just bought two hundred of these for Christmas presents. Now I've got to put it together, it's a little tricky, just takes a minute."

He moved quickly in the small, jerking movements of the very skinny, pulling open drawers of dildoes and plastic titties; cards showing babies with huge male organs boasting "Me at 2"; and finally grabbing out a small series of plastic lumps pressed together in some undefinable mass. His scrawny yellowed fingers pushed the bits apart, dismembering the lump.

Hannah watched in cynical child-wonder as he pushed the bits and pieces into shape. Two forms emerged. A tiny erected male positioned in back of a tiny pink female. Below them was a lever, half the length of a child's finger.

"I'd better do this for you, it's a little tricky at first. You start slow, then you pick up speed."

He moved the lever, and the little pink man's body thrust itself forward, the penis disappearing between the little plastic legs of the woman, and he moved it faster. His eyes twinkled, tongue moving over his slack lower lip.

Hannah stood behind him watching these two tiny plastic people thrusting, building in perfect sex rhythm, and she felt excitement flood her, passion lost for so long from her life, lost with her husband, triggered by bits of cheap pink plastic. She ached to take the toy in her own hands and work it herself.

"Want to try it?"

"Oh, no, thank you. I don't think so." She longed to buy it.

"Here you keep it. Free of charge. It'll make you remember the place."

He dropped it into Hannah's purse.

"What's that over there?" Hannah pointed to a box on the floor, not caring what it was, trying to protect her pride, endangered by the acceptance of the gift from this decaying little man. Knowing that by remaining, she was losing her right to judge him.

"Oh, now this is our best item, no one else carries it." Hannah moved toward the box, saved from having to acknowledge the exchange of the pretty plastic fuckers. She looked down into the face of a deflated rubber girl.

"Manuel, Manuel! Get out here and blow one of these things up for the little lady."

"Oh, no, really, that isn't necessary. I was just curious."

"No, no! We need one blown up for the decor, anyway. Manuel!"

A soft-faced Mexican boy shuffled in, his eyes lidded in coagulated boredom. He put a small bicycle pump into the deflated, overpainted face and began to pump.

WHOOSH. WHOOSH. WHOOSH.

A phone was ringing. " 'Scuse me, honey, that may be important."

The skinny little man slithered past her, making his way between miniature electric crap tables and horseracing games, cocktail glasses shouting "FUCKIT OR SUCKIT" at the thirsty, and disappeared.

The boy pumped lethargically, head down. Hannah turned away, embarrassed to watch, as the lady's face filled out, her breasts popped, her arms began to tighten. WHOOSH. WHOOSH. WHOOSH.

She found a revolving cocktail tray with a little plastic cherub set on top. Alone, a child now; alone to do forbidden things.

Remembering all the magic forbidden things she had done. Unrecapturable, lovely things, made magical and perfect by the danger and the aloneness. She pushed his head. The little cherub peed water into the little glasses.

"Great gimmick! Isn't that something? People die over that one. Fill it up with beer or wine or anything, people love it!"

Hannah pulled her hand away quickly.

WHOOSH. WHOOSH. WHOOSH.

She turned to see the deflated lady's legs pop out.

The phone rang again. "People drive me crazy, can't get enough of this stuff." He skittered around her and disappeared again.

The boy took the pump out and stood, holding the lady in one limp arm. His head straightened and their eyes met, passing some secret, some moment of understanding of what they were and what was real in this place.

"It's for the old men. The old men, they like thees."

He looked at her again, quizzically. The absurdity rising between them. Two strangers from unfriendly worlds, conversing between a garish rubber dummy with three real rubber holes for old men and traveling salesmen to relieve their sex-yearnings into.

"What did I tell you! Great, isn't it?" His voice lowered, he brought straggly graying eyebrows together. "Got the mouth and the front and back, ya know, like the real thing."

"How much is that?"

"Fifteen ninety-five."

"I'll take one."

And two Box Lunches for Ethel and Sophie, a couple of dildoes for Estelle and Louise and an uncircumcised cherub for Morley.

"Manuel, wrap one up for the little lady. Terrific party gag.

"I'm buying it for my father. He likes party gags."

She smiled mockingly, feeling ashamed at the bitter, sickening irony of her choice, her Christmas greeting to her father.

The boy shuffled back. The lady, all deflated now and thrown carelessly, befitting her station, into a used, brown market bag.

"There you are, young lady, you come again and tell your friends."

"Oh, I will. Thank you."

Hannah walked rapidly to her car. She tossed the lady in the back seat and slid behind the wheel. Ignoring the car waiting to take her place, she opened her purse, grabbed up the little pink plastic people and sat, smiling and excited, moving them back and forth in precise, rugged sexmotion.

CHAPTER 13

"Okay ladies, let's get that circulation going. Take a deep breath in and hold it, now let it out! And again. In and out.

"Now jog! Get those knees up! Higher! Faster! Tummies in! Now get those knees all the way up! Up and down and up, up. Tighten those tummies harder!"

She was sweating already.

Deep breaths, I haven't been able to take a deep breath in days. Oh, God, I may die here, thirty more minutes. Look at her, never sweats, never pants, talks while she's jogging, never misses a step. It's not human.

"Okay now ladies, bend those knees and let's do some elbow touches. Stretch those spines! Come on now. One and two and three and four..."

I hate that one. That's the worst. She does it on purpose. That's the killer, loses half the class with that one. All the old ladies start fading. One of these days someone's going to croak during that one and they'll send ol' taut tummy to jail, killed an old lady, toe-touched her to death, in front of twenty witnesses.

Hannah rolled and sweated, her legs thrashing, arms stretching, mind and body in deadly conflict. Thoughts invading the mindless activity almost like dreams. Bits of images rolling around in her, straining.

Got to talk to Nick. Got to stop taping. Better call home,

see how Charlie is. Got to stop thinking about it. Christmas is coming.

"Very good ladies. Okay now, roll over on your tummies, let's do some swan dives. Now get those legs up and tighten and hold. Hold iiiit."

Sweat poured down her face.

Oh, I hate this. Why do I do this? What's a little flab? Nick likes a little flesh. Look at her! Not a hair disturbed! Swan dives. I'm not a fucking bird, no swan alive ever did this. All the old ladies are gasping. One of these days— Murder! Good story line. "The Health Spa Slaughter." How crafty. Tight-tushied gym instructor swan-dived the wife of her lover to death.

Bad thoughts returning, morning panic. That voice echoing behind her motions, her constant preoccupation.

"The police can't do anything to me. Don't you know that? Where's that big brave husband of yours? You can't hurt me. You're the one that's going to get hurt."

Rage flashed, flushing her face.

I could kill her. I don't want to hate anyone, it's making me so bitter.

"Okay now, everyone on all fours, let's do some nose-to-knee kicks! Get those legs up and in and out! Get them high, watch out for your neighbors! Don't kick anyone! Breathe deeply, and one and two and in and out. Kick 'em! Kick 'em higher!"

Oh, shit.

Hannah's knee crashed into her nose. She stopped, crouching on all fours, body smells washing over her, sounds whirling, the moans and puffs of the unwounded, the still fighting. The young, the strong, the unafraid, struggling onward against the enemy. FLAB! FAT! OLD! SAGGY! More dreaded than the German Army. They valiantly fought on, past strength, past sense, higher, tighter, faster, harder! Till they broke. A kick in the nose.

First casualty this week for the Nicoli regiment. A pulled muscle. One out in the rear flank. Old lady dizzy in the front lines.

Wounded. Hannah crouched, sweat dripping from her lowered, throbbing face onto the feet-scented floor. Her breath came in gasps, stomach heaving in an effort to regain composure, remove pain.

Probably broke my nose, always wanted a nose job anyway.

She got up, snatching her locker key in fury, feeling unreasonable anger at the smiling, remote being, nose-to-kneeing before her.

It's not fair, Mommy I try so hard.

Long-ago sobs melting into today's pain.

I'm a good girl. I try so hard.

Hannah stormed from the room, ignoring the exhausted eyes following her retreat in agonized victory.

Hot steam, cold shower. Lipstick. Comb the hair. I'll be okay.

Hannah opened her locker, stripping off her soaking gym clothes and tossing them nervously into her bag; reaching for her robe and slippers in hasty, snatching motions.

She slammed her locker shut and moved quickly past the wilted army of survivors emerging from the gym.

As she passed the bulletin board, she glanced casually at the assortment of health messages—ginseng treatment, rooms for rent, Poodles for sale—and reached for the shower room door.

Something caught her eye. Something that did not fit there. She released the door and returned to the board. In the lower left-hand corner, pinned between an announcement for Transcendental Meditation classes and water ballet instructions, was a front-and-side photo of a small child.

Missing from Worcester, Massachusetts since August 10, 1978: David Jordan Freeman

Age—6 years
Height—3 feet 9 inches

Weight—42 pounds
Skin—olive
Hair—curly brown
Eyes—hazel
Distinguishing features—small scar on right cheek from dog bite.

FAMILY WILL GIVE $25,000 REWARD FOR INFORMATION LEADING TO WHEREABOUTS.

Hannah swallowed, batting at tears with sweat-lidded eyes. The baby face of a nice, middle-class child, stuck there 3,000 miles away from his home. Stuck there, without thought. Passed by. Scanned by hundreds of restless eyes looking for health, looking for bargains, looking for instant beauty. Eyes grazing by a child's mug shot. A family, shouting behind him, shrieking out across the country. Pleading for an end to a nightmare. Hannah stood frozen with emotion. The faces of her children covering David Freeman.

I want to go home.

Hannah brushed at her eyes and pulled in confusion at the shower door. Home, now invaded like a diseased body by the unseeable.

Home. A child skating after dark away from the cold. Smells of buttered bread and beef. Skinned knees bandaged, bullies thwarted, bathtubs waiting, mothers hugging. Safe and sound and kept from trouble. Nose running, feelings punctured. I want to go HOME.

It was already dark when she pulled in the driveway. She had tried, driving too fast, to beat the dark as if the light offered some arcane security. But it hadn't worked.

Still red-cheeked and flushed from the gym, Hannah, blood pounding in her temples, locked her car, knowing that she had never done such a thing in her own driveway in her entire life.

"Mommy, Mommy, Charlie kiss. Charlie cookie, cookie."

A sigh escaped. He's alive. Another reprieve. Children eating cookies and taking baths, while thousands of mothers moved around harboring dreaded, uncontrollable fantasies.

Tina appeared in the doorway, her dark brown eyes sad, the family tension now part of her own separate burdens.

"Tina, todo is bueno?"

"No, Mrs. La mujer negativa telefoneó muchas veces."

Nerves shattered. Like a captured spy given no rest, no chance to regain strength. Hannah felt her body tighten and tension lock every joint, every muscle. She felt herself moving beyond humor, beyond the civility she so cherished, to blind, overstretched emotion. Atavistic, primal lashing in the mind took hold of her. A hate so powerful, a fury at all helplessness, all the angers: Children bullied, leaders lying, baby food with metal splinters, drunks driving into school buses. Trusts betrayed, betrayed endlessly. Milk-rich dairymen pouring surpluses like white murder down city drains. Nuclear power plants. Handguns sold like toys. Oil on the beaches. Ozone layer disappearing. Politicians lying and lying and smiling and lying. Stupidity and ignorance and acceptance of Armageddon. All of the impotence she had ever felt, all of the anger it had ever caused, every betrayal and disappointment hit.

And in that moment she joined everything she hated.

I'll kill her. We'll have her killed.

The phone rang.

"Don't touch it, Tina! ¡Yo, yo!" She put down the baby and raced the stairs two by two to her room, slamming the door. The phone by her bed rang on. Hannah fumbled with the tape, moistening the earpiece with her tongue and pasting it over the receiver. Her hand was trembling. She pushed the record button and picked up the phone.

"Hello."

Drunken breathing hissed against her ear.

Hannah's throat was ice cold, hate tightening her mouth. "I will not permit you to continue this. The police are looking for you and they will find you. You're a sick, cruel person...you."

Shrieks of laughter, drunken snorting filled her head.

Hannah slammed the phone down, unable to communicate, unable to think.

No cunning, I never did have any cunning! I don't know what to say, don't know how. I need help.

Tears came, washing the hate.

Katharine Hepburn would know what to say.

The phone rang.

"Hello." Hannah pushed frantically at the machine, trying to restart. Giggling, babbling noises. "We're coming to take your kids."

The phone closed.

Hannah threw it on the bed, panic spreading.

She heard Neilie come in from school.

"My father picked Neilie up!" She was up, moving for the stairs.

"Dad, will you come up here for a minute, please?" His face paled. "Well, I have a dinner date."

"It's important."

"Mommy, is the bad lady calling again? Did she say bad words to you?"

"Yes, she did, sweetheart, but it's okay. I just want to talk to Grandpa for a minute. You go in and have your dinner and then we'll play War."

"Okay, Mommy. You tell that lady if she calls my mommy bad names again, I'll punch her in the nose."

Her father moved up the stairs, head lowered.

"She's been calling all day. I just got home and she started. She said she's coming tonight to take the children. I can't stand any more of this. Did you talk to the police? Have they found anything? I want to kill her!"

"You're getting hysterical. She's just trying to upset you. I talked to Hudson this morning, they haven't found her yet." He paused, looking away from her. "She's been calling me, too. She's drunk. Now, just calm down."

"I can't calm down! How the hell do I calm down? It's a

nightmare. When we tell someone about it, they look at us like we're diseased. It's so ugly. How can you stand it? How could you let this happen? After what she put Mother through! You don't give a damn about us, you couldn't. If she comes here, if she touches this house, I'll kill her, I will."

She paused, panting with hurt. "I'm ashamed you're my father! I loved you, I trusted you, despite everything, I did. You don't care that I'm innocent, that I haven't done anything and this creature is trying to destroy me!" She was sobbing, doubled over on the bed, holding her stomach. Words never said. Anger, betrayal, pushed back forever behind the good girl's mask; needing the love and approval of this man and so terrified of his anger; holding her own, pushing it down in fear of losing the last thread of her childhood, her child-self. Justifying him and endlessly forgiving. Converting the reality of his character, his sickness into fantasy and self-hate. Refusing to accept him as he was and so, refusing to accept herself, grasping at her dying fable like a drowning child.

"That's not true!" Her father's face was purple with fear. "Whaddaya want from me! I'm trying! I made mistakes! I gave what I could! I'm not an emotional man; I can't help it. I'm weak, I know that, but I'm tired of being the bad guy. I did everything for you and your brother. Everything! You always had a beautiful home, new cars. I sent you to college. I helped you buy this house, gave your husband a job, helped him learn a business, what do you want from me?"

It came slowly, as he spat the words in the fury of his frustration, spat them like animal venom thwarting the enemy, it came to Hannah that for him, what he said was solid truth. And it was all he knew. All he had. And all he could or would ever have. He would never be able to hear or understand her need or her anger. And he would *never* change. He had devised his defense system, his fort against guilt and the emotional demands of the wife and children he needed but could not love, with the strength and precision of the true survivor. He could no longer see over the wall or beyond the warning signal, the threat of a demand to perform as the person they wanted him to be, and without his fortress he could not survive.

"Okay, Dad. You go on. I'll call Nick, see if he can come home. I am upset. It's okay."

He stood, hands in pockets, face mottled as if he had been suddenly sick. He had lived his life the only way he could and he did not understand what she wanted.

"Okay, okay, I'll call those bastards tomorrow. Yeah, I, uh, better go. I've got to pick up this broad in the Valley."

He hesitated, as if part of him wanted to touch her, take her hand, kiss her. He leaned forward on his toes, hands still thrust deep in his leather pockets, and then he turned and quickly left the room.

And then Daddy Warbucks sits Annie on his knee.

Hannah sat in the dark listening to the sounds of her children playing below.

The phone rang.

"Hello."

"Well, well, well...don't have enough on your little tape machine yet, poor little rich girl?"

She slammed it back, slamming it into the receiver over and over as if the instrument was the form, as if by destroying the instrument she could hurt the voice.

Neilie stood in the doorway, eyes wide with child-fear of the bizarre, the slightest alteration in the structure of their lives.

"What's the matter, Mommy? Why are you smashing the telephone?"

Oh, God, what do I do? What do I do?

"Neilie, baby, come here, Mommy wants to talk to you."

"Don't cry, Mommy, everything will be all right. Would you like to play with some of my toys or something?"

Mothers, mothers, motherrrrs.

"No thank you, darling. Listen, I'll tell you the truth like always. Okay?"

The child nodded, her eyes blinking, bracing to understand, to be brave.

"That bad lady, well, she keeps calling Mommy and saying bad words, and finally Mommy got so angry that she got mad at the telephone. It's like when you want to hit Charlie and I tell you to go sock your pillow or pound on your drum? Well, I can't hit the lady, so I hit the telephone."

Tears edged out of the huge, baby-clear eyes. "I don't want that lady to hurt your feelings. I don't like it when you hit the telephone. I don't want the pleecemens to come here anymore."

They held one another, stroking in love, passing warmth and courage.

"Don't worry, darling. Mommy's going to call Daddy right now and see what we can do. Maybe we'll all go on a vacation for a little while. Would you like that?"

"To Palm Screams?"

Hannah laughed softly, kissing away her child's tears.

"Maybe. Now don't you worry, no one is going to hurt any of us. You go and have your bath and I'll call Daddy."

The child rose, shoulders straight, head level, moving away from inclusion in things she did not really want to know, back to the bubbles and color of her innocence.

Hannah snatched at the receiver. Driven by the need to reach someone, to share, to relinquish.

You take over, just take over.

To unload on her husband what she was not able to settle for herself.

"Oberman Incorporated."

"Did Mr. Nicoli leave a number where he could be reached?"

"No. I'm sorry, no message."

Rage washed her. He never left a number. And she always reacted the same way. She knew that game, part of the "I'll show you" routine. "Passive-aggressive hostility" was the label she had neatly attached and taped on his forehead. It fit all the things that drove her crazy. Leaving her the car with an empty tank, coming in an hour late when they had a dinner date, letting the health insurance lapse, never leaving a phone number. Each a small, silly thing, but building like drops of stale water, until one too many falls and the stagnant tub spills over.

Her anger frightened her. It was not what she wanted to feel, or who she wanted to be. She was there guarding the good guys and he was nowhere. She could not solve the anger, and so she began to dial numbers, places where he might be. He was not at the tennis club or the health club. He was not at the accountant's or at the house of his football buddy. Her despair grew with each failure. He is never here when I need him! She wandered around the room, turning on lights, the TV, running water for a bath. Disjointed, like a broken doll, her mind and body disconnected. Memories, that slide show again, clicking inside her aching head.

It was two weeks before her wedding and they were taking a day off, whizzing up the coast past Malibu, past Zuma Beach, soaring around the miraculous solid-rock curves, heading for Santa Barbara. "Honey, we have so many things to talk about. Have you called New York, how are you going to tell your daughter about us? Can we have her come soon and visit or go there?"

He drove faster, silent for a moment. "She can't come here now. It's best if we just leave them alone for a while."

"But why? Carol's remarried already, what's the problem?"

"I signed adoption papers, Hannah. It's better for everyone, they were putting a lot of pressure on me."

She had not been able to speak. It seemed to Hannah, with her fierce family instinct and rigid adolescent view of how humans should be, as horrible as if he had just confessed to murder or child molesting.

I can't marry someone who would do that, give his child away without *even* talking to me about it! How could he do that!

But it had come too late for her to look at; she had gone too far for too long, and so she pushed the feelings away, stored them in the cedar attic of her delusions.

Her mother's attention now went into the daily battle of living with a mutilated body and a husband so terrified by her disability that he was unable to touch or hold her, and so at the time that Leah most needed to be held and made love to, she was discarded and rejected. Norman could not touch her, and he cried into his pillow because he was ashamed of himself, but he could not do it.

And so Hannah's mother turned to her for love and Hannah turned to Nick. And so there was no turning back.

After her bath, she felt better. She played with the children and locked the house tight, leaving lights burning in every room; restoring her sense of order, of control. She put the children to sleep and returned to her bed.

In the quiet, eyes not focusing on her book, ears not deciphering the television script, a new rage began to build.

Maybe I can strangle her with Neilie's jump rope. Nick hasn't opened his mouth once! Never confronted my father, never talked to the Monster. Me! I do it! Who needs this? I do everything alone anyway.

Anger stormed—and despair.

She stopped, thoughts snapping like whips in a cage.

A car. She rose, heart pounding, and turned out the light, grabbing a flashlight from the closet. Slowly she moved to the window. Fantasies flashed. An overpainted, drunken woman with three armed men. It was her husband.

Relief mixed with the anger that returned with safety.

Hannah replaced the flashlight and sat back down on the bed, waiting.

"Hi, everything okay?" He moved to the closet, taking off his jacket and slipping out of his shoes simultaneously. His face was haggard. Eyes, Neilie's eyes, eyes that had broken her heart when she first loved them; eyes filled with life, now lidded with strain and fatigue.

"No, everything is not okay."

"What happened?" He stripped off his clothes, folding them neatly and carefully over proper hangers, an eight-year-old slum kid keeping house for his mother. He undressed slowly, as if movement brought him closer to something he knew was waiting but did not want to meet.

"My mind happened. We happened."

He sighed, knowing that again he had done the wrong things for her.

"What do you mean? What did I do now?"

"It's what you didn't do. You didn't come home and you left no number. You know what's been going on here. How dare you not even leave a number or call and check in with me? I'm always left to do it, face it, whatever the problem, alone. I thought we were a team now, you and me and our little family, but you don't want to come home and sit here with this fucking machine and the fear. 'Let Hannah do it, tell her she's too emotional and she'll do it!' I'm so damn sick of hearing that! Don't you realize what's at stake? If there is even one chance in a hundred thousand that she's dangerous and we don't do everything we can, do you know what that means? That's our lives, baby. That's it! I need your help and you just want to play tennis and pretend nothing's changed. I don't expect you to be my daddy, but I expect you and me to be equal! I don't *want* to handle it alone! You let me get you off the firing line and you know better! You never even call...to see, to see."

She was crying again, feeling her life being split apart, torn into pieces by a voice without shape, stretching each of them beyond their ability to cope with the compromises of their lives and their relationship.

"I didn't think you were that upset. I think you're overreacting."

"Well, then tell me *that!*\ You can tell me *that*. Give me some input to help me! You don't even do *that*. What do I have to do to let you know what I need? How many times has this happened with other things and I always blame myself, and then all of a sudden tonight I thought, wait a minute, maybe it's not that you shouldn't *need* to need him, maybe it's not *your* weakness, maybe it's his!"

She had gone too far; gone beyond the boundaries they usually set, the playing by the rules, make-up-in-an-hour boundaries. His anger, kept hidden for months, for years on end, behind those large, blue, un-Italian eyes, was seeping over the container, too full to stop the overflow.

"I've had it! I've had it with all of this crap! I've had it with your lousy father and you! you! you! that's all I hear! What this is doing to *you*. I'm sick of it all, do you hear me!"

"Then help me get us away from here."

He held her arm, his hands digging into her skin, pressure so firm she was frightened to move or speak. His anger, now unfurled, uncontainable.

"You're hurting me! Let go of me! Get out of this house! Just get out!"

His face pushed upward in fury, grabbing her harder, shaking her; the rage of helplessness, his vulnerability making him victimize what he most loved.

"I'm sick of your criticism. I'm not your fucking father! Do you hear me? I'm sick of your tension and your overreacting! Sick of it! You want me to handle that bitch?

I'll handle her! I'll go out, I'll find her and I'll twist her fucking arm off! I've been trying to stay calm because I didn't want to do anything stupid. I bought a gun today; want me to kill her? We have a gun now. Okay? Is that okay!"

He released her, pushing her back on the bed.

And he left the room.

She lay there in the dark, listening to him move about, knowing lie was suffering and wanting to reach out. When he came upstairs to bed, he was drunk. And he fell down beside her, shaking the mattress, and slept and she couldn't reach him to bring them back together.

CHAPTER 14

What amazing creatures of habit we are, Hannah thought, balancing a paper coffee cup in one hand, morning paper in the other, as she climbed the stairs leading to her office.

Spend the whole stinking night fighting, screaming, kicking the cat, but morning comes—make the coffee, wash the face, take the car pool, business as usual.

She opened the door, tossing the paper on her desk cluttered with pages of discarded words, and sank into her chair.

I must need my routine. It must make me feel safe. Well, if I'm mutilated or get a divorce or my children are kidnapped, I always have my "career." She smiled to herself, sipping her coffee. She felt better. The week of emotional strain resolved for the moment by the decision to change phone numbers. The hope, with silence returned, that the woman had lost her connection and would refocus somewhere else. Please God. Hannah sighed, hoping for a second chance, knowing damage to her life had been done and praying for time to sort, examine, try to find a better way, a new level of communication.

FUCKING OFF WHEN I SHOULD BE WORKING
NOTEBOOK

Back to immolatable material. Here I sit listening to traffic outside my beloved little office window, suffering from acute writer's brain cramp with a side order of inner tension. I am still so tired (and sounding more like Aunt Louise every day). I AM ESPECIALLY TIRED OF THE FOLLOWING: Being thirty-two. Getting stuck right in the middle. Growing up with all the old values—got to get married, got to have babies, security, money—and then, when we had already done it all, made the commitments, POWEE—Feminism! All the ladies jumping up and down telling us, "Hey, you don't have to do that anymore, you're free!" Uh, yeah, swell, but, uh, we already did it, hit us a little late, so what dowedonow? Easy, HAVE A CAREER! Career. Guilty when you're home being a mommy, guilty when you're working, not being a mommy. Only screws us up more, perfect women all. Got to do it all.

"I worked through both my pregnancies. Yeah, but I know a woman who handed in a TV script on the way to the labor room. Oh, well, guess I'm not as worthwhile as she is." BOO YOU. "I'm a doctor and I have four children and I teach at a leading university and I plan to have four more children and I breast-fed all of them; and I have a perfect marriage and I'm brilliant in my field; and I have a terrific personality, a great figure, do two hours of yoga every day and I'm gorgeous."

"Oh, yeah? Well, *I* know a woman who has *eleven* children, she's married to the King of Baghdad, she's a Pulitzer Prizewinning journalist, a Nobel Laureate in science, she was Miss Universe and she swims the English Channel every morning before breakfast..."

"Oh, guess I lose." BOO you.

Also exhausting is:

Relating to other human and semihuman beings.

Conversation.

Exercise.

Being healthy.

Watching what I eat.

Watching what I drink.
Washing my hair.
Having hair.
Cleaning clothes.
Having clothes. Thinking about wearing clothes.

Married Sex. There I said it. I am tired of it. I want a new balloon or I don't want to play. Hitting the marital muggies—being so touted in current fiction (that, too; I am very tired of current fiction). And I'M TIRED OF STATUS. God has a Gucci belt. Jesus is a rock star. Moses "published." FUCK it all. WHAT DO YOU DO? WHO DO YOU SCREW? WHERE DO YOU GO? WHO DO YOU KNOW? YOU PASS. YOU FAIL. THE BIRD TO ALL OF IT.

I'm tired of being afraid.
I'm tired of being a good girl.
I'm tired of believing that my life should be happy.
I'm tired of caring what it will be.
I'm tired of improving my mind.
I'm tired of feeling guilty when I'm not improving it (which is most of the time).
I'm tired of conflict.
I'm tired of trying to find answers to end the conflict.
I'm tired of being tired.

When Neilie was three, we bought her a turtle for her birthday. And she loved that horrible little green creature for about a week, carried it in a little cup all day, waddling about, and then one morning I couldn't find her anywhere and finally, in a panic, I opened the door to our sun porch and there she was. She had climbed out of her window onto the balcony. And I grabbed her and took her inside. "Where's Myrtle?" I asked. She pointed down, indicating that Myrtle had taken an instigated nose dive off the balcony.

"Why did you do that?" I demanded, picturing the revolting result of Myrtle's plunge waiting below on the terrace.

She shrugged her fat little shoulders. "She just wasn't any good anymore, Mommy."

No good, give it a toss. Makes sense. 'Sense me, dear, I'm not feeling much like screwing you anymore, going through a conflicting period, what with inner growth and kidnap threats and marital conflicts and all. Ya see, what I really want is to just bug out of here, it's easier that way, ya know, but being a responsible, monogamous, middle-class lady, would you mind a leg up off the terrace? No divorce, no guilt, just a spot of green squish, swept up in a minute. 'Scuse me, Dad, having a real tough time with this anger and hostility I'm feeling toward you, wasting a lot of energy and emotion on it, lots of money in shrink bills, would you mind stepping out on the sun porch? Just take a second. Just wasn't any good anymore, Mommy. Nothing clearer; freshest thinking in town. Nobody want to make it easy for me? Want *me* to be the one, huh? Take a little fly to the Redwood Deck, eternal victim that she is. Sorry, babe, I'm not *that* tired. Yet.

Phone ringing.

Hannah shut off her machine and leaned back, grateful for the interruption.

"Is this Hannah Nicoli?"

"Yes, it is."

"This is Sergeant Dodd at the Beverly Hills police station."

Hannah's breath stopped. "What is it? What's happened?"

"Do you know a woman named Agatha Howard?"

"Yes. Yes, I do."

"We have her in custody. She has no identification with her and she told us that you could vouch for her."

Relief flooded her and guilt at the relief that it was not her turn, not her life. "Certainly. Of course I can. Why are you holding her? What happened to her?"

"She was arrested last night on a five-oh-two. Drunk driving. We couldn't get anything out of her until this morning."

"Can I post bail for her? What can I do?" The thought of Agatha sitting alone in a jail cell, Agatha, whose life was motivated by the need to be free, to move, to not be enclosed, sickened her.

"Well, ma'am, she wanted to know if you could call a lawyer and come pick her up. Her car was destroyed."

"Oh, God. Is she all right?"

"A little bruised and shook up. Wouldn't be a bad idea for her to see a doctor. She could have a broken rib. Can you bring some identification for her? We can't release her without seeing some identification."

"Yes, yes, of course. I'll take care of everything. I'll be there as soon as I can."

Hannah flew on automatic pilot. Calling the attorney and racing to Agatha's tiny apartment with the permanently unlocked door. She sifted through the private places of her friend, the places that were none of her business, the secret pockets of identity that belong only to the possessor, keeping the most intimate friends and lovers, strangers. The things we never share or know. She was five years old again, sneaking into her father's drawer, looking for pennies and finding condoms and pictures of naked girls, private treasures, more personal than a fingerprint. She rummaged through the jasmine and tobacco smells of her friend's dresser, finding bottles of strange potions from Switzerland and Mexico, love letters, unpaid bills, Polaroid pictures of exotic men, looking for something that would prove that she existed. She grabbed Agatha's passport, alien registration card and an expired California driver's license, and raced across town to free the captive.

She parked in front of the Beverly Hills Post Office and walked down the street to the police.

She had never been inside a police station.

But this was Beverly Hills and even the police station looked beautiful. Disguised inside, sparkling Spanish architecture, flowers growing in front, shiny new patrol cars glowing in the driveway. A movie star's lock-up.

It served its people well. No unsavory character or vehicle got more than a block. Anyone walking the streets after dark was stopped. Until, that is, the police knew your habits. The police were less paranoid here, protecting a community where it was illegal to park on the street overnight in front of your own home and garbage was seen only in alleys and Arab millionaires gave quarter-million-dollar block parties to meet the neighbors.

There were murderers here and drug dealers, and robbers and muggers and drunks and con men, but somehow they did not seem important. Beverly Hills still presented the facade of a town where jaywalking and expired parking meters were as serious as the police problems got, and Hannah believed it, too.

"I have talked to more policemen in the last three months than in my entire life," Hannah thought as she waited in the cold cement lobby for her friend to be freed.

What is all this? Some weird energy force is surrounding me. Maybe I *should* call Louise's psychic. Police stations, firemen, violence. What am I doing here? Things like this don't happen to women like me.

She had never felt so raw, so vulnerable.

Sure, Hannah, and mothers don't shrivel and disappear, either.

Metal doors banged in the background. Footsteps echoing down corridors. Heavy, steady, black-shoed steps keeping harmony to Agatha's quick, tapping heels.

Hannah stood up and walked toward the wire-glass door marked "No Admittance!" Out came policemen, looking serious and important, and Hannah's father's lawyer, looking arrogant and well dressed. Agatha stood behind them, fur coat clutched tightly around her small, slender body, large dark glasses covering her face, holding on to her thrift shop chinchilla as if she were naked underneath.

"Hello, darling." Her voice sounded slurred, heavy with sobered emotion and shame.

"Hi. Are you okay?"

Hannah stood in the midst of the stern-faced men, signing papers, reading documents, passing cash over and receiving in return Agatha's confiscated belongings. A worn alligator bag, a string of paste pearls, a pack of French cigarettes and a red-velveteen change purse with three dollar bills and two French centimes.

They walked to Hannah's car without speaking.

"I made a doctor's appointment for you, right around the block. Okay?"

"Fine, thank you, darling."

"Want to talk about it?"

"Later."

"Okay." She felt hurt, left out and unappreciated. She unlocked the car, helped her friend inside and drove two blocks to the famous street of medical miracles, the great white way of medicine that was as much a part of her hometown as the department stores lining Wilshire Boulevard.

Hannah walked Agatha inside, filled out the meaningless forms for her and kissed her cheek. "I'll walk around for a while. I'll be back in half an hour. I love you."

"I love you too, darling."

Agatha pressed Hannah's arm and, holding her emerald-covered hand over her face, walked crisply toward the door to relief.

Hannah walked aimlessly—Agatha's face flashing before her—up and down Bedford and Roxbury Drive, home of doctors, lawyers, banks and boutiques.

Better stay off Rodeo or they might mistake me for an Iranian and put the hook out of Van Cleef's.

She smiled. Without thinking, she had led herself to the building that her mother's doctor had been in. She stood filled with memories, overwhelmed by the unreality of this city.

People do not die in sunshine. People do not commit crimes. How can you die next to a palm tree? How can cancer crawl into a tennis dress?

It had not been a good dying place.

Unapparent Wounds

When I go, I'll go in Boston or at least San Francisco.

She sat on the steps to the entrance, not caring that she must look silly, and remembered. She saw herself fat with child, leading her mother, frail and morphine addicted, her legs like bent sticks, down these luscious streets; past the golden girls and the heavily made-up shopping set and the healthy, tan jogging set, everyone carrying leather purses and shopping bags from Giorgio's or Neiman's. And right alongside all this health and wealth and beauty were the medical buildings. People being wheeled in, carried in. Pale people. Frightened people. Sick people. Dying people. Some of the dying people had deep suntans and came wearing tennis shorts or jogging suits, but Hannah had gotten very good at telling who was dying and who was denying.

She sat, chin resting on her knees, feeling the sun on her white, freckled face; watching beautiful, unreal women strut by. Not feeling intimidated like she used to guiding her mother and feeling somehow defective, shamed by the sickness, feeling the distance between the winners and losers and hating herself. She felt, clean. She felt, okay. It was a nice, rare, new feeling and it warmed her like the sun. And she watched the Bentleys and the Mercedes and the Sevilles, and the handsome men all looking like movie stars parade by with their little shopping bags.

A man on crutches, one leg gone, came down the stairs beside her.

Fiorucci and fractures, Gucci and gallstones, Hermès and hemorrhoids, Courrèges and cancer. Carry your urine specimen home in a Tiffany shopping bag!

Hannah moved over, making room for the victim.

Who told me that when they came here they always felt as if they would walk into a building, go through the door, and be outside in an empty lot like the whole city was a sound stage? How can you get sick by a swimming pool? How can you get old wearing Adidas? How can you be depressed in a pure-silk Saint Laurent blouse?

Hannah sighed. It was time to go.

So long, Beverly Hills, you punk-rock nightmare.

Agatha sat on the waiting room couch, tears falling from inside her dark plastic glasses, racing down her firm, sharp chin into the folds of her fur.

Hannah wanted to hold her, let her cry against her shoulder, but she knew better. Agatha would not be able to receive such an offering.

"Are you okay, sweetheart? Was your rib broken?"

Agatha shook her head, fighting for control. "No. Just bruised. But I fainted. I always faint. I'll be fine."

"Okay, let's get you home and into bed."

Hannah helped her up and guided her out of the office and down the street, slides clicking through Hannah's head, helping her mother down the same litter-free path, avoiding disapproving glances.

People turned to stare. Hannah wearing old jeans and sandals, half-carrying delicate Agatha masquerading as a contessa in soiled black satin and chinchilla down the piercing morning-sun-filled street.

"Oh, God, darling. Could there be a more shocking place to be sick? I'd like to machine-gun the whole bloody town."

Hannah paid the parking. "They're getting two dollars for two minutes now." Settling Agatha gently on the back seat and driving slowly up Rodeo Drive and away. The ride seemed endless in the silence between them, so many questions that she wanted to ask and dared not. Finally, they were there. She helped her inside, up the elevator past the seamy day clerk and the out-of-work actors sharing lies in the lobby, and into her Art Deco hiding place. She ran a bath and left her alone, respecting the fierce privacy which separated Agatha from everyone else and allowed her to live a life that demanded endless performances at the center of the stage. She could see them, but they couldn't see her, not the real her. That was only for Agatha and she shared it with no one.

"Hannah."

Hannah went to her. She lay in bed fresh from her bath, covered in second-hand silk, her face looking fresh and rosy, a little girl's face that she did not love, hidden forever under hats and glasses. A dark purple bruise was growing on her eyebrow.

"How do you feel?"

"Fine. It's so good to be here. My God, jail. Hannah, you can't imagine the feeling. Being closed in a cage and no one cares, no one comes. It was horrible. I'll never have another martini as long as I live."

"I can't stand it anymore, tell me what happened?"

Agatha reached for a cigarette, sitting high against her cream-satin pillows.

"You'll think I'm over the edge."

"I'm hardly one to judge."

"All right. Remember that attractive Count we met at lunch?"

Hannah nodded, eyes child-wide, waiting for the fairy tale.

"Well, I went to that dinner party and we started an absolutely mad affair. Too high, too fast. Just my style. I went off my trolley for him. He'd pick me up in a chauffeur-driven Rolls with a full bar stocked with Louis Roederer and Beluga and whisk me off to dinner, parties, you name it. I had my bags packed and my name changed. You know me. I was already redecorating his villa in Rome and his apartment in Milan. We've been inseparable since that night. And he was *fabulous*. If he could turn me on like that, you know he was good. I've been half-living at his rented house, up on Benedict for two weeks now.

"Then yesterday morning he called my office and told me that he had to work late, and why didn't I go to this party we were invited to alone and he'd try to join me later?

"I don't know why, but I didn't believe him. Something wasn't right. And also, I've never been able to find out what the bloody hell he does or why he's here anyway. He's always out socializing, and suddenly he's working late.

"Well, I was crazy all day and I went for drinks with some friends and got a bit sloshed and decided to go up there and see if he was lying. I stopped on the way and bought a bottle of Heublein's martinis, and there I was in hat and gloves and a dinner dress and my chinchilla coat, crawling around in the yard between garbage cans, slopping up the martinis and whimpering like a wounded pup. I *knew* he was in there. And I climbed up a fence and onto the roof and crept along to the bedroom window and braced myself with my arms and lowered my head down, and there he was—going hot and heavy with some bitch—and my hat fell off and he looked up and saw me! Well, I flew out of there. I was so humiliated and upset. I started driving up and down, slugging those damn martinis like a madwoman. Another dead end. J really thought he was going to be it. I was crying and carrying on, and I smashed right into a lamppost. The whole windshield was in my lap. I don't know why I'm alive. Someone called the police and there I was. So much for love affairs."

"Oh, Agatha, I'm so sorry."

"Oh, darling. I'll be fine. It's all just a ticket on the merry-go-round. Actually, it was probably the best thing that could've happened to me because it helped me make a decision."

"What?"

Agatha lit a fresh cigarette, the nicotine sparking her, rekindling her restlessness. "I'm going home, darling. I'm going to write my mother for a ticket, and I'm going back to Melbourne. I'm so tired of this life I'm living. I need a fresh start."

Hannah swallowed hard, feeling three years old with everyone gone. "I think that's a very good idea, but God, I'll miss you."

"I know, darling, me too. I'll be back. I just need to make some changes now."

They sat together quietly, assessing the information.

Agatha lit another cigarette. "God, enough about me. Tell me what's happening with you. Has that monster been found?"

Hannah sighed deeply. "No, but it's more than that. I feel like, since these calls have started, that something is beating in my head, in our lives, beating on my head to listen, beating me down as if I had been playing some game with my life and now everything's splattering. I *feel* myself changing." Tears filled Hannah's eyes. "Last night (after OUR FRIEND called to say she was coming to take the children), I called Nick and I was very upset and I couldn't find him anywhere, and I realized that he doesn't want to be with me, doesn't want to face any unpleasantness. If he can get away with deluding himself and making me or the kids or the world the scapegoat, he will, and I feel so betrayed and so angry." She sighed.

"It's like all the things that I haven't been facing for years, all the nights I don't want to sleep with him, it's like all of a sudden I thought, hey, Hannah, it's not only you! It's both of you. Something's wrong, Agatha, and all of this pressure is just blowing the lid off and for the first time in our marriage, I'm peeking into the pot. I blamed *him* for something. I didn't blame myself. I may not even have been right, but it's like that didn't make any difference. I'm scared, Agatha. I don't understand what's happening to me."

Agatha watched her. "I know you are, darling. You've had too much for too long. Just try not to live anything before you have to. You're very special, Hannah, and you're very strong. Trust life a bit. You take everything so damn seriously. It will all work out. Just try to be very good to yourself."

"I will if you will."

"It's a deal."

Hannah stood up awkwardly, knowing they had finished. "Go to sleep. I'll make you some lunch and leave it in the refrigerator, and I'll talk to the lawyer and find out where we go from here."

"Thank you, darling. I'm not going to worry about it. The worst they can do is deport me."

Hannah smiled. "Now that's a positive attitude. I'll remember that."

Down the hall and down the elevator and across the pool

terrace and into the parking lot Hannah went, lost in twilight images, feeling life changing, Agatha leaving, aloneness, new information fighting for acknowledgment. She was sinking in the sands of change, but it felt warm and alive around her and she was not panicky, she was able to breathe.

CHAPTER 15

"I don't believe I'm doing this. How did I let you talk me into doing this?" Hannah sat next to Kathy on a weather-beaten, ocean-stained bench lacing up a pair of freshly rented roller skates.

"Oh, quiet. It's good for you. You've got to get out of Bullshit Hills once in a while and mingle with real people!"

"Drunks, junkies and middle-aged roller-skaters, that's real all right."

"Come on, Hannah, follow me. Just pretend you're ten years old again...it'll come right back to you."

"Whadda ya mean, pretend?"

Her friend skated ahead of her. Six feet of pioneer legs and blond frizzy curls.

This is ridiculous, we look like *Gong Show* rejects.

Hannah stumbled, almost falling over.

My God, do I feel old.

She caught her breath and began skating slowly down the boardwalk. She was beginning to enjoy herself.

Where were you when your child was kidnapped? "I was roller-skating with the Hare Krishnas."

She glided along, stopping to let old people cross and dogs and mothers carrying infants and fathers riding their babies on bicycles and black dudes skating backward with fancy transistor radios plugged in their ears. A drunk whistled at her. A Chinese weight lifter called her "Red." She was into it now. She *teas* ten years old. Gliding down Oakhurst Drive, fearless and happy.

"Hey, Momma. Slow down, honey…" Hannah turned and saw a funny-looking black boy of about twelve skating close behind her.

"Hi. You live around here, Momma?"

"No. Just skating through."

"All right. That's some pretty hair you've got. You got a boyfriend?"

Hannah blushed. "No, but I've got a very strict father."

"All right. How about going down to the beach with me? I've got some very fine dope."

"No, thanks."

"Hey, come on, baby, we'll have fun, hang out a while."

"Listen, I can't talk and skate at the same time, I'll fall down. You're very cute, but I think I'm a little old for you."

"How old? I like my women mature. You look real young from the back, Momma. From the back I'd say thirteen, from the front,…"

"Listen, I'm not interested in an estimate. You're making me very nervous. I don't want to fall down, so please just go on."

"All right. Don't get all bent out. Later, Momma." Kathy waved at her. "I'm gonna skate to the pier, come on!" Hannah shook her head and stopped, almost crashing into a little old lady with five dogs and a handful of tangled leashes.

"Excuse me."

"Isn't it a lovely, lovely day!" offered the dog lady as a Chihuahua ran around her ankles, trapping her.

"Yes." Tears filled Hannah's eyes. She wanted to grab the old lady in her arms and hug her. She skated back to-' ward the parking lot to wait for Kathy, stopping to buy a frozen yogurt cone and settling down on an empty bench to people-watch. A handsome tan man whizzed by her backward on bright purple skates. He stopped, looked at her and skated on. It made her uneasy.

This never happens to me, what am I sending off? What are these people sniffing out?

And then he was back, skating slowly back and forth in front of her and smiling. He was very good. His strong body moved over the pavement as if it were ice. He twirled. He coasted. He stayed. Hannah tried to ignore him, but she could feel her face flush and her heart pound. She played with her hair. She threw her half-licked cone in the trash bin. She relaced her skates.

Jesus, why doesn't he go away? Jane Fonda would tell him to piss off.

She said nothing.

He skated up to the bench, his purple wheels clicking against her plain brown ones, and looked down at her.

"Hi. You're beautiful. My name is Damian and I'd like to fuck you."

I can't think of anything to say. That's crazy, never in my entire life have I not been able to think of something to say.

He sat beside her. She could feel the warmth of his long, lean thigh against her bare leg. And she liked the way it felt. And she liked what he had said to her.

Omigod, what is going on here?

"You want to, too. Don't you? I felt the vibrations. Your antenna is all the way up, lovely lady. Come with me, don't think about it and get all uptight, just do it. I live right across the street. Come with me." He stood up and took her hand.

Hannah Oberman Nicoli, the roller-skating Jewish nymphomaniac.

She let him take her hand and lead her slowly across the parking lot, gliding alongside this tall blond stranger, roller-skating off into infinity. It was will-less. It was mindless. She felt drawn toward the power in his body, in his voice, in his sureness, in a totally trusting way. It was unlike anything she had ever done. It was terrifying. But it felt safe. She let him lead her and she trusted him.

"I live up here, just follow me." He bounced up the stairs of an old Venice walk-up. A student's room. Indian pillows and incense burners. Straw-mat rugs and Chinese lanterns covering bare bulbs.

Like her room at college. Tears were in her eyes, again. She was nineteen, again. And so, she belonged here.

"Take your skates off, I'll get some dope." She did as she was told. She watched him unlace his skates, his hands moving surely, strongly. He lit a joint and handed it to her. She took it, inhaling deeply. Not resisting, as she usually did, always afraid of losing control. She didn't need any control here. It was safe, here.

"Come on, I'll show you something." He took her hand and led her up another flight of stairs and out onto the roof. She was in the sky, and she saw the ocean stretching farther than Japan and the gulls flying. It was quiet and powerful and it felt like heaven. In the middle of the roof was a large redwood tub.

"Come on, take off your clothes."

He stripped off his shorts and eased his golden-tan body into the tub. He lay back in the hot bubbling water, watching her. She lifted her T-shirt over her head, stepped out of her shorts and undid her bra. Then she stepped out of her panties. She was naked, rising over the ocean, Aphrodite in the Afternoon. It was the first time she had been naked with anyone but her husband in almost ten years, and it felt fine. She got into the tub, slowly, the water covering her like warm wax.

He passed her the joint. She inhaled deeply, feeling herself floating away, off on a cloud, safe from harm. She did not exist here and yet she only existed here. There was no yesterday or tomorrow. She was twelve and she was eighty, and she was no one's daughter or mother or wife or friend. She was a goddess and she was a cloud drifting by. He kissed her, tasting of sweat and dope and sun oil, and she kissed him back. "My name is Hannah," she said. And kissed him again. She felt her whole body yield. Felt all the tension, the deadness leave. Felt lust and heat and yearning. Felt life.

I'm not dead. I'm not frigid. I'm not!

She had found out what she needed to know, and it brought her back to herself. She stood up, almost pushing him over.

"I'm sorry...I'm really sorry. I have to go. I..."

She ran from the roof, not waiting for an answer, grabbing up her clothes, pulling on her shorts and shirt-leaving her underwear. She picked up her skates and ran down the stairs two at a time, barefoot and panting. He didn't follow her.

She found Kathy sitting on her car, looking angry.

"Where in hell have you been? I was just about ready to call the fuzz. Did you go swimming? You're all wet."

"No." She stopped, relieved and exhausted. "Let's go home."

"Not until you tell me what happened to you." Hannah stopped and looked right into Kathy's nearsighted blue eyes. "Okay. I was making out in a hot tub with a beach-bum doper wearing purple roller skates."

"Oh, Christ, Hannah, cut it out, tell me!"

Hannah hugged her, feeling laughter pushing up from the new warm place inside her belly. And she put her head against her friend's breast and laughed till it hurt.

When Hannah got home from the beach, it was dark. She skipped up the driveway feeling wicked and elated and totally unlike herself. The phone was ringing inside and she ran to it, expecting no danger for the first time in months.

"Hello?"

"Hello, stranger."

"Oh, hello, Sophie. How are you?"

"The same. Where have you been? I've been calling all day. Everyone could be dead there."

"No such luck. Sometimes Tina doesn't hear the phone and I've been gone all day."

"Not good for the children. What's so important?"

"I was roller-skating." Hannah stuck her tongue at the receiver.

"I didn't hear you. I must have wax in my ears."

"You heard me. What can I do for you?"

"Well, I originally placed this call because Ethel and I wanted to invite you and your father (if he's still alive) and the children for dinner. But since we decided this morning, Ethel and I had a disagreement and so, I don't know. Also, I called before I knew that you had gone crazy. So, now I don't know what to do."

"Well, Sophie, when you make up with Ethel let me know. But I should tell you that my father and I are having some problems, so it would be better if we waited a while."

"So? What kind of problems? He's not getting married again, is he?"

"No."

"Is he still seeing that woman with the face-lift?" "Yes."

"God forbid."

"Well, whatever. Anyway I don't want to discuss it."

"I won't ask again. I know when I'm intruding."

"Thanks, Sophie. I'll talk to you later."

Hannah ran around the kitchen, peeling potatoes, making hamburgers, rushing to finish, returning to her good-girl world. The phone rang again.

"Hello."

"So, what's this about you and your father? Why would you tell that big mouth, Sophie, and not tell me?"

"Ethel, dear, I didn't tell her anything. She just happened to call and I mentioned that we were having some problems. That's all."

"None of this would be happening if Leah hadn't died and left him alone with all those shiksa golddiggers running around."

"Yes, it was really inconsiderate of her. Listen, I'm fixing dinner, I'll call you later."

Ten minutes later it rang again.

"Hi, dear. It's Louise. Your aunt Sophie called me and woke me up to tell me that she was worried about you. She said you were fighting with your daddy. He's such a difficult man. I had a nightmare about him last week. His presence has been in my room for days and I can't sleep. I bet it's because of your trouble."

Hannah sighed. When would she learn?

"It's nothing, really. I'm sorry you haven't slept. I'll call you next week. I'm very busy right now."

"Don't call before two."

"Never."

She set the table, watching the clock, the children appearing bathed and sweet and ready to eat supper.

"Charlie hungy. Charlie eat."

"Soon, darling, soon."

Nick came in, looking tired, watching her quizzically, anticipating gloom and finding cheer; humming Hannah, waiting with a drink in her baby-blue jogging suit, breaking into the pattern of their depression.

She told of her day and the phone calls, and he laughed in spite of himself.

"Nick, let's go away. Let's go to the desert for a few days." She could not believe her own voice; who was this person filled with optimism, reaching out of her isolation?

He looked at her sharply. Their wounds still so raw, so unsealed. "Okay. Let's do it this weekend."

She let out her breath, knowing she could change her mind and choosing not to.

CHAPTER 16

Spontaneity in marriage is a craft, one that Hannah and Nick had prided themselves on perfecting. Of course, Hannah had always added, having a live-in senorita helped keep the rhythm moving. Spontaneity, sometimes also known as escape from reality, had moved them that Friday. The change in phone number coddling them. And so, pushing against the depression of their personal breach and the flashes in the mind it had released, they had gone, running from the post-Christmas blues and the tension, leaving their children and maid-in-residence with Hannah's brother and sister-in-law playing their parts.

They had packed, made the arrangements and departed before they could reconsider the decision. The drive was quiet. They talked of playing tennis and where they would eat and ride their bicycles and make love. Or Nick talked about it. Hannah sat, tension crushing her chest as if she were being carried off by some dreaded stranger against her better instincts and unmovable responsibilities.

"Are you okay?"

He had seen. She had reached into her purse for a tranquilizer, hoping he would not see, wanting the privacy of her tension; wanting to avoid the disappointment in his eyes at seeing her real feelings, the loss of the euphoria of the early week.

"Yep, just a little tense. I guess I'm feeling guilty about leaving the kids. I'll be all right."

They drove mostly in silence, their car finally swishing around the giant thrust of mountain that was nature's mark at the entrance into the Valley. Hannah felt her heart dip, remembering all the years of swinging around that mountain from child-frenzy at the certainty of pleasure to her first weekend with Nick. Now, the pill lessening the sadness, she thought of all the past swings and all the future swings, till she grew too old or life changed courses for her or she died.

"Look, Nick, Colonel Sanders finally made it; next month McDonald's, and the circle closes."

"Yeah, terrible, isn't it? But we always have fun here anyway."

"Yep."

They reached the hotel, which leaned against the mountains in the old section of town, and Hannah felt better, cheered by the sun and the change in situation.

They unpacked quickly, trying to catch the day before it disappeared, cram swimming and tennis into the last hour of light.

"What's that, Nick?"

Hannah pulled on her tennis shoes, her eyes falling on a black leather case flung hastily on the bed.

He avoided her, gathering up the slender leather pouch and putting it quickly into the dresser.

"It's the gun I bought. I want to take you out into the desert tomorrow and teach you how to shoot it."

"Oh, no, Nick. I can't! You know how I feel about guns. I won't do it. I don't even want it in here. Put it in the car. I can't even stand having it so close to us."

"Hannah, you're being silly. You're the one who's so frightened that creep is going to come to the house. What would you do? You knew I bought the thing; I want you to learn how to use it. Just trust me. It's not dangerous once you know what to do with it."

"Yeah, sure. How can anything that kills people be dangerous?"

She shuddered, her eyes scanning the drawer as if the very existence of that small leather thing threatened her life and her security. She tied her shoes carelessly, wanting to leave the room—

the gun and the intimacy of her husband somehow both threats to her stability.

Nothing has changed here, you see!

But, buried in her tension beneath the tennis clothes and the sun oil and the visor hiding her face, she knew she was lying.

The pool was crowded. Hannah and Nick waited, dripping sweat from their tennis game, feeling self-conscious, being sized up by the other guests, waiting for the pool boy to find them a chair. Hannah scanned the faces, recording images.

It was quite a crowd. New York divorcées wearing diamonds with their bathing suits, escorted by bored young fags carrying their Bendel pool bags in gold-wristed hands. Middle-aged widows with sun-shielded faces and desperate eyes pretended to read paperback novels. A group of good-looking men in tennis clothes, with tans cultivated like rare orchids, slouched in director's chairs sipping beer and trading sports stories. Now and then a beautiful girl would prepare herself for a panther prowl of the eligibles.

There were always girls like that at the better hotel pools. Starlets, models, of eighteen or twenty. Prowling. Using their beautiful, lean young bodies as bait. A tall blonde sat up. She oiled her legs and put fresh lip gloss on. She angled a cowboy hat forward on her long, straw-colored mane and pushed up the bottom of her purple Danskin leotard to show the cheeks of her buttocks, and then she stood, sucking in her already concave stomach, and insouciantly swayed past the good-looking men to the bar. The widows watched her. And Hannah watched her, not minding the heat or the wait.

"Look, Nick. Those gorgeous guys and those beautiful girls, all getting off on themselves. That blonde did her whole act and not one of those guys even glanced at her. God, I remember when guys fell out of windows over someone like that; now all any of those beauties need is a mirror. Kathy went to that new roller disco in the Valley, the one Cher and all that crowd goes to, and she said it was like walking onto the set of *The Stepford Wives* or something. All of these gorgeous young girls, done up to the molars...makeup, hair all perfect, no bras and those skin-tight leotards cut to the twilight zone...and all of these macho guys, and they just skate around all night and never look at anyone. Then they all take their skates off and go home, alone! Strange new times, these."

"Yeah, hey, there's a seat." Her husband picked up their tennis bag and moved ahead of her. She felt lonely, cut-off and bored with him, not having the energy to draw him out, break into the moodiness that he was wearing lately like a favorite shirt, grabbing for it because it was comfortable.

Hannah took off her tennis dress, feeling shy and conscious of her freckled whiteness against the blackness of her swimsuit. She sat in the shade watching, feeling invisible and removed from everyone. She counted five copies of *Cosmopolitan* magazine being read, and six self-help books. She smiled.

Answers, answers, find those fucking answers, ladies. Why was it she never saw men reading self-help books? She felt lazy and relaxed, the tension dissipated by sweat and exercise. "I think I'll swim, Nick." She rose, sucking in her stomach ("and here we have the over-thirty prowl"), and walked to the edge. She dove, feeling the water cover her and surrendering to its magic clearness. Cleansing her, separating her. She swam, eyes closed, eavesdropping on conversations.

"Her son's twenty-one and he's going with a thirty-five-year-old actress with a thirteen-year-old son!"

"Well, maybe she's a very nice person."

"Oh, sure! She's had brain cancer and been married to two Hell's Angels; she's the salt of the earth! It's about sex, that's what that's about!"

"I'm having those cellulite massages and the bulges on my hips are *melting* away. It's agonizing and expensive, but it's working! I've stopped my acupressure and the bodywrapping, and I'm not even taking my ginseng capsules, it's changed my whole life!"

"So, they took mother to the hospital and X-rayed her lungs, and they called us in and said, 'There's something there and it doesn't look good.' So we said, 'Okay, operate,' and they opened her up and found all of these hard white globules and they said... Cancer! You know what it was? It was oil. Mineral-oil deposits from all the crap she drinks to keep regular, and they were all ready to cut her lung out!"

"Doctors!"

"Lawyers!"

"Real Estate Agents!"

"Mechanics! The whole world's going to hell."

Hannah swam on, feeling full of people. Absorbing the chatter and not thinking about herself. Needing no mirror to reassure herself with. She swam to the side to catch her breath. An old woman with dyed black hair dog-paddled up to her. "You know who you look like?"

"No."

"Yes, you do...you must...you look just like what's her name!"

"Oh, her. Thank you."

"No. No. You know, what's her name. The redhead. She was in all the old movies. She played Mrs. Roosevelt. You know! Gloria Greer!"

"Greer Garson?"

The woman hugged her. "That's it. That's the one! See, I told you, you knew! I'm losing my marbles, I'm not a well woman."

Hannah laughed, looking over the lady's shiny black head, trying to make contact with her husband, to share. But he had gone. Leaving her room key and the sun oil. Hannah left the pool, wrapped herself in a hotel towel and moved back into the tension.

He was asleep when she came in. She stripped off her wet suit and hid in the hotel tub. Hot bubbly water covering her like fur. She closed her eyes, moaning softly in pleasure at the comfort and the warmth. Warmth earned after straining muscles.

One of God's gifts, Hannah murmured to herself.

God gave us hot baths to help us get through all the things he fucked up. Little afterthoughts from up above. Booze, Valium, hot baths, sleep and religion, Uncle Morley! Religion! And sex.

The word stopped the calm. Sex. As she had hurried in her restless need to escape the gun and the nearness of her husband, she hid now, covered with bubbles, knowing that when she emerged, clean and naked and without diversion, he would be waiting to make love to her. And she knew that she did not want him to. And she knew how she had used every possible excuse, her mother's illness, the baby, the calls, every conceivable rationalization to hide from herself the consequences of this avoidance.

It was easier, at first, to think that it was neurosis. A freezing of self, some congenital infirmity that had suddenly taken hold of her previously arousable person. Better me than him, better me than us, but Venice had changed all that.

Afterward she had gone to see her therapist. Gone against her will, propelling herself toward danger like a mouse to the cheese. And she had told him the truth, told him of the caller and the ecstasy of the rooftop, told him of her anger and disappointment, sobbing out her confession and begging for absolution. And he had listened.

"Hannah, it is not neurotic not to want to sleep with someone you don't trust and are angry at and whom you may no longer love. It's just been easier for you to blame yourself. If you were defective, then you wouldn't have to look at your relationship or jeopardize your marriage. But this woman is saying things to you that reinforce your own doubts, and it's opening you up."

She had not been able to stand the words, "I have a man who loves me." She kept chanting to herself, neutralizing the truths. It was too much to believe. Better me than us; who cares about sex anyway? But she couldn't stop the memory of the rooftop. Naked and alive and free.

She hid in the water, afraid to leave. Knowing the only person left living who loved and accepted her was waiting to hold her and she did not want him to.

"What took you so long?" Her husband put down his magazine and handed her a glass of wine. "I ordered some champagne to celebrate our being friends again." Nick smiled at her, his face soft and looking removed from the tumult inside Hannah's head.

"Oh, honey, that's lovely, but I think I'll wait a little. I'd like to just lie down and read for a while. You had a nap, I'm exhausted."

"Okay." He put down his glass and reached for her. "Take off your robe and let me feel you."

"Okay." She moved slowly, her heart pounding like a virgin afraid of failure, rejection, disappointment.

They made love as they had for years now. Without kissing, using mouths and vibrators to create a sectional passion that had once come just from the touch of a hand or a look. Two veterans, pushing the right buttons. Hannah stood outside her body, watching herself climax without ecstasy. And they settled down beside one another, murmuring love notes. After a while they picked up their books, each one knowing something was wrong, something that could no longer be denied. And hoping that the other did not feel it, too.

Hannah threw down her book and reached over her husband for the wine. "Come on, let's get dressed and get out of here, go hear some music or something." And she rose, glass held like savior's blood, and put on her makeup.

"Allan?"
"Yeah, hi, Hannah." Her brother's voice sounded sleepy.
"Did I wake you?"
"No, no, just kind of lying here, talking. How's the desert?"
"Oh, fine. Hot. How are the kids?"
"Fine. Tina's giving them breakfast."
"Everything okay?"
"Yeah."
"You don't sound like everything's okay. What's going on?"

"Well, nothing really. I don't want to make a big deal out of this, I don't want you to get uptight." He sighed.

"She sent a telegram last night. But everything's okay. We'll be right here, so I don't want you to worry."

"What did she say? Allan, was it a threat? What?"

Her husband came out of the bathroom, face still covered with shave cream.

"Nick, she sent another telegram. I knew changing the phone wouldn't stop her! I knew it."

"Hannah, don't get excited. All she said was that you couldn't get rid of her and a lot of crazy mumbo jumbo, couldn't really understand it, no sentence structure, just crap."

Nick stood behind her, his tan face solemn with the invasion.

"Oh, God. I knew it. We'll be home today."

"Hannah, really, it's okay, just relax, there's nothing you could do that we can't do."

"Maybe, but I can't really relax and forget about it. We were leaving tomorrow morning anyway, so we'll leave tonight. If you hear anything, call the police. Please."

"Don't worry, we will, you enjoy your day. Everything's going to be okay. We'll see you tonight, or tomorrow, if you change your mind."

"Okay."

She put down the phone and turned to her husband. They stood, not speaking, looking at each other for a long concentrated moment. "Why did you call, Hannah? You promised you wouldn't call. Goddammit!"

"I'm sorry, Honey. I couldn't help it. Nick?"

"Yeah."

"Get that thing and let's go out into the desert."

"Okay, Hannah, whatever you say."

They decided to take their bikes. Riding for miles, away from the motels and the restaurants and the all-night liquor stores. Past Frank Sinatra Drive and Eisenhower Medical Center and Bing Crosby Road, past streets named after cactus and Indians. They rode hard, sweat tickling their noses, stopping occasionally to wipe their faces and drink water from a flask.

About five miles away from town, they rode to a place where the street ended, stopped abruptly like a horse in a stall, just stopped in the sand and turned into desert.

It was not a pretty desert. Skeletons of old cars, pieces of carpet and decaying furniture, broken bottles and rust-rimmed beer cans. Things abandoned, left to die by their owners, no longer needed, or wanted. Used up and dumped in the vast, silent, barren desert to be taken by the sun and the wind and people with guns to shoot.

They left their bikes and walked into it, feeling the silence and awesomeness of the place, the way it was, before. The way it would have been if no one had ever come here. The way it really looked— like a mannequin without her makeup. The way it looked under the golf courses and the tennis courts. Naked and plain and frightening in its truth.

"God, Nick, can you feel that quiet?"

They sat on an old inner tube and listened to the desert.

"Okay, want to shoot a round now?"

"No. But I will."

Hannah watched as he walked back to the bikes, eagerly, forgiving her. He unlatched the bike bag and pulled out the gun. She watched him move confidently, his fingers removing the instrument. So small—such a tiny little thing, a toy gun. He placed shiny little gold bullets in the chamber. How could something so cute and innocent hurt anybody? It seemed absurd.

As he moved closer to her, she realized how afraid she was. The isolation, the raw reality of nature and human waste without society's bindings, making the possibility of finding some blaring, irrevocable animal madness in oneself, viable.

"Here."

Her husband handed her the gun. It was wet with sweat.

"Oh, Christ, Nick! You're scared too, aren't you?"

"A little."

See, he does feel. He can share.

She breathed deeply, trying to stay close to him.

"All right, now point it at one of those tin cans. Don't tense up. Aim a little low. When you fire, it will kick a bit. But first, check the safety and cock it, that releases a shell into the chamber and then it will fire five shots without your having to touch it again."

She was making noises deep in her throat. It was as if here—unthinkable things happened. Masks of civilization ripped off, and, worse than in battle, the lack of structure, of any form of authority, made the nightmares real, like being afraid of jumping out of a window; it was almost likely, with this tiny, sweet-looking toy in her hand, it was possible and easy and so perfectly rational to turn it on one's husband or put it between one's eyes. It seemed almost unavoidable.

She pressed the trigger, shouting out at the enormous sound of the thing, as it kicked against her hand.

"Oh, Christ, Nick, take it away! I understand. Really, I see how to work it. Take the bullets out of it, please! Please!"

"Okay, okay! Just let me shoot the rest."

He shot at the can, enjoying the power of the thing. Heroes in the movies, cowboys and Indians.

She stood behind him, holding her ears and not believing they were living this, standing together in the middle of the desert, learning how to prepare themselves to kill another human being.

CHAPTER 17

They left the desert that night, returning with tan skin and new tension. Hannah went through the motions of her life without concentration, preoccupied and remote. Reading was impossible. So was listening to her daughter's questions, or her husband; even watching television, her old escape, was not working. And working was not working. A heaviness held her as if she were very old and knew there was no future to hope for. As if age had taken the reason for growth. Growing, then, being a step toward death rather than toward a future, better self.

Letters were coming. Terrible, rambling letters. Unsigned and typed.

She gathered them all like greeting cards, taking them in neat piles to the Xerox place and making copies for her new friends at the police department who didn't really want them. She moved through her days trying to avoid contact with anyone who would demand anything of her, screaming at her children with the voice of an enemy and glad that her husband was working late. She passed her nights curled up on her bed, eating jelly beans and watching crime shows; knowing that somehow, something must happen soon, and knowing she could not make it happen. As with all of life's changes the rhythm cannot be controlled or it will slap back at you in some penitential rage at your impatience, your egoism.

But the restlessness held and she wandered within it, behaving oddly, lost in herself. She began driving around the streets of her past, searching unconsciously for an answer, a path. Every morning now she drove Neilie to school and then wandered, listening to Beethoven and accelerating slowly up and down the roads of her childhood.

In the neighborhood where Hannah grew up, between Santa Monica and Sunset Boulevard in Beverly Hills, she had seen all the families as perfect and invincible, roller-skating around in a warm-muffin fantasy, with each house a giant crock pot simmering with security. But while she whirled by, comparing the bitter reality of her family with the illusory glory of the gardener-wet lawns and four-car garages of her perfect friends, things were, in fact, happening inside. Now, she retraced her childhood; roller skates and bike tires replaced by the wheels of a Mercedes. Up and down the streets she had known better than the curve of her own body; Hillcrest, Oakhurst, Sierra, Palm, Maple, Foothill, up and down these streets she cruised, twenty years later, house by house, braking before memories. And she found a new reality.

In a ten-block radius, a sack-race radius from Hannah's own door, people had not been safe. Mrs. Milner next door had died of cancer, before her fiftieth birthday. Her mother had done the same. Mrs. Feldstein, four doors down, in the house that always had a full refridgerator and lots of cars in the circular driveway, had, too. She could see them all in their black leotards having their exercise class in the Obermans' cork-floored den. Holding on to the sides of the polished oak bar, leg-lifting to the music. And they were all dead.

Mr. and Mrs. Cohen, who lived directly across the street, had both died within one year of each other of heart attacks, leaving their high-strung adopted daughter an orphan at eighteen. The Golds, next door, were divorced. Mr. Foreman, two doors down, went into a major mid-life depression and was hospitalized. The famous bandleader down the street dropped dead one morning. Mr. Gottleib had a cerebral hemorrhage and was left a vegetable, despite his elegant wife and two homecoming-queen daughters and a couple that lived in and all the parties they gave. Next to him, Mr. Lipton, who had a shiny bald head and always handed out homemade cookies, put a gun in his mouth and blew his face off Around the corner, the Plotkins's oldest son, one of three gorgeous boys, idolized by every girl in Beverly Hills High School, was sued for divorce by his teenage wife after infecting her with syphilis, contracted during what turned out to be one in a plethora of homosexual encounters. (Hannah still remembered his bar mitzvah.)

The Hellers were divorced and she had a nervous breakdown, recovering in time to marry a gigolo, who she referred to as her "cigarette lighter." ("Where's my cigarette lighter? Oh, there he is.") Mr. Baker had an affair and lost all of his money, and they moved from a mansion, since occupied sequentially by several famous film stars, to a small apartment below Santa Monica Boulevard, an area known as the poor section (shame on shame).

And then the Freemans. The most envied family in the radius. Who always had a crowd of friends watching ball games on the biggest color TV, and played golf at Brentwood Country Club, so normal, so secure, so wealthy, so wanted. One night, three years after Mr. Freeman sold his business and lost the profits in bad investments, he walked into their wondrous kidney-shaped pool with all his clothes on and a load of barbiturates in his stomach. The pool man found him in the morning. Mrs. Freeman, who had up to that point been a pleasantly neurotic hypochondriac, had a breakdown and spent the next ten years of her life crawling out of the hold. Their sons, who had been part of the golden-boy squadron of Corvette-driving, nightclub-going heirs of the "Haves," were left, without a meal ticket or a goalpost in sight, and took to selling real estate and hanging around private discos with drugged-out starlets.

Mrs. Goodman on North Rexford criticized her cook, who overreacted by hacking her to death with a cleaver and stuffing parts of her in the meat grinder.

One of the hardest truths for Hannah, cruising around in her red-leather time machine, was seeing the Powerses' old house. Her parents, her brother and she had gone there for swimming parties and summer barbecues. She loved going because Mrs. Powers was sexy and beautiful and wore a bikini (none of the mothers in the ten-block radius in the fifties were very sexy or beautiful, and no one wore a bikini; they were just mothers). Mr. Powers was sexy and handsome and also wore a bikini. And they had two sexy and handsome sons, whom she was simultaneously madly in love with. Within the six-year period after they all graduated from high school and moved on into the world, Mr. Powers surrendered to alcohol and pills and lost his money gambling. Their oldest son dropped out of medical school, got married, had a baby, took a job with the city and blew his brains out with a shotgun. Two years later their younger son died suddenly and mysteriously from a lung infection. Mrs. Powers is currently a middle-aged woman, with no resemblance to the lady in the bikini, who has survived to sell "better dresses" at a Wilshire Boulevard department store.

The Steins' oldest son had cancer of the testes and was castrated; pretty Margo Peters, whose father was a famous heart specialist, OD'd on heroin in the powder-pink bedroom; and then there were Jerry Miller and Mike Adams and Tom Andras who died in Vietnam. But they were really outside the radius; no wealthy Jewish boys went to Vietnam.

And still, driving up and down those quiet, lovely, vegetating streets, she flinched in resistance to this truth.

Hannah had grown up thinking that money protected you from life, and so, also, do a lot of ghetto people, and that's the danger. The only thing money protects you from is being poor, she thought, realizing how silly it sounded and yet knowing how many people living there didn't know that. Money had been her father's only scale by which to judge success, and she realized how many of those poisonous fumes she had inhaled.

As she drove, doubting herself and her value, a palpable, moaning need began moving through her. Rising in her belly sensually. A ravishing heat in her cold body that could not be described. That she felt so fully and so fiercely she relinquished all control and let it take her. A need to love. A need to hold another human being, to smother that person with her need and her passion to be free, to be herself. A need to be taken over by feeling, pure, raving feeling. In the heart, in the gut, in her breasts and the entrance to her sex. Hold me, love me, carry me. Let me feel, let me spread, let me out. Feeling without focus; a need for some shadow figure; a need crackling up through her body, hitting at the carefully arranged life patterns in her head like waves on a rock and loosening pieces of herself, loosening her fears, forcing her to admit that she had not felt the agonizing beauty of this feeling in years, and, whatever the cost, she did not want to lose it again.

She pulled her car over and turned off the engine, closing her eyes, the feeling rolling through her, covering her. I need. I *need*. A phantom figure darting before her heavy-lidded eyes. Purple roller skates and warm water. She regained at that moment the ecstasy of her girl-self, before it had turned into the fears of the committed. The lies of security and control.

"In ten years we'll move to Europe and put the children in a Swiss school."

"Giving your daughter up was an act of love."

"It's just bad luck that none of your deals ever work, honey."

"If I get sick like my mother, Nick will stand by me."

"Children give you a purpose, a reason for living."

"Let's start putting money away so we can go skiing next February."

"Marriage gives you closeness with one human being."

I need. I need.

Nineteen years old and mad with sex yearnings, Hannah sat, heat rising in her cold body, long-buried heat, long hidden from herself under the daily rituals of her snug little life. Death and a madwoman, tears and terror, fear and hate and pain and atrocity, fear of her father and the loss of her child-trust, the loss of her passion for the comforts of home. A madwoman. Whispers on the telephone had broken through the beehive in her head and released at last—as if returning from the dead, free from her history—released the blood in her body and let it dance.

CHAPTER 18

FAMILIES ON FILM: NOT MANY LAUGHS

With the aid of movie cameras, scientists seeking to learn what makes the American family tick have found a lot of talk, not much laughter and little special zest for living.

According to the study done by scientists at the University of California Medical Center, "There has been a theory that people don't talk much in a family setting. Our data shows there is a lot of talk, a lot of interaction. But not much laughter is going on in the family setting. There aren't many belly laughs. Our most joyful family was all deaf."

Among social scientists, great debate is developing over whether the family as an institution remains viable.

Hannah tossed the paper on the sink, giddy with the lunacy of the Sunday news.

The phone rang.

"Hello."

"Uh, hi, Hannah. How's everything, how was Palm Springs?"

"Fine, Dad."

"Uh, I thought, that if it was okay, maybe you and Nick would like to come with me and Patsy for brunch and we could take Neilie to the pony rides later."

"Well, I don't know, Nick's still playing tennis. Oh, I guess it's okay."

"Good, well, if I don't hear from you, we'll pick you up about twelve."

"Alright."

She regretted it immediately, furious with herself, at her regression from the ecstasy she had felt just days before in her car, returning to the race from reality; brought back into the bog by the steady sameness of Sunday mornings.

There had been no more telegrams or letters. Nothing. And so, she, Saint Hannah of West Hollywood, would forgive. "I forgive you, oh father, what you have brought to bear. Saint Hannah will go to the ponies as an Act of Grace."

"Mommy, Mommy, Charlie's drinking the mouthwash again."

"Oh, damn, where is he?"

"He's standing on your sink in the bathroom. You'd better hurry before he gets dead. I told him it was poison but he just won't listen. He's acting like a one-year-old."

"Yeah, wonder how he got the lid off," she whispered, dashing up the stairs, her daughter, the innocent murderess, trailing behind in big-eyed guilt.

"Charlie brush the tooth, Mommy, taste good."

Toothpaste trailed in thick white streams down the basin and onto the carpet. The baby stood, mouthwash reddening his nose, toothpaste mashed into his cheeks and between his fingers and around the soft tissue of his lips.

"Damn it, you two! You know better! Neilie, you know you're not allowed up there! Grandpa wants to take you to the ponies, but if you two don't behave, we're not going, understand?"

They nodded. Accepting passively, the price for their dangerous venture. Knowing it would come due and still, in the frenzy of their reach toward freedom, proceeding. Freedom being the forbidden, the touch of something magic in its consequence, and knowing also that they would continue to risk despite lost treats and slaps on the hands and tears and love withheld; despite the TV snapped away and the lights clicked off before they were tired and the agony of isolation behind the closed doors of their pretty prisons, they would continue drinking the mouthwash and playing with matches and climbing to the sun porch and stealing cookies from the freezer and knocking each other down and throwing milk on the floor until there was no more danger to it, till it became silly and they accepted the death of their need as growing up.

Hannah cleaned up the thick, oozing white mess, crouching on the floor with towels, pushing against the stains in hapless motion.

The baby sat, sticky and stained red and white like a melting valentine, watching her anger through the pristine channels of a primary mind.

"Charlie no more brush the tooth, Mommy. Charlie no good. Charlie yugly fatso. No cute."

"Charlie's not an ugly fatso." Good old Neilie, she thought, putting more water on the towel. "Charlie's just a pain in the ass." She laughed and looked at him.

The sudden acceptance of that truth. Of her love for these children and her confusion as to their place in the changing rhythm of her life, released. It was true. He was a pain in the ass. And she smiled.

Noise below. She turned, hearing her husband's key in the door. Sounds of Sunday. Tennis bag tossed on the stair. Whistling in the kitchen. Sounds of the trap reclosing around her. Pony rides. Saint Hannah at home.

"Daddy's home. Neilie, go on in and get dressed. We have to get ready for Grandpa. Hurry up now."

"Okay, Mommy." The child ran, relieved. Getting off easy. Charlie blamed, but not really dead. Privileges threatened, but, for now, not ruptured. Close calls. Little kids knew all about them.

"Hi."

"Hi."

"What the hell happened?"

"Charlie was at the toothpaste again."

"Where were you, why didn't you stop him?"

"I was screwing the Sparkletts man. Where were YOU, why didn't YOU stop him?"

They both stopped. Cutting off the conversation at the edge of the tension, knowing that it was unworkable and had no direction. Blames from hidden secret places moving without connection into words over ridiculous happenings.

"My father invited us to brunch and then we'll take the kids to the ponies." She looked up at him from the white-stained rug, braced for reaction.

"Great! Why the hell did you do that?"

"I don't know. I felt guilty, I don't know, I'm crazy, that's why. He sounded so vulnerable. I just did it. I can call him back. We don't have to go."

She waited again. Waited for him to resist, to lead her.

The Strong Angel who would lay his hand on her head and say, No, dear Hannah, we will not follow that path. I will show you the way. There will be no brunch, Saint Hannah, no ponies with that man. Today we will walk in the meadow and talk of truth. Take my hand and I will help you.

"Okay. I'd better take a shower. Can you clean that crap up later?"

"Yes. Come on, Charlie, Daddy's going to take a shower."

She picked up her melting valentine, heavy and warm in her arms, tension, closing her chest, and left the room.

He didn't do it. He never does it. He can't do it. Why should you want him to do it. You big baby. Ball-breaking bitch. Help yourself. He can't do it. And he doesn't want to; he wants you to do it.

And she loathed both of them.

At twelve they were ready. Fresh and clean and hungry. Happy-looking, Sunday-perfect family waiting in the sunshine for the person they would someday replace.

"Mommy, look! Here comes Grandpa, he gots the Rolls-Royce!"

Hannah and Nick exchanged looks.

Jesus, he really does want me to forgive him.

She smiled. The Rolls-Royce. Car of her father's dreams; dreamed of like their long-ago trip abroad, from the day he had first worked.

Tagging along with his drunken father, selling junk in Indiana. Money. Money. Success. His whole life he had worked. Worked and been afraid and worked and been greedy, and relentless and angry and making the people who worked for him shrivel under his fear and his unsatiable distrust and need to succeed.

And then, finally, he was there. And he was only thirty years old, and he fell apart.

Clinging to her mother like a dying animal, never leaving her side. And her mother, eight months pregnant, nursing the succeeder. Sleeping jammed together, Daddy crying, three-year-old Hannah waking to the sobbing and searching for comfort and full-bellied mother, all jammed together in a single bed, clinging to mother love to keep from falling off.

But her mother kept score. Her mother never forgot. Her mother gathered interest for what she had given, and he paid. Businessman's gamble, bad debt. He paid till the day her mother died, for the fury of his fear.

When he had recovered and was no longer afraid that his heart was about to stop every morning and could drive a car by himself, he started to work again. And he worked with the same singular spur of the driven that he had had before.

He denied himself pleasure and the experience of his days.

When Hannah was nineteen, full of romance and plans for New York, he decided, after sixteen years of rebuilding his courage, to take the trip of his dream. To take his family to Europe. Magic danced in the air. Summer vacation from college. Grand tour. Europe.

For three months they traveled. Her brother, furious at being taken against his will from the beach and his puberty, and she, dancing down a night sea of melting candles and the heat of her girl-passion intensified by being alone and unquenched. Better for giving her the phantom of love.

And they traveled. Her mother—weak. None of them knowing that disease was already unpacking in her body. Her father, screaming in the airports at the overweight charges. Screaming at the ticket people as if, so deep was his terror of new experience, he wanted them to subdue him and keep him on the ground.

The S.S. *France*. Hannah danced all night in tourist class and necked with a Mexican real estate agent behind the water pipes. She went to the Louvre in her Ohrbachs copy of a Chanel suit, and walked by the Seine and met a homely, rumpled student, who spoke no English and smelled of sweat and took her to Montmartre and kissed in a cafe. And she felt that she was fire and clouds, and life was a fresh fruit, a new thing, that she could stroke and it would make her beautiful. She moved about with her family, immunized to their misery, in a world of her own strength and she saved herself that summer. She had known, very young, how to save herself, and then she had married and life had dried out and she had forgotten.

The night they came back, she had been awakened by a sound floating down the long side halls of her parents' house. A sound that fizzed in her head like a smell one cannot place. A sound of being three and sleeping jammed together in fear in a single bed. And she had risen, pulling on a robe and moving will-lessly toward the sound.

Her father sat alone in the huge paneled den with his face on his lap, sobbing as if he would splinter and crack beneath the strain. And she sat next to him and tried to understand. And what she understood was that, again, he was crying because something he had worked his whole life for was over. And he would never be able to have it again. It was dead now. And he had lived through it.

It was the closest moment they had ever shared, and she had forgiven him everything, aching with love for this man who did not believe that anyone could love him and so was unable to accept what she offered, sitting beside him, wanting nothing but the privilege of sharing his pain.

And then the Rolls-Royce. The last thing. Huge, licking, lush machine with lamb's-wool carpets and black, real-leather seats that made you feel tiny and enormously powerful all at once and smelled richer than mocha cream—a car like that.

The price of a person's house. A life's savings. A pension for old age. A beautiful, unreal thing, built to be enjoyed and knowing it was a special, ridiculous thing for the gods. And he was afraid to drive it. And he hated it. He would not admit that, but he did.

It sat in his carport, shining. Washed by a black man every Thursday. It sat, like a beautiful woman put on a plate, wanting to be tasted and not just admired. He was afraid of it.

The dirty junk peddler's son, carrying his books home from Hebrew school in the snow to screaming sisters and boiled potatoes. Shame on shame. A little broken-nosed Jew boy with a drunken father, sin of Abraham. Only Jew drunk in the town.

He hated his father. And he loved him. And he was ashamed of him. Now he had children who hated him and loved him for all the same reasons. And $600 suits and a tennis court. And a Rolls-Royce car that he could not love. Still dragging his feet in the snow, not wanting to go home.

Her father honked. They picked up diaper bags and car seats and waved toward the car. A treat of treats, to ride in that car. People watching you, treating you with reverence. Movie Stars without a screen.

They drove to the restaurant using the children for protection.

"Neilie, did you tell Grandpa and Patsy about the puppet show they're having at school?"

"Uh-uh, I forgot. It's from a long time ago."

"Charlie's learning Spanish, isn't he, Neilie?"

"Uh-huh, Tina's learning him, but she doesn't understand when I try to learn her, uh, what language do I speak?"

"English, and it's *teach* her."

"Yep, I try and try, but she doesn't understand nothing."

"Anything."

"Anything. Charlie, say *mañana*, Man-ya-na."

"Magnanga."

They all laughed.

Hannah continued the placation, hating herself, hating the aggression of her despair as much as the passivity of these people. This husband. This father. This manipulating, slack-faced woman who had moved into all the dark parts of her father's need. A woman who would gobble up such crumbs, so abused had she been by herself, riding beside him wearing her dead mother's jewelry in spite of Hannah's protests and rage at her bad taste.

Her mother had left her nothing because to do the opposite would have been to admit that she was dying, and she had never done that. Never. And so, Hannah had sat beside her on the last day of her life exchanging recipes, unable to give her a proper good-bye. She had taken nothing but an old photograph and a black-wool blazer, which she had cut down but could never wear, and her father let Patsy have the few pieces of good jewelry— which killed Hannah and she knew would have killed Leah if cancer hadn't.

Hannah hated these contacts. She and the children performing for the dour egoism of these people, tongues lapping like dehydrated dogs, who took from her, sapped her energy. Her husband letting her give, placate, dance on her broken toes. Knowing what it cost her and never offering his help. Sitting, sullen. Doing her a favor like the rest. Letting her demean everything good in herself, but too filled with his own resentment and disappointment to help.

And then later, when it was safe, when he would not be called upon to ease the burden of her need to reach this father/man, he would blame her. "Why do you do that? You use those kids to please him. You don't have to entertain everybody."

Bullshit. When she stopped, they all stopped.

The fact was that Nick was as afraid of her father as the rest of them—all of them performing for the golden carrot—dangling just out of reach.

When they got to the restaurant, she stopped. So tense, so exhausted from the effort and the need to pretend they were still a family. She sat quietly and asked for a glass of wine. Which her husband did not order. And she asked again, desperation rising, the need for some release from this mounting burden, this lie she had created. The corner into which she sat painted, trailing the brush behind her; knowing it would lead here and unable to stop herself and with no one to lift her out.

He snapped at her. "Just relax, Hannah, we'll get it."

She met his eyes.

He cannot look into my eyes and not know I am dying here and not help me. Talk, Nick, *please* talk to them. Get me my wine and help me do this.

But he was sullen.

I will not entertain them. I will not. I will not use the children to entertain them. I will not.

So they sat. The unloved woman, chain-smoking, eyes shifting around the table, like a thing caught under a rock. They talked in tense dribbles about the service and the taste of the omelets, watching the children enjoy themselves, unaffected by the emotional havoc around them.

The wine arrived like morphine to the wounded, cold white liquid flowing in her throat.

They finished their eggs and toast and wine, and wiped up the sticky baby hands and faces. They freshened their breath with spearmint gum, and rose, the movement a thrill of freedom, so tight had she been stuck into the red-vinyl corner of her self-abuse.

"Are we going to the ponies now, Grandpa? Please, please?"

"Yeah, yeah, sweetheart, right now."

Her father moved ahead of them, holding her daughter's hand; holding it the way he might have held her own hand all that time ago. But she did not know that, she could not remember it, could not remember ever sitting on his lap or playing with his glasses or running to him in tears, or being held by him. Would Neilie remember? Do you remember because it happens? And not remember because it didn't?

Her father bent and kissed her child. The way he could not kiss her. Part of her was sad, and part jealous of the gift; part of her was her child and received the kiss, also. And part of her did not want him ever to touch her or her child again; wanted to run from these people as if she had borne herself and had no past.

They pulled into the driveway, jammed with Sunday parents, horns honking, restless children jumping and pulling toward the pleasures.

"Mommy, I want to ride Thunder. That's the fastest. I want to go a hundred times."

"Just relax, Neilie. Grandpa has to park the car first."

"Why don't you get out, Hannah, and I'll wait for the car in front to pull out."

"Okay, Dad."

She wanted to get out, restlessness making her feel trapped in the big, sweet-smelling machine.

She reached to open the door, holding her daughter's hand. Her husband turned away to help the baby out of his assortment of straps and safety bars.

"Come on, Mommy, let's go get the tickets!"

"Wait a minute, Neilie, just calm down now, we're in a driveway."

She pulled the handle, the door swinging slowly, the heaviness of its cost buried in layers of metal and leather.

Her daughter pulled on her arm, slender legs reaching for the dust.

And then her child was thrashing, ripped into the air like a kite in a bad wind. The car shot forward, bucking like a pokered bull. Her child was down and the wheels were moving toward her head and Hannah was screaming. She was shrieking for her father to stop the car, while eternity held her there and the car did not stop.

She clutched her child's hand, dragging her foot and holding on to the coat hook, knowing that her child was being killed. She pulled her daughter forward, seeing the wheels coming, knowing that she must pull the child faster than the machine to keep her head and body in front of it, screaming and pulling and clutching the tiny, wet hand like a lightning bolt frozen solid.

It stopped. People were running. Her daughter was lying on the ground, and then her husband was grabbing her up and a man was shouting: "THE CAR RAN OVER HER LEG! PULL DOWN HER SOCK! IT RAN OVER HER LEG!"

And her father was crying and screaming something at her, but she could not understand. The resistance, overpowering. She was standing next to her husband and shaking her head. "No, no, it didn't run over her. I kept her in front of the wheels, it didn't! IT DIDN'T!"

Then he pulled the sock down and she saw the crushed bone.

Without hesitating, conditioned like a lioness to protect the weak and helpless, Hannah turned from the sobbing, purple-lipped child and put her hand on the shaking back of her father's head.

"It was an accident. It's nobody's fault."

But that was a lie. It was somebody's fault.

And they were back in the car. The shame overwhelming. People standing around the silken chariot, shaking their heads. Her husband held their child while the baby screamed. Her father babbling, accusing her of something...not watching her child... something, so desperate was he to shift the burden of his guilt.

Something; her fault? Hitting the wrong pedal? Why didn't she have Neilie by the hand? She could not speak, knowing that it was not true, that she had saved her life. Knowing even in the moment of accepting that damage had been done; seeing the bone, blue and crushed against the bright yellow sock, that she had tried to spare him, and he could not even accept that.

Her husband was screaming now, confronting her father for the first time, raw injustice giving him the courage he so badly needed and had never found.

"You leave Hannah alone, you dirty son of a bitch, or I'll break your fucking neck. YOU did it! YOU did it! Don't you dare try to blame this on her! You never drive this goddamn thing. You told her to get out and then you stepped on the gas, you stupid bastard! I'll kill you. If you say one more fucking word, I'll knock you out of that seat!"

Her father was whining deep in his throat, like a drunk at midnight. They were somehow in the hospital. She was filling out forms.

"How did the accident happen?" The doctor stood over them; her little girl asleep from the shock and terror, lying against her breast, succumbed to pain.

The words stuck like poles in cement.

"My, her, we were, a, car, ran, we were getting out of a car and it jumped and...

"Good God. She's a very lucky kid. That's terrible."

Shame. Shame flooding her soul.

My father ran over my daughter with his big Rolls-Royce. You see, I wanted to forgive him because no more calls were coming. You see, one of his whores has been threatening my family. So we were going to the ponies to forgive him. I didn't really want to, but my husband said okay and he works for him after all. And so I thought, well, that must be the thing to do. See, the calls had stopped, so I thought, he's still my father and he doesn't want to hurt me, he really doesn't, but he almost killed my baby so it doesn't matter, you see, if he does it on purpose, it just doesn't matter anymore that all these things aren't on purpose.

The doctor set her daughter's leg. The child never waking, still purple-lipped and shivering. They sat watching. Her husband holding the baby, and she, her daughter in her arms, shame reeking from the clean walls and the clear, purified air.

Then they were back in that car. Now it was a monster, a horrible, menacing thing. Nero's chariot, all the sweet beauty of its richness lost to them forever.

They rode in silence. The passive outsider who had replaced her mother, looking around from face to face, unable to assess the damage to her position.

They were home. Her daughter was put to bed; carried up the stairs with her small leg jutting out in the plaster cast. The children went gladly to their beds, a safe, familiar place.

CHAPTER 19

"Well?"

"Well?"

"How was yours?"

"You first."

"No! Not possible. You first."

"You won't be able to top it, I promise."

"Good, that means yours was worse than mine. You go first."

"Wait a minute, Agatha, I need a cup of coffee before I start this one. Hold on."

Hannah moved quickly to the stove, refilling her cup and almost dropping the kettle in her rush to make Monday morning contact.

"Okay, ready?"

"Absolutely."

"Okay. Friday night we went to a dinner party and Nick got drunk and fell backward in his chair through a sliding screen door. So Saturday we didn't speak. And then Saturday night we made up and went out to dinner and talked a lot of fairy-tale shit, what we're going to do when we grow up sort of stuff that I don't seem to be able to handle anymore, and Sunday my father ran over Neilie's leg with his Rolls-Royce."

"What! What! Oh, my God! I don't BELIEVE THIS!"

"Told you you couldn't top it."

"How is she? Is she all right? Is she home or did they take her to the hospital?"

"Home. She has a broken tibia, cast from her hip to her toes, but the doctor said she'll be fine. She's already driving me crazy. She knows she's got a lot of cookies coming from this one. If I suddenly start screaming hysterically, don't pay any attention, it will pass. My life seems to be turning into a Joan Crawford movie."

"I don't even know what to say. How did he do it? How did it happen?"

"Basically, we were getting out of the back seat and he stepped on the wrong pedal, he never drives that thing, and somehow I pulled her forward and kept her spine from being crushed and that's about it. Except that Mommy may lock herself in the closet and start eating spiders."

"You poor darling. I'm so sorry. Have you had any more letters?"

"HA! NO! The irony is that I went with them yesterday because I felt guilty about being so hard on poor old Dad because the calls and letters had stopped. I never learn. If there is one piece of poop in the whole park, I'll step in it every time.

"Anyway, I have lived. Neilie has lived. And it's Monday morning again. Tell me about you. Tell me something amusing, make it up if necessary...but make it funny."

"Oh, God. I couldn't be funny. I stayed in bed all day Sunday with violent pains in my stomach and of course I was sure it was cancer; luckily I still had some marvelous Mexican pain tablets left."

"Oh, those are just great when your stomach hurts. What's wrong with it?"

"Well, I'm not sure...but Saturday night I had a mad sex thing with that little Indian sculptor I know, and I thought maybe he pushed my loop out of place or something, but the top of my stomach is sore, too."

"The TOP OF YOUR STOMACH! What the hell did he use, a chisel? The Little Sculptor...with the three-foot cock!" They laughed together. It hardly mattered whether it was funny, it was that kind of laughing.

"Oh, God, I don't know, it may be something else."

"Well, listen, if you'd like me to try him out...sort of a second opinion."

"Anytime, my darling, you can have them *all*. I most certainly hope I never, ever fall in love ever again."

"Do you really mean that?" Hannah stopped. She knew that she longed for the risk of loving again, and she did not want to admit it to herself or anyone.

"Absolutely. Never." Agatha paused, "I'm leaving for Australia tonight. Got a hot ticket from my Mafia travel agent. Talk about rotten timing. I hate to leave you now."

"Oh. I won't even get to see you."

"I know, darling. I'm so sorry. I can't wait any longer. I must go. They suspended my bloody license for three months, so it's really a perfect time to leave, except for you." Tears filled Hannah's eyes. She sat, legs tucked under her, feeling lost.

"Kathy's got a part in a play off-Broadway. She's leaving, too."

"Come see me. We'll have fun."

"I'll hop the next kangaroo. Write, please."

"I will, darling. Don't worry. Remember it's just a ride on the merry-go-round, not so serious any of it. Say goodbye to Nick and the children for me. I'll write as soon as I get there. Wish me luck."

"I wish you everything. I love you."

"Bye, darling. I love you, too."

Hannah put down the phone, cradling it quietly like an opened present, empty of its surprises. Broken connection. Lines going nowhere. She and the telephone. All alone. Waiting for a ring-ting-a-ling-a. A, what? She sighed. "The act's breaking up."

"Mommy, I can't go make a pee pee. I keep getting my wooden leg in the way. Help me, Mommy."

"Coming, darling, just a minute."

She rose slowly, knowing it would be a very long day, that there was no reason to rush into the stretches of empty space, and moved toward the stairs.

"Mommy, hurry, I've got to go real bad. I can't hold it inside anymore."

"Yes, baby, I know the feeling."

It was a long day. Neilie clung to her, questions finally pouring out, wide eyes blinking away the fear. Questions dragging Hannah down; tensing her in impatience, angering her with her own impotence of answers. "Could the Rolls-Royce get me dead? When they take this thing off, will my leg still be there? Did Grandpa try to kill me like on TV? If a truck runs over my head, would my brain squish out? If your brain came out, would you be dead? If the Rolls-Royce runs over me again, will I get another wooden leg? What's an accident mean? How come Charlie didn't gets no wooden leg? Does the Rolls-Royce like babies better than little girls?" On and on and on.

Hannah fed her lunch on a tray and took her to the bathroom and sponged her small round body and helped brush her teeth. She read stories and played War. The baby threw up on the carpet and turned very pale and cried on and off all day and into the evening. When she and Tina worked together, preparing them for the night, they clung to her, the baby copying his sister's need, pushing against her for a strength and warmth which she did not have left. And, finally, as if the cell door had opened, the day ended. They were asleep and she was free.

"Hello."

"Hi, how's it going?"

"Okay, got the kids down. Neilie almost drove me crazy with questions. I hope she's okay, she seems awfully anxious. Are you coming home soon? She kept asking for you."

"No. I thought I'd go hit some balls at the club, so don't cook anything for me."

He stopped, braced for her reaction. She was silent, feeling again the pounding loneliness that had followed her all day.

"But, Nick, I really wanted Neilie to see you. I promised her."

"I'll see her in the morning."

She battled her anger and lost. "Okay. Never mind. I know how important your backhand is. I'll tell your daughter that. She'll understand."

She stopped. She was breaking the rules again—going too far.

"Don't do a number on me, Hannah, I've had a hard day. Your goddamn father is driving me crazy. I'll be home early. I love you."

"I love you, too. I'm sorry."

She put the phone down. Feeling guilty and relieved that he was not coming home. That she would be alone.

"I love you." Words they said now like "pass the mustard." Words she had lost touch with. Words that had no meaning.

She ran a bath because she did not know what else to do, lying back in the water, humming under her breath as the hot, oily warmth climbed her body.

The phone rang again.

"Dammit."

She leaped forward, almost hitting her head on the wall, and reached for her towel; racing down the hall to her bedroom, leaving a trail of soggy marks in the carpet.

"Hello."

"Well, hellooo, bitch." Giggles screaming in the room.

Oh, God, no, it's not true.

"How did you get this number! How did you!"

Laughter crackling up her spine. "I told you, stupid, you can't get away from me. Never, ever, ever."

Laughter crawled up her scalp.

"I'm ready, dearie. Tonight's the night."

She dropped the phone, whimpering like an ancient creature.

Oh, my God, please, no more, please.

Tears mixing with sweat from the bath, images flying in her head. Neilie and the car and Nick and knives and screams.

She dialed frantically.

Be there. Please, Nick, be there. No answer. Call the club. Oh, God, the number, what's the number?

"Information."

"Yes, please, the number for the Westside, uh, Indoor Tennis Club, I don't know the street."

"Just one moment, please."

Oh, my God.

"Is that in Los Angeles or West Los Angeles?"

"Uh, West, I think."

"I show no listing."

"Then LOS ANGELES! It's *got* to be listed."

"One moment, please."

"The number in Los Angeles is 234-1545."

"Thank you."

Frantic dialing.

"Westside Tennis."

"Yes, has Mr. Nicoli come in? It's an emergency!"

"No, not yet. Can I take a message?"

"Yes, please. The minute he gets there, tell him his wife called and said to come home immediately. Please don't forget, it's very important."

"All right, I'll tell him."

She walked the room, throwing the towel on the bed and grabbing for a robe. She moved through the house, bare feet slapping on the wood floors, testing doors and window latches and pacing the hall.

"Call the police, better call the police, too."

She tore cards from her wallet, her frustration rising, hands fumbling together like unrelated objects.

"Calm down, Hannah. Dial the number, Hannah, okay, okay." She held her breath.

"West Hollywood Sheriff Station, Lieutenant Stuart speaking."

"Yes. Yes! My name is Hannah Nicoli and this is an emergency. I want to talk to Detective Hudson."

"What is it in regard to?"

"It's in regard to threatening phone calls that we were having and we changed our number and she's got it and she just called to say she was coming here to hurt me and take my children, that's what it's in regard to and I want some help immediately!"

What would Myrna Loy do?

"I'm sorry, ma'am, but Detective Hudson is not on duty tonight. Now, I'll be glad to file a report."

"I don't want a report! I want the police to come here, immediately!" She knew she sounded hysterical, knew that she must not offend this person, this distant, calm, protected, black-clothed person, or he would not help her. Myrna Loy would have William Powell.

"I'm sorry. I know I sound emotional, but this woman is crazy, there's a warrant out for her, and I'm all alone here with my children and she said she's coming here."

"Well, chances are it's just a threat, but I'll try to get an officer out there as soon as possible."

"Please, please try to get someone. My children are asleep and my little girl had a serious accident yesterday. I hate to move them. I don't want to frighten them, but I'm afraid to stay here alone."

"All right, ma'am, now you lock your doors and try to relax a little."

"Thank you."

She paced the floor—jumping at shadows.

The phone was still. She sat holding her knees and rocking in the darkness.

What should I do? Call Agatha? Agatha's not here anymore. No one's anywhere. Oh, God! I can't wake Neilie up now after yesterday and scare her again! Goddammit, Nick, come home! Why is it always when I'm alone!

And then she felt something. Not a sound. A thing, which conquered the senses, moving through her like a sip of something cold. A feeling of someone. She got down on the floor and crawled to the window, lying in the darkness with her ear against the open frame, too frightened to breathe. There was someone down there.

"The gun. I've got to get the gun."

She crawled along the floor, dragging a chair behind her. And then she was up, stretching on her toes to the storage cupboard high above their lives where they had hidden that little toy thing and forgotten its presence.

"What did he say? Where do I put the bullets? Oh, shit, it's worse than the damn Cuisinart."

Her hands shook. The touch of the thing, all alone with it, like a dream of something too horrible, a deadly, sinful thing to do alone. A man dressing like a woman, sticking a dildo inside yourself, picking legs off flies.

Her hands felt like spastic wings. She fumbled.

"Oh, God! Safety! Got the safety on, okay, okay, Hannah, it's okay, put the things in...be cool now. It's just a moving picture now. Gonna call 'Cut' any minute now. Okay, cock it, okay. That's all. Okay."

She crawled back to the window, the feeling of something there, filling the space.

Slides clicking in her head, standing on her pink toilet seat, afraid to look out.

And something moved—or slipped. And her fear vanished. And she became ice. She rose and moved to the stairs, poising herself, knees together, gun pointed outward, like a Hollywood Frontier Woman.

Lights, camera. "If she comes through that door, I'll kill her. I'll blow her fucking head off."

Protector of her home. Her life. Her children. *She* could do anything. She *could* do *anything*. By herself. She could even kill.

I should comb my hair.

And the giggling started outside the door. Soft, drunken giggles, haunting her porch.

"Dear God...it's real. She's there."

She sat frozen, filled with separated, dispassionate fascination with this presence, this force that had moved into her life and exposed her to herself. She sat, shoulders hunched forward, aiming the evil little toy at the door, listening to the sound of cruelty, of perversity, while she and the presence traded places, and for the first time that she could remember, she did not feel like the victim. She was the power. Sitting high on the stairs, listening to the sound of evil and realizing its weakness.

"Relax, Hannah, John Wayne's riding up the driveway right this minute."

Steady, rhythmic, open-palmed slapping hit at the door. A drunk's attack. Open-handed smashing, slow and sloppy. It went on and on.

John Wayne's dead.

"Oh, God, please don't let Neilie wake up, please."

She did not move.

"I should call the police again. I've got to call them."

But she did not move.

Thudding in her head. Chimes clanging. Pressure on the bell.

"Mommy, what's that noise? Mommy, I woke up. What's that noise?"

Neilie stood behind her, eyes lidded by half-dreams, staring down at her mother crouched on the stairs, holding the golden gun.

"Mommy, what's you got? Is that a present for the baby? You said no guns, guns are bad toys, remember, Mommy? Mommy! Someone's at the door."

The baby, sensing danger, began to cry.

She rose, thrusting the thing into her pocket, and took her daughter's hand.

"Neilie, baby, you know that bad lady that was calling us? Well, I think she's sick or something and she wants to come in our house, but Mommy doesn't like her and I don't want her here. Now, I want you to go back to your room and I'll go get Tina and you can all play the record player and stay up till the lady goes away. Okay?"

"Okay. I'll punch her right in the head if she comes in this house."

"She won't, darling, really it's all okay."

James Bond will be here in a second, dear.

"Open this door, you dumb cunt, or I'll burn your fucking house down."

"Mommy! Mommy! She said the F word! She's got matches out there, Mommy!"

"Neilie, get inside, please! I'll get Tina."

She was running down the stairs past the presence.

"Tina! ¡Inmediatamente! Tina, emergencia! Mujer negativa. ¡Por favor, tome niños!"

The girl followed her, eyes squinting in the dark, staring back at the door as if it had suddenly sprung from its resting place in the air.

"Los niños en el cuarto de Neilie. Cierre la puerta. ¡Y no abra!"

She grabbed the baby, pushing them all into the small, yellow-flowered room, closing them away, muffling the children's voices, the baby whimperings hidden inside her own.

She tripped over her robe, falling into her room on her knees, scrambling upward toward the phone.

Where's goddamn Superman when you need him. "West Hollywood Sheriff Station."

"This is Mrs. Nicoli, I called earlier, the woman I called about is here! She's here! She's banging on my door, she says if I don't open it she'll burn the house down. Send someone quick, please, please!"

Too shrill, Hannah—much too shrill. Anne Bancroft would be throaty. Meryl Streep would be pale and vulnerable. Where's Spider-Man? Where's the Hulk? Come on you guys, next scene already!

"All right, Mrs. Nicoli, I'll send someone right away." A window shattered.

My robe's got mustard stains all over it.

She moved from the room, not even replacing the phone. Grabbing for the gun instinctively now, like reaching for a tissue to thwart a sneeze.

Marlene Dietrich, Lauren Bacall, gun in one hand, French cigarette in the other.

Calm returned with the gun. Power. She sat back on the stairs, waiting for a hand, a face, something she could hurt.

But there was nothing. Quiet giggles. Murmurs of madness on the porch.

Hannah felt her enter.

My God, it's real!

Broken window glass, grinding under foot pressure.

Just waxed the goddamn floor.

She's in the living room. God, my God.

She stiffened. Both hands tightening around the gun.

"I can't move. I can't." Come on, 007.

A lamp crashed to the floor. The piano keys rattled against some force. A body. Tripping and balancing. And the giggling started again. Terrorizing baby giggles. Demon sounds in her pretty party room.

Drunken humming in her house. Stumbling, heaving noises.

She's drunk. I should lock myself and the kids in the bedroom and wait for the police. But I can't. I can't move. Help me, Moses; doesn't work, need Jesus! I knew it, if I was Catholic, Robert Redford would run in and...

Her arms were numb. She didn't breath. She was, in some primal way, setting a course. Invaded by the enemy. Territory surrendered.

She can have the living room, but not the stairs.

Lines drawn. Points of honor. Things one would die for. Bad little boys, testing, waiting.

The house was black. She saw with her nerves, every breath the creature took, she felt.

Audrey Hepburn was blind.

She heard bare feet—heavy, thick feet slapping across the living room to the hall, moving toward the stairs. And rage over the trespass flushed her. She caught her breath and half rose, knees straining, legs spread, balancing the gun between her thighs.

"Not the stairs."

The threats, the fear, were no longer considerations. She had traded in her game of helplessness for her honor. A tattered bum with a perfectly knotted tie. Her territory had been invaded. Mother birds, mother bears, queen bees, underdogs.

"Not the stairs."

She was white hot. She was steel.

Bare feet flapping over crushed glass. Drunken grunting. The thing pushed itself up the hall landing and moved toward the stairs.

The crystal vase on the hall table, her mother's vase, shattered. A foot moved forward.

She's on the stairs.

Neilie screamed at the noise. "Mommy!"

Her head jerked toward her child's door and back like a palsied doll. "Mommy!"

Ingrid Bergman...

Her knees collapsed—spreading her legs wider and screams tore from her throat. "No More!" and the gun fired and fired, over and over. She screamed in anger, terrible, billowing rage pouring through her, cleansing her. Raising all the deep-rotten knots of her anger and unclogging her soul. It came and it came and she shot and she shot, arms locked, shooting like she had prepared her whole life for this, teeth bared, eyes squinting for focus, ignoring the moans—the blood and bits of bone and flesh spattering around her bare legs. Without horror. Without pity; propelled by her hands. Brainless, mindless rage. A breaking point. The place nice girls never think they'll visit. Somewhere frightening and rudderless inside. Covered with trendy clothes and good manners. Hidden from themselves even in dreams. A primal scream without a guide, beyond the rules of the parquet-tiled road.

She had broken. "NO MORE!" The gun stopped. Emptied. And then sirens. Contorted safety. She rose, arms still locked. Face shattered with tears and sweat and fury.

A thick-bodied woman lay dead on her stairway. Black hairs

springing from white, broken-veined legs. The soles of her feet, dirty and crusted with splintered glass and dead skin. She lay, face down, greasy brown hair pressing against Hannah's polished wood floor, a knife beside her. A vial of acid broken and searing into Hannah's carpet. Blood, released into the darkness, forced out of its protected place inside the creature's warm skin, exposed to judgment, purple in the darkness, racing aimlessly, spider-tracking down the body.

She moved forward, sidestepping the creature without interest. The gun, still frozen in her hands, she moved toward the noises. More sirens. Cars appeared. Lights flashed with authority. She opened the door and stood— one bare leg wrapped around the other. A twelve-year-old's stance. An ice-cream-licking posture. Standing like a child—wide-eyed and hidden in the shadow of the whirling lights, feeling the circle close.

Ingrid Bergman would have lipstick on.

A man moved toward her.

"Mrs. Nicoli?"

"Yes."

"Can I come in?"

She left the doorway, holding herself with her arms— forgetting the thing on the stairs, the gun in her ice cream hand, the tears on her cheeks.

They sat in the darkened living room. And she, no longer the victim, feeling deep, heaving anguish for the poor creature, surrounded by black, heavy-breathing men in her hall, being photographed in all her naked ugliness, poked and tagged and wrapped up like spoiled food. And the black, hairy-armed men, gasping under the strain, lifted the spoiled thing and carried it out of her life.

Bette Davis would have made tea and talked her out of it.

The detective cleared his throat and began. She answered his questions without hearing them. Not listening, but knowing the answers, needing the comfort of his precision, his warm smell in the chill of her house.

The officer, who is Clint Eastwood, falls madly in love with this brave, fearless woman and carries her off in her mustard-stained robe.

Her husband's key in the door, his face immobile, eyes snapping over them, the guilt of exclusion filling his face.

"What happened?"

They talked around her. Her exhaustion moving into her need to tell him, to reach him. Her anger was gone. She searched around for it, but it was all gone. She had been shaken dry like sap from a stick—feelings wrung out and beautiful, uncomplicated exhaustion, covering her like the arms of a lover, protecting her from any more.

And the questions ended. And the crisp, warm-smelling man, who seemed for some perverse reason proud of her, shook her husband's hand and left them alone.

"Oh, my God, Hannah, I'm so sorry I wasn't here." His face flushed in confusion. "It's all your fucking father's fault." Tears covered his broad, tan cheeks.

"I don't want to talk about it, I have to see the children. Neilie heard it. I've got to see my children."

Liv Ullmann in *A Doll's House*, she had found her own weapons.

"Our children." He took her hand.

And she looked at him. Stopping for a moment dead on the stained, silent stairs.

"My children." She said out loud, not even knowing she was speaking it to him, thinking she was talking to herself.

She moved away from him up to the light and noise of the yellow, sweet-flowered room.

CHAPTER 20

NOTEBOOK (VOLUME III)

HANNAH NICOLI, THE WORLD'S FIRST JEWISH MURDERESS, PAGE 2001 OF *RIPLEY'S* (ALSO *WHO'S WHO IN AMERICAN WOMEN*). I AM NOW THIRTY-TWO YEARS, THREE AND ONE-HALF MONTHS OLD.

I have had my name in the newspaper and my face on the six o'clock news—fame at last!

I have lost five pounds—which is good. Perfect diet. Take one gun. Shoot to death one crazy lady. Just watch the pounds melt away!

I have lost most of my illusions about sanctity and executive privilege, which is, I guess, good.

I have almost lost my daughter—which is what you would expect.

I have been abandoned by my relatives. Not a "Hello, stranger" in sight.

I have lost my father, or will as soon as I can face the fact that I never had him to lose in the first place, which is good for the noodle but lousy for the central nervous system of the average neurotic child-woman.

I have my husband. Don't want to write about that, sorry Hannah, sorry eternity.

I am still tense as tensile.

Still have no patience with my children.

Still bitter about "The Past."

I have learned about police stations and guns. And how to tie-dye a mustard-stained terry-cloth robe with blood and acid!

I am overburdened with self-imposed responsibility to make it up to Neilie for that horrible weekend. And furious that she's manipulating my guilt. Little SHITS. Will they grow up to be BIG SHITS? Save that for my forty notebook.

Eight more years. A hundred more crow's-feet. Three thousand leg shaves. Twenty-five hundred yoga classes. Loss of ninety billion brain cells. Midriff bulge. TITS TOUCHING THE TUM-TUM. Husband having first coronary and/or first affair with tasty-teeny. Kids beginning to realize you are not Super MOM. Not even worthy of time or attention. A "thing" that lives in their house and goes to the market. One hundred twenty-thousand roast chickens. Eighteen orgasms, HA! Elevated blood pressure. Hysterectomy. "What you could have done with your life if" fantasies. Fifty-thousand Dry Cleaning bills. Twelve hundred breast self-examinations. Eight Pap smears.

Two hundred million glasses of white wine—same sawed-in-half Valium.

Forty. Yick.

So, okay. Hannah. So the moon didn't rise at thirty-two. So it's been a lousy, unspeakable, unreal three and one-half MORE months. So? Thought you settled all that in the bathtub. SO? The lady is really dead. Your mother is REALLY dead. And, worse, you don't *really* want her to come back either. Ouch—that one hurt. Will God tell her? When I get up there, will she sulk like she did down here and not talk to me for eternities?

I have suddenly realized that I am surrounded by sulkers. All my life I've been following a bunch of sulkers around, trying to snap them out of it. "Uh, please, Mom, come on, tell me what I did; uh, come on, Dad, come on, Mom, she didn't mean it, he didn't mean it, they didn't mean it. Uh, come on, Nick, tell me what's the matter? Don't say nothing! You've been sitting in the dark drinking gin for three hours! Give me a break—tell me! Come on, Nick—it's been three days now—gimme a clue—is it me? Are you broke? Terminally ill? Bad backhand? Aw, come on. Come on, Neilie, don't pout, tell me what's the matter? Don't say nothing! Come on, Charlie, even *Charlie*. A two-year-old sulker! Pushes me away and stands himself in the corner with his fat cheeks all poked out. What yo' lips poked out about, boy? "No touch me," he says. SULKERS. GODDAMN IT! I need a fighter, better a down-out dirty fighter than those GODDAMN SULKERS. I'm not a sulker. I'm a murderess, an aggressive person. Susan Hayward. Simone Signoret. Forty. Six thousand hours of sulking. Would you tell our TV audience what you were thinking about during the gruesome attack? I was thinking how Ingrid Bergman would play it.

Hannah stretched, pausing only momentarily. A week of frantic working, pages of ideas, rambling thoughts, half-finished articles, stacked in folders around her. Words beaten out of her machine, her only place of self, keeping her away from the edge of her fear, since what she had begun to refer to silently as "The Attack." "The Attack" was not over. Police were coming and going, statements, overstatements being given. She hugged her children tighter and her walks grew longer, but she had no nightmares and no remorse. She had taken to her machine sensing that something, some Ingmar Bergman finale, was still coming. And, in her own way, she was preparing.

She wrote all day, until her shoulders were rigid with tension and her stomach hollow. Her heart, pounding from shots of caffeine.

"Hello."

"Hi, honey. I tried you at home, you're really putting in a day." Guilt hung on the line. "Want to have dinner out?"

"Okay, great. Where?"

"How 'bout Chianti at seven. I'll meet you."

"Okay, I'll call Tina. See you."

She sat staring blankly at the phone and shuddered with memories.

Okay, Hannah, things aren't so bad. Not too goddamn bad, considering. Could be in Bangladesh, blind, kid with Down's syndrome, a boat person.

She smiled to herself, feeling new feelings. As the spiders had been swept away from out of the deep dark corners, emerging from the angel hairs, new feelings had arrived. First, horror, despair, terror at the imperfect; strangers. Not monstrous any longer, but still appalling. Black and ugly and angry, wriggling in the light. The bottom of her, swept from the corners and into the sun.

Then, she had accepted them enough to be curious about this spider-self. She had dared to look, slowly removing the bloodless hands from her eyes and peeking.

With this tentative and fragile new awareness, other feelings had appeared. Love and compassion, sponging the guilt and fear, caressing her.

She was late. Her husband was sitting at the small, marble-topped bar in the back of the restaurant, waiting. Hannah paused in the door, nearsighted eyes naked of glasses batting around the room, not recognizing her own husband. People looked up casually, in this chic neo-bistro place, an In place, where no one ever talked too loud and pasta was served on little plates and everything was more Florentine than Florence. A perfect, quiet, expensive place in which to be seen eating slowly. People watched her and whispered. She was used to that. People had always looked at her. She never knew if it was because they thought she was pretty or because she had, as someone had once told her, pluck, an attitude, a presence. She didn't care anymore—she liked that they looked.

Nick waved to her and she made her way down the narrow, dimly lit central aisle, ignoring the eyes.

Eat your little under-$100,000-a-year hearts out.

"Hi." Nick smiled at her, his eyes puffy with sadness. "Hi, I didn't see you." She smiled back, wanting to reach out to him, to hold him in her arms and comfort them both.

"You never see me. You should get contact lenses."

"Are you kidding? Can you see me farting around with those tiny little things. I can hardly butter bread."

"Well, then, wear your glasses."

She sighed. Tension moving between them.

"Nick, we've probably had this conversation a thousand times. I can't walk around with my glasses on, I get nauseous. I don't wear them enough. I only need them for movies and driving and seeing famous people's pimples and wrinkles when I'm sitting down. Fell over on the tennis court because I tried to play with my glasses on, remember? It's just something I have to live with, not recognizing my husband in Italian restaurants. May I have a drink?"

Nick sat up straight, the barrier created. "Don't get uptight, love. I was just trying to help."

"I know, I just hate repeating myself. I *don't* need contacts, I like not seeing good, well? Whatever. I NEED a drink. I've been in that box for nine straight hours and I didn't do anything usable. I don't know what I'm doing. I feel like my brain is scrambled. I'll have a vodka martini."

They sat silently for several moments, waiting for her drink.

Easy, Hannah, easy. What's there to be afraid of?

"Relax, Hannah." He reached for her hand. "I know what you've been through, but it's all over. So relax."

"Yeah, yeah, easy for you to say." Hannah had said too much. She caught herself, shifting their focus. "How was your day?"

"Okay, same shit." His face softened—relieved that she would not pursue the subject or blame him—and she hated his relief even as she granted it.

"I'll tell you, I'm going to get out of that garbage pit. I've got a couple of investors interested in starting a film studio. Your father and I can't go on after what's happened. It's worse than ever. If I can put this deal together, we'll be out of this town in two years, tops. No more creeps. No more worrying about money. No more taking shit from your father. We'll be free."

She moved her hand away.

Relax, Hannah.

She was fighting his words like an old lady with the neighbor's mad dog. Tired of the theme. The plans. The delusion of it almost, now, an architectural achievement.

As if God had written, "Nick and Hannah Nicoli, in two years you will be rich and free, you will find a world where you will dance in the wheat fields and take no shit." She didn't care about that and she didn't believe it. Somehow, more and more as he talked about tomorrow, worked on sketches of "THE HOUSE" they would someday build, the Bentley they would someday drive, the places they would someday go—as if the reality of the world, inflation, energy supplies, the disappearance of the endless potential of the American Dream, did not exist—she became more and more resistant. She found herself humoring him, snapping at him, phasing him out like one of the children. They were not in the same place. She in truth—he in myth. She wanted to be in the same place with him.

What was that story?

She remembered a story by Sartre about a woman whose husband was insane and she stayed in the mad room with him, never leaving, hoping she would absorb his madness so that they could be together.

She gulped her drink, too restless to sip. Thoughts she had never admitted.

I hate when he starts that stuff. It's not real, it's not important. Not after what I've seen. It's not controllable, and if it doesn't happen, he'll feel his life is a failure. I know him, he will. And it's not going to happen. He is not able to make those things happen. My father is right about that. He doesn't tell himself the truth—and you can't get where he wants to go without it. He wants *me* to get us there.

She listened, trying to control herself, not respond, not manipulate his words to make them less threatening to her life-game. But she couldn't stay still.

I used to stay still, I used to dream with him; when I loved him, I used to believe it, too.

The thought hit her stomach like clear, cold juice.

Oh, God. What did I say?

"Excuse me, sir, we have your table."

Hannah looked up, the quiet, elegant phrasing of the maître d' cutting through her thoughts.

"Great, I'm starved."

She finished her drink quickly—reaching for her purse almost in unison and moving swiftly away from the bar —following the clean, smug, perfectly poised shoulders of their professional host.

"Madam," the small, crisp man bowed slightly, indicating the table and touching the back of the chair ever so gently.

"Thank you." Hannah, self-conscious of her movements beside this neutered, unreadable elegance, feigned effortlessness as she maneuvered down the tiny aisle and into the small, straight-backed seat. Her husband, moving slowly toward him, eyes darting around the room, stopped.

"Don't you have a booth?"

"I'm sorry, sir, not at the moment."

"I don't like sitting out in the middle of the floor like this. I asked for a booth when I made the reservation. I see two in the corner over there, man—come on."

The slick little European man stiffened imperceptibly. Hannah stiffened with him.

"I'm sorry, sir, but those tables are for four people. If you want to wait, we should have something in twenty minutes or so."

"Nick, it's okay, I'm starved, I don't really want to wait anymore."

"Okay, okay, but I don't like this crap."

The man moved away as if from sickness or a bad smell, his face and posture unreadable from years of encounters.

"Was that really necessary?"

"Yes, I don't like these assholes taking advantage of us. Saving those booths for someone more important. I'm sick of that crap."

"Then why do we come here? You know it's like this. These places are always like that. It's not worth getting upset about, relax—ha! now I'm telling you. Let's order some wine and an appetizer or something and talk awhile."

"Okay. If I can get a waiter back."

Something was going wrong here. Something was happening. She knew it, knew the pattern, felt his hostility, the "Bully Brigade" she had named it long ago—pick on the little guy, the kids, the porter, the gas-station attendant, anyone safe. Your wife. Stay away from the real anger, stay away from the self. She hated it. The mixture of passiveness and aggressiveness of her husband's moods, now, because of the winter's madness, more real and disturbing and unpalatable to her.

Her husband caught the busboy by the jacket on his endless march with the silver water pitcher.

"Hey, could you get our waiter, please?"

"Hokay, jest a meenit."

"Goddamn it, I hate waiting just to order a lousy drink."

"I hate it too, Nick, but we're here. So let's just let it go. Okay?"

"Yes, sir. Ready to order?"

"No, we're not ready to order. We would like a bottle of the Bolla Soave and two mozzarella marinaras, and bring the wine now. We'll order later."

"Certainly, sir."

The man backed away, feeling the tension. Hannah backed away. Her husband leaned forward.

"What's the matter?"

"Nothing. I just hate that tone in your voice. It's really not the waiter's fault or the busboy's…it's not worth ruining our evening over."

"Oh, come on, Hannah. Don't be so stupid. I didn't do anything."

"You know, Nick, I cannot figure you out. Either you wander through situations like the ninety-pound weakling or you flex muscle when no one's pressing. Which are you? Are you flexing because you feel like a big shot now and that's the way THEY act? It's not like you, I don't know, it makes me nervous."

Shut up, Hannah, shut up. What are you doing? Why don't you shut up—if you don't, you know what's going to happen—he'll blow. It wasn't a big deal—give him some space—be quiet, he's suffering, too. Look at what he has to put up with every day just to take care of you and the kids.

But she could not stop; like the pounding on her machine, beating away the fear, she was propelled toward some confrontation, toward the ripping off of the mask of this relationship, the pretense of loving, of no anger or disgust; propelled toward the release.

THERE NOW! YOU SEE IT! THIS IS WHAT I AM! THIS IS HOW I REALLY FEEL! THIS IS WHAT I LOOK LIKE! THERE, THERE! LOOK AT IT! SEE ME! THIS IS WHAT IT IS. THERE! The cat from the bag, the troll from under the bridge, the makeup in the sink, the baby from the belly. THERE! THERE! THERE! THERE! THERE!

"Drop it, Hannah. I mean it! Just drop it."

"Can't we talk about it? Can't we discuss it? Don't threaten me. I want to know why? What's going on in your head? Talk to me. If I can understand it, maybe it won't upset me. Why don't we ever talk about what's bothering you? We only talk about me. Talk to me, *please*. I need to know what *you* feel. I don't need you to be perfect or whatever the hell it is you think I need. That's a game. We're too old to keep playing that game. It's not the damn table, but it *is* something. For chrissake, admit it. It's something else!"

She was pleading—despair rising in her voice.

Let me in, please let me in. I don't want to be out here all alone. I don't want to go away, let me in or I'm going to have to go away. PLEASE.

His face was tightened with the rage of uncertainty, of having no map and finding oneself suddenly lost, nowhere to turn to find the old path—the trail to safety burning behind.

"You're so full of shit, Hannah. You're so wrong. You and your psychology, it's so much shit. I do talk to you, sometimes I don't *want* to talk to you. You and your whole goddamn family and all of this complicated shit, I'm sick of it! Sometimes a cigar's just a cigar!"

She felt her body go cold with anger. Cold and hot and hot and cold and desperate and unsure.

You're WRONG, HANNAH—everybody knows that, you've always been WRONG. You and your whole nutty family. WRRROOONG. Let it go, Hannah, just let it go.

But she could not stop. It was where she had been waiting to go. The violence which had looked like the end was only the opening— the motor turning on, allowing her finally to move forward. Finally, move into her life, to thaw the frozen center and breathe.

"That's not true. You're bullying me. How dare you tell me what I feel is WRONG! That's all you ever say to me! We never have an argument that leads anywhere. We can't discuss anything because all you care about is winning, proving me WRONG! Don't you know I don't care about being right? I care about getting closer to who you are and growing in this relationship, that's all I ever cared about! I tell you...you tell me. There is no winner. There's just two losers. Us."

The waiter moved between them. Hannah sat straight— pride replacing emotion. Did he hear? Fighting in a restaurant.

Oh, God. I hate this.

Nick sat back. His mouth edged white with tension.

"That's fine, you can open it now."

"Right away, sir." They focused on the silent efficiency of the man, watching him with protracted attention, feigning interest, diffusing their anger. His clean, hairy fingers twisting the corkscrew, popping the cork, sniffing, backing up ever so slightly to wrap the bottle and pour a taste.

"That's fine, you can pour it."

He poured. They watched every movement with diffident attention. Wanting him to stay between them. And then he was gone.

They sat without speaking. Sipping wine. Lonely eyes wandering the room. What kind of people don't talk in restaurants? MARRIED PEOPLE.

Cool it, Hannah. Cool it.

"This is delicious. Nick, I don't want to fight with you, don't you know that? I just hate to see you lying about what you feel. It makes me distrust what you say and it's destroying us."

Did I say that? God.

He sucked in breath, letting it out with barely controlled hostility, another mask slipping down onto crisp linen tablecloth. Whoops! Sorry, dropped my facade, pick it up in a minute.

She saw it. Saw it slip, the anger he almost never let out, afraid of its violence.

He hates me. He really hates women.

She gulped down more wine.

"Don't turn those cold blue eyes off on me, please DON'T do it."

"You better shut the fuck up, Hannah, I mean it. I'm getting mad."

"So get mad! Don't threaten me with your anger. Why can't we get mad without it being so frightening? What will you do to me if you get mad? Murder me? Strangle me with a piece of fettucine? *I* do the killing in this family." The words froze them.

"Nick, what's happening to us?"

"You don't know what the fuck you're talking about, it's the wine, baby, you ball-breaking bitch, you're going too far now."

"It's funny, all of your wives go too far sooner or later."

And then, she knew it was too late to turn back. The unmentionable—buried. The other marriage—the other child. The past failures. All unmentionable. Lowered and covered with dirt, exhumed by the dead woman and wandering the earth of their nights.

Suddenly, for the first time since she was a kid in college at her first New Year's Eve party, she was drunk. Drunk not so much from wine, but from the shock of truth.

"You should have come home."

"What the hell are you talking about? You're drunk."

"I am not drunk. You should have come home. I begged you, Neilie needed you, I told you. You went to play tennis. And I excused you. I ACCEPTED IT. I needed you. You didn't want to come home. That's not what bad little boys do...they run off with the guys and play stick ball. Let Momma take care of it. Maybe you are what that crazy woman said. Are you? Weak...a weak pimp? Leaning on me, leaning on my need to please everyone, copping out with my father because you're afraid of him...letting him humiliate you and turning it on me, bullying waiters and your kids but never standing up to an equal. *I* talked to the police, / sat on the stairs with that fucking gun, you were too busy playing tennis! 'It's okay, dear, she doesn't mean it.' You didn't WANT to come home and face it and help me. I killed someone with *your* gun. I don't respect you anymore. I don't trust your judgments, I don't want you to screw me, I can't come with you inside me, only a finger or a machine or something that's not part of you...not me relinquishing myself to you. I lost that. I had it; oh, God, you know how much love I had for you, how I could make love-to you, touch you, never stop. I loved you so much. I don't like you anymore; too much past, too many lies. We're too different now. I've grown up and you've stayed the same. I see you differently. And, I don't love you anymore. I can't help it! I don't!"

She was gasping. Her chest heaving with the penetrating force of her words. Springing out of her mouth—epileptic in intensity. A fit of truth. A truth tantrum, oozing up out of her soul, coursing down from her brain. A dam of truth bursting through the honeycomb of her world.

Their eyes were locked together. Locked in a moment of absolute togetherness. For the first time in years. Seeing into one another's hearts—beyond loving—hate breaking through the game of love and freeing them to face one another.

He did not speak.

"I want to leave. Nick, take me home, please...now."

She rose, grabbing her purse and moving, head straight, eyes averting the glances of the people in the room, tasting trouble.

She pushed through the door to the street, weaving slightly in the air from the wine and the terror of her words, forgetting they had arrived separately.

My God.

"May we have our car, please?"

"Yes, ma'am...just a minute."

The attendant ran, moving loosely free in his body. Hannah ached to be him.

Her husband stood beside her, his face grim, eyes clouded with pain.

They waited.

The car screeched around the corner with the boy's enthusiasm.

"Thank you." Social necessities. Form. Manners. Her mother in a coma—Hannah still wiping spittle from her lips.

Who the fuck cares if you drool when you're dying? Comb your hair, brush your teeth, say thank you. Say please. But I'm dying! Tsk, tsk, that's no excuse for rudeness. If I choose to die, I will jump naked from a window with my legs spread apart—FUCK YOU!

Hannah's head reeled.

They pulled away from the curb like a horse from the gate, her husband ripping through traffic, using the machine as a weapon against his anger and fear.

She was crying. "Stop it! Please! Nick...stop it! You'll kill somebody, for chrissake, stop it!

He ignored her. His face set in the new mask, the one beneath the placid self-covering she had known. Seeing it slip occasionally—

just often enough for her to need to deny to herself that underneath there were hidden things that frightened her.

"Please, Nick, stop it! Stop it!"

He swung the car around the corner down a dark, deserted street and slammed to a stop. Grabbing her arms before the gears had caught.

"You want me to stop it. Okay...I'll stop it."

He held her arms in his hands like two bird wings, squeezing into her skin, past the blood and flesh into the bones of her body.

"You dumb bitch! I thought you were different! You're not! You and your tension and your mouth. When we got married, you said you had so much love to give me, you hadn't even begun, and for years all I've had is an uptight, critical bitch! I know how long it's been since you wanted to make love...you think I *like* that? You think I don't *know*! What happened to all that love you had for me? You dumb Jewish cunt, you're no different!"

"That's not true. It's not fair. I loved you. I tried to do everything for you. I did try. And then everything started to catch up with us...all the past, giving your child away and taking money from my father and everything, and not ever helping me or talking to me and blaming me for every business deal, everything that didn't work out. I was nineteen when I met you. I fell in love with who I thought you were. It's not your fault and it's not *my* fault. I'm thirty-two now! I'm different. That maniac started calling and she said things about you and me and my family and everything started breaking open and now I can't put it back.

"I didn't want it to break open, I wanted us to go on. Oh, God, Nick, I'm so scared of us not going on! But I've lost myself. I always loved to make love and I was calm and I've lost both things, my best things. I've lost them! I haven't felt like a woman in years. You want me to be your mother. I don't want to do that anymore. I can't! The bad boy will play tennis and Hannah will wait for the nasty lady with the gun and protect the children and earn a living and be a grown-up. Well, I do all of that *alone*. If you can't share yourself with me, then I might as well live alone and not feel like a failure all the time. I'M NOT A FAILURE; I'M NOT!"

His hands dug deeper into her arms and he was shaking her.

"Loving you isn't enough, what do you want from me?"

"Your loving makes me feel terrible about myself...

that can't be loving, it can't! I can't live this anymore, I want some peace. I want myself back. I don't know who I am without you and I can't keep pretending to care. I care about how what you do affects me and the kids, but I don't really care about *you* anymore. Oh, God...Nick, I can't help it. Please let go of me, please. You're hurting me, please! I don't want to feel like this, I can't help it. Neilie got hurt and everything went crazy and I saw things I didn't want to see and I tried to put them back, BUT I CAN'T."

She was screaming now, the pain and fear overwhelming her. "LET ME GO! LET ME ALONE! I WANT TO BE ALONE! PLEASE! PLEASE!"

He held her firm, his teeth clenched in fury, raising her half out of her seat and staring at her as if she were everything terrible and frightening that he had ever known. And then, the moment of flooding, the brick wall at the end of the alley, the dead end accepted, his face relaxed and he released her.

They sat in silence in the car—spent. Limp from the wringer of their words. Their fit of consciousness. "I forgot my car."

"Screw your car." He put his hands over his eyes, bowing his head forward. "What do you want to do, Hannah?"

Of course—let *Hannah* decide—let Hannah make the decision.

The thought cooled her, strengthened her to face him—without her game. Without justifying or discounting herself. She swallowed hard, the words closing in her throat.

"I think we've got to separate. We need some time...there's just been too much pressure. Too many changes WE...I need to be alone for a while."

They looked at each other, their eyes holding them up, raising them like a high. A slug of reality.

He nodded. "Okay, but let's do it fast. I'll go tonight. I don't want to have the kids see me leave. I just want to go."

"But I think you should sit down and explain it to Neilie. She's had so much, Nick, please."

"I can't handle it. Not now."

"Okay, Nick. I'll tell her tomorrow."

"Okay."

They sat again without moving. Breathing sounds filled the car. The stillness throbbed around them.

And then he started the engine, driving meticulously now, trancelike, down the late night streets. Home.

They walked to the door, like a thousand other nights, coming home together nights. Coming from movies and parties and dinners. Coming home to a bed and a cup of coffee, to a toothbrush and Johnny Carson, to sleeping children and half-read novels.

Habit controlling, they turned off the kitchen lights, locked the door and moved up the stairs, past the acid stains and the memory. Hannah sat on the bed, not moving, watching him change his clothes and pull out his suitcase.

This is not real. This is not my life. This is not happening.

"I'll call you tomorrow and tell you where I'm staying."

"Okay."

She followed him with her eyes, his large, strong back stooped slightly forward. He turned in the doorway and smiled at her, breaking her heart.

Barbra Streisand would say something spunky.

"I'll get my clubs and stuff on the way out. I've got a game Wednesday."

"Okay."

And he was gone.

Gone were his razor and toothbrush and bathrobe. Gone *Time* magazine and his tennis racquet. Gone the leather jacket she gave him for Christmas and the new watch and the thirty-dollar tie she had bought for no reason. Gone his flute and his briefcase and the transistor radio. And his best suit.

He had gone.

She sat on the bed like a disciplined child-eyes following as he gathered his most needed things.

What would you grab if your house was on fire?

Once on a television show where young married people won prizes for revealing the more personal embarrassments of the people they loved, the host had asked a young man what his wife would say she would take first if their house was burning. The man smiled proudly. "Oh, that's easy, we have a beautiful six-month-old baby girl, she'd take the baby." He relaxed, victory secured.

When the wife returned from her padded, silent room, they repeated the question. The husband rocked forward, snugly confident. "Well...I'd, uh...gee; I guess I'd take my photo albums and my new camel coat, oh, and our cat."

The husband's face froze in betrayal. "What about the baby!?" he demanded of this sudden stranger.

"Oh, I forgot about the baby."

And he was gone.

She sat, laden with the numbness that covers new truth. The unbearable moment when we must relinquish a deception. Of self, of one another. Like a death sentence, the happening was unacceptable. And impossible to bear.

She sat bearing it till she could bear no more. And the numbness lifted and was flushed by anguish.

She carried herself to the bathroom, the survivor of the dogfight, holding herself together, a step at a time-limping toward the safety of her private room.

Only it was not safe. He had been her safety and *he* was not safe.

Liza Minnelli would sing now.

Again, startling her, as if she could not believe it was possible to grieve more and live—the tears came.

Hannah sat on the bathroom floor, muffling her sounds to protect the children's sleep. "Nick...Oh, Nick...This can't happen to us. Somebody help me." Her eyes caught her face in the mirror, naked of makeup, fine hair hanging in tangled strands, fair skin mottled with red emotion.

"Oh, my God, I'm so ugly...I'm so frightened. I'm a freak...a freak...who would want me? I'm a failure and a freak. I'm not even a woman anymore...oh, God, help me, I write and no one wants it and it's all I have left. All I am, an ugly rabbit-eyed woman with nothing in the world that doesn't scare her. I'm a fraud, my whole life is just a fraud. We thought we were so happy...it was just all the outside things and it was *us*\ Oh, God, it was us and I couldn't face it! I couldn't look at the truth. You've gained nothing...nine years of marriage and you've gained nothing! Look at you! And now you're alone, all alone. Oh, God, somebody...make it stop!"

She hugged herself, gasping in grief at what she saw. And somewhere, deep from the loneliness and terror that she felt, she knew that she had always been all she had and that would have to be enough.

"Mommy, Mommy, the mens are here!"

Hannah gathered her papers and pulled the plug on her typewriter. She lifted it gently, and put it in its case and carried it downstairs, the rooms of her house careening back at her from tear-clouded eyes.

The house of her growing. Of her marriage. Of her babies. Flowers painted by hand on the crib. Curtains hung. Pillows sewn. Plants potted. Her space. Her place.

She looked out at it with strained child-eyes and took her favorite seat on the stairs. Her stairs—those stairs. Boxes stacked in the hall. Furniture gone. Dust on the shiny wood floors. A house about to be rejected, discarded, left alone to be taken by strangers.

Who will take care of me? How can you leave me? They may hurt me—break my windows—paint me orange. Don't you care? I thought you loved me. How can you do this? She and her house talking together.

She patted the stair rail, wiping her eyes.

The children's voices reached her from the lawn.

"Mommy, Mommy...they're coming inside, Mommy!"

She swallowed. The reality of what she was doing squeezing through her. She stood up, unsteady on her feet—seeing herself leaving—comings and goings of a life. Waving good-byes. College and marriage and movings. Apartments and houses. A child's fear—moving on.

"It's time, Hannah," voices whispering in her head.

"It's time. Bye Nick, bye Dad, bye Agatha, bye telephone,...bye Mother, bye house. Hello, Hannah, whoever you are. Big grown-up lady with her own moving van. Hello there, Hannah."

The phone was ringing—calling her back.

She tripped over a box of dishes, stubbing her toe.

"Hello?"

"Mrs. Nicoli?"

"This is Detective Hudson."

"Oh, hello."

"I'm just calling to let you know that we have stamped the case closed. We won't be bothering you anymore. The court ruled self-defense and the department apologizes for not being able to, uh, prevent the, uh, whole thing...get to you sooner."

Irony, my dear. Ironeeeeee.

"Oh, well, I'm glad to hear that. Thank you for calling, I appreciate it."

"My pleasure. Hope everything goes better now."

"Thank you. Good-bye."

She recradled the phone, standing there rubbing her toe with one hand and stroking the shiny white instrument with the tips of her free fingers. Feeling it, as if it were alive. Her daughter's face, the baby's funny soft ears, a friend's hand, someone who lived in her life.

Drunken phantom ladies, crushed bones, mutilated spirits, broken hearts, ruptured families, tears and tearings—parts of a life.

"Mommy, the mens are taking our furniture out! Come and look, Mommy, come quick!"

"Okay, sweetheart, I'm coming. Just a minute."

She moved her fingers slowly away from the phone, resisting the urge to kiss it good-bye, like not knowing when to kiss a person. Do I love them? Do I hate them? Did they help or hurt? The telephone of her nightmare, ready to be replaced. Leading her down a ringing trail of changes and losing her, to herself.

Good-bye, stove. Good-bye, linoleum.

She stopped, rubbing her foot, and relaxed in one deep, whistling sigh against the door of her kitchen, releasing all of the tension into the walls of her house. Relinquishing the fear, to the place of its nurture. And pushing herself forward, she turned abruptly and left to face the movers.

EPILOGUE

NICOLI NOTEBOOK (VOLUME IV)

AND NOW THE NEWEST EPISODE IN THE ROLLICKING ADVENTURES OF HANNAH OBERMAN NICOLI—THE ROLLER-SKATING JEWISH MURDERESS... THIS EPISODE ENTITLED: "HANNAH LEAVES NICK, SELLS LOVE NEST AND MOVES TO CONNECTICUT TO START AFRESH AS AN OVER-THIRTY SINGLE!"

So, hello, Gorgeous. Not quite shaping up like we thought, fourth decade, but—that's how some decades go.

Anyway, I'm still here and the mob hasn't broken my fingers or anything. I am now thirty-two years, nine and one-half months old. My husband is currently producing an X-rated movie and living on his newly purchased cabin cruiser in Marina del Rey with, as Neilie describes her, "A great big, huge brown lady with big fat muscles," that's what the kid said, Charlie Brown. That song is entitled: "Life Goes On."

I am waiting for the moving men to take me away. The good news is, I have a two-year lease on a house in Roxbury, Connecticut, and a book contract! (So long, suckers!) The other news is, I'm a swingle (sort of an acronym for swinging single). And the odds are:

I am broke. I have two highly visible, rapidly growing children.

Fifty percent of all the men I have met are gay. Twenty percent want Bo Derek, a little younger. Twenty percent are married. And 25 percent are too Creep City to swallow a Big Mac with. That adds up to 115 percent. Sure you want to sign on for this cruise, my brave little Friend?

Could end up going the whole distance all by myself. (Well, at bloody least, I now have a *self* to go with!) I'll be okay. Just sort of a transitionary period. (Of course, that could be said for the entire last thirty-two and three-quarters years.)

No one in my family is talking to me. (That goes on the good news list.) I mean murder is one thing, but DIVORCE...Morley sent me a Bible and said he was praying for my soul. Candy sent me a hot-pink see-through blouse (for my new social life, I guess). Louise sent me a nude watercolor of my mother (she did it from memory, which is probably why it is my mother's fifty-year-old head and a twelve-year-old body). Ethel and Sophie wrote me a letter (my theory is holding). The letter began, "No one in the history of our family has ever had a divorce." At least, she left out the killing part, or maybe there is another fiend in the closet?

My father and Patsy went to Europe, but it doesn't hurt. I seem to be filled with heroic portions of acceptance and forgiveness of myself and all.

I went to the movies by myself. I went to a bar by myself.

I went out to dinner by myself.

(This is not a life I know how to lead.)

I cannot settle for life with a human crutch anymore. But this is not a world I know anything about.

I am not trading in a used man for a new man.

I am on my own freckled feet.

And I will learn how to live this life. But—isn't this the place where I take two aspirin and meet Alan Bates?

www.ingramcontent.com/pod-product-compliance
Lightning Source LLC
LaVergne TN
LVHW040735250326
834688LV00031B/314